DEMON THRONE

MORNINGSTAR

DEBBIE CASSIDY

Contents

Cover by Sanjar Gombar

Chapter One

Vampires suck.

And not in a nice way.

The breed I tangled with were ugly too, twisted, pale, scrawny, with severe cases of halitosis. We called them sucker rats because they lived underground, occupying the sewers and network of catacombs beneath the city. The Fringe, my home, had our fair share of sucker rats. They usually kept to themselves, feeding on *actual* rats and other rodents, but sometimes they got brave. Sometimes they got organized, and when that happened, people went missing.

And when *that* happened, people like me were called in.

Hunters.

We were an antisocial breed, preferring to work solo, but going up against what was probably a nest wasn't something to do alone. Because *that* would be stupid.

"Fuck, it stinks down here," Orina said.

We sloshed through inches of shit water. "Breathe through your mouth."

"Yes, let's taste the shit particles, shall we?"

I bit back a smile. "You didn't have to come with me."

"What? And miss out on some vamp slaying? Like hell. You know I hate suckers."

Yeah, I did. I also knew that the Order she worked for didn't take vamp slaying jobs. Their main duty was to keep the city safe from the cold ones. Huge, wolven-looking beasts that fed on human organs. They nested in clusters and preferred to lay their eggs in a human host—food for their offspring as soon as they hatched. Only angel-blessed people like Orina were able to kill them, and don't ask me what being angel-blessed meant. The origins of the term were a closely guarded secret, a need-to-know basis only, and according to Orina, I didn't need to know.

I suspected that the Order of Helsing was affiliated with House Dracul, the not-so-ugly vampires of our city. Turned out that having royal blood from a bygone era no one recalled made them acceptable. Still, Orina refused to either confirm or deny my suspicions. My buddy was tight-lipped when it came to the inner workings of the Order. The stuff I'd learned came from deductive reasoning—one of my fortes.

The Mageri who ruled the city had even given Dracul their own territory over a decade ago. I'd watched the world change from my favorite spot in the tower of the Magisterium where I'd gone to school. It wasn't just the vampire royalty who'd gotten their own territory; the demons and the shifters had been granted land too. Our city was now split into Dracul, Morningstar, and Raventhorn. But the Mageri had accidentally left a section of land unclaimed. We'd named it the Fringe, and it was home to many humans and supernaturals who didn't want to be affiliated with either of the three houses.

People like me and Orina.

The Fringe also attracted the dregs of society, and the

criminal footprint was strong here. It was up to people like us to clean up the messes and keep the Fringe safe for all.

Today we were on a rescue mission. A coach, stopping to fuel up on its way to Dracul territory, had been hijacked by sucker rats late last night. The driver had managed to get away and reported it to the Fringe PD. The PD had outsourced the job to yours truly. Not the first time they'd done that either. Apparently, they didn't get paid enough to deal with sucker rats, and from the amount they'd offered me to clear out the nest, neither would I. Only problem was I needed the cash more than they did.

I stopped and pulled out my phone to study the map of the sewers. "Should be a set of steps up ahead."

"I see them." Orina picked up speed toward the tunnel exit. We climbed out of the crappy water onto a ledge, then through an arch and up another flight of steps onto a maintenance level. The city's sewer system was vast and elaborate, linked to a network of ancient catacombs that were off limits. Not a problem, as I had no intention of poking around in them. Being in the sewers was a major concession for me. I hated being closed in, and being under the earth gave me the fucking creeps.

"You okay?" Orina asked.

"I'll be better once we're out of here."

"Me too," she said.

We'd entered a narrow tunnel. "Hold up." I checked the schematic on my phone. "This is where we go dark."

"Good," Orina said. "Means we're on the right track."

The underground systems were only half mapped due to the risk of getting your jugular ripped out and your bones picked clean. It made sense for the sucker rats to make their nests in the uncharted territories. Aside from the fact that this tunnel wasn't on the maps, it was also unlit by the anemic strip lighting that illuminated the mapped sections of the sewers. I pulled glow sticks from the thigh pocket of my cargo pants, then cracked and shook them to life before looping one around each wrist. I handed two to Orina.

She smirked and drew her sword from the holster at her back. It glowed softly, casting enough illumination to make my puny glow sticks redundant.

Not everyone got gifted a magical sword by their employer. "Show-off."

I tucked my phone away. It was going to be mental mapping now. Not a problem. I had an excellent memory. Not as photographic as my shifter buddy Quinn. But good enough.

It didn't take long before we picked up a soft buzz of sound. Voices?

Orina's sword glowed brighter, the light pulsating. She froze and my heart leapt into my mouth.

I locked gazes with her, blood pulsing in my head, because her sword only glowed like that for one reason.

When a cold one was nearby.

"It can't be," Orina whisper-hissed.

"Your sword begs to differ."

"Damn it." She pulled her phone from her pocket, stared at it, then put it away. "No cell reception."

Which meant no backup. "We're talking a double whammy here, babe. Sucker rats and cold ones. It's a suicide mission for just the two of us."

I mean we were fast, skilled, lethal, but we were also sane.

She nodded curtly. "We retreat and come back with reinforcements. It's the best course of action."

It was the smart move, the best decision, but then a

child's cry drifted down the tunnel toward us. We froze, heads tipped to one side as we listened.

"No, Mummy! No! Stop. Leave my mummy alone!" The distinct sound of a slap was followed by a scream and sobs.

Ah, shit. Not a kid. They had a fucking kid.

Orina and I exchanged glances in an unspoken agreement.

There was no way we could leave now.

Time to do something insane.

Chapter Two

The tunnel opened onto an upper-level balcony and the action took place in a concrete chamber below, dotted with tents and sleeping bags. There was a five-foot hole in the wall partially out of view from our position crouched on the balcony.

Another entry route for the sucker rats?

This was their nest, and the stench of fear and death was strong. Unsurprising, considering the pile of dead, desiccated bodies by one wall, and the group of fresh humans shoved up against another. I scanned frightened faces, zeroing in on the little girl with the bloody mouth and swollen red cheek. A man crouched beside her, his arms around her, but her teary gaze was on a spot out of our view.

Anger tightened my chest. I was so gonna rip these suckers' heads off.

Orina gripped my arm in warning.

I glanced her way, seeing my rage reflected on her face. She shook her head slightly, a caution to keep my shit together.

I returned the nod and focused on the enemy. Six suckers. Not the whole nest, if the number of tents and sleeping bags was anything to go by, but an easy take-down for us.

They were silent, watching whatever was going on out of view.

Orina's sword continued to pulse in warning.

Where were the cold ones?

She jerked her head left. Yeah, if we shuffled over a little, we'd be able to get a view of our blind spot.

We moved slow and stealthy, keeping below the barrier to stay out of view. Finally, we came to a halt. I blew out a breath, nodded at Orina, then cautiously peered over the ledge.

Three humans covered in silver residue were stuck to the far wall.

Two of them, males, looked like they were sleeping with their mouths wide open, but the third, a woman, was wide-eyed with panic, paralyzed not with fear but by a toxin that only one kind of creature produced.

Orina sucked in a sharp breath as the cold one padded into view. Its large silvery body exuded lethal power and the scrape of its thick reptilian tail trailing behind it was loud in the sudden silence. It approached the woman and opened its jaws to release a silvery appendage from between its five-inch-long teeth. It was about to inject the woman with its eggs through her mouth, and when that happened, she was as good as dead.

My gaze flicked to the males, noting the slight bulge to their torsos. It was too late for them, they had minutes before their skin burst and the thick membrane sac containing the cold one's young pushed out to kiss the air. It would remain attached, feeding on the life in its host's blood until it was ready to hatch, after which it would feed on its host's flesh.

A job like this needed a plan. Needed shit to be executed to perfection. But there was no time. If we waited, this woman, this mother, would be taken from her child forever.

I locked gazes with Orina, seeing my determination reflected in her eyes. My lips curled in a wicked grin.

"Count of three?" Orina whispered.

"Fuck that."

We vaulted over the barrier in unison, bodies cutting through the air like bullets, and landed in crouches that would make any superhero proud.

The air spiked with shock as every eye turned to us, including the big ass cold one's.

I raised a hand in greeting. "Hey, is this a private party or can anyone join in?"

"Demon blood," one of the suckers hissed at me. His gaze tracked to Orina, confusion clouding his features. Yeah, my bestie was a bit of an enigma.

I pointed my dagger at him. "You must be the resident wanker."

He pulled back his teeth and hissed. "Get them."

Orina ran for the cold one, sword already cutting through the air.

She could handle herself.

I had suckers to behead, and my handy short sword was made of blessed steel, perfect for the job. I yanked it from its holster at my hip and attacked with dagger and sword.

Fighting came naturally to me, like breathing, or eating, or basically any regular function, as if my muscle and sinew were attuned to the dive and dip, jab and spin of a good old-fashioned rumble. Fists worked too, but not on suckers. The only thing that took one of these fuckers down for good was knocking their heads clean off their bodies or incinerating them.

With no fire to hand, the beheading would have to do, and I was more than happy to get those heads rolling.

Four down, two to go. Orina had the cold one on the defensive, hissing and spitting acid, but my buddy was a pro when it came to tangling with these creatures; no need to watch her six.

Shit, fangs coming at my face.

I brought my arm up in front of my neck to block the attack and shoved the sucker back. "Dude, you need a breath mint, or ten."

He bared his teeth and rushed me again.

He never made it. The thud of his head hitting the ground was accompanied by the gurgling death cry of the cold one.

The final sucker backed away toward the hole in the wall.

I canted my head and pointed my dagger at him. "Don't even think about it. You run and I *will* chase you, and when I catch you, I'll gut you and pull out your entrails before I cut off your head."

One of the humans whimpered.

Shit, I needed to hold back on the graphic descriptions —there were kids present, and parents may have covered eyes, but ears were still flapping.

The sucker rat looked torn.

I took a step toward him, adjusting my grip on my dagger so I was anchoring the hilt to my palm with my thumb, fingers up in a surrender-and-stay-chill gesture.

He glanced at my dagger hand, then at my face.

"Answer my questions and you can go."

Orina joined me, chest heaving with exertion. “Why are you feeding a cold one?” she asked him.

The sucker rat looked to me.

I arched a brow. “Answer her.”

Its eyes were wild. It opened its mouth and made a mewling sound.

“Fuck.” Orina tucked her sword away. “He’s a renfield.”

Shit. I looked closer, noting the blackened skin around his mouth and the mottled state of his skin. He was a human feeding bag, a minion for the sucker rats, and he had no tongue.

They usually ripped those out.

We’d get no information out of him. “Go. Get out of here.”

He looked confused.

Orina took a step forward, stamping her boot. “Get. Go on.”

This time he turned and fled through the tunnels.

I turned to the humans still huddled together. They watched us warily, which was weird because we’d just saved their asses, so where were the thank yous and expressions of relief?

The woman who’d been stuck to the wall was crouched before the little girl, sobbing softly. Not hugging the child, just staring at her and sobbing.

My scalp tightened. Something was wrong. I took a step forward and the man who’d been comforting the child earlier moved to stand between me and the group.

“Don’t.” He held out his hands. “It’s not her fault.”

What the fuck?

“It’s okay, Mummy. It doesn’t hurt anymore,” the little girl said.

The woman sobbed harder.

Oh, shit. I looked to Orina. "I can't."

She nodded. "I'll do it."

"Please, don't. You can't," the man pleaded.

I stepped forward, forcing the guy back. "You know the law. You understand why."

He began to cry. "It's not her fault. She didn't ask to be turned."

My heart ached for him. "I know. I get it. But she isn't your little girl any longer."

Several of the other humans stepped up to help me, blocking him off from his child so that Orina could...

Fuck, I hated this part.

The kid screamed and bawled, activating every latent maternal instinct in me to intervene and help her. But it wasn't real, and any moment now—

"Bitch, stay the fuck away from me." The kid's tone dropped to something gravelly and inhuman.

"And there it is," Orina drawled. "The monster within."

Suckers were a breed of their own carrying a bio-mystical infection in their blood that could make more suckers out of humans. The infection had no effect on supernaturals, though.

Turning a human without written consent was against the law, and turning a child was prohibited not because the infection stopped them maturing physically and fucked with their mind, even though that was reason enough. No, it was prohibited because in children, the infection ate away their soul and replaced it with another entity, one we knew very little about. All we knew was that the infection in a child acted like a gateway for this entity.

The little girl who'd inhabited that body was gone. I needed to remember that and block out her screams as Orina dragged her away from the group and into the tunnel.

The screams turned to growls that cut off suddenly.

My shoulders sagged. It was done.

The man fell to the ground and covered his face, and the woman scrambled toward him and pulled him into a hug.

Humans stared at me with exhausted eyes.

I sighed and jerked my head toward the metal ladders leading up to the balcony. "Come on. Let's get you guys to safety."

Chapter Three

The bar buzzed with conversation. Patrons trading jibes and curses or merely sharing a laugh created a soothing, familiar atmosphere. The Hole in the Wall was one of my favorite haunts. I'd spent many evenings in here nursing a pint of ale and shooting the breeze with fellow hunters. We might not work well together, but we loved to share stories about our exploits.

Tonight, I'd dragged Orina with me. The humans were safe with the authorities and the Order was busy figuring out what the hell sucker rats had been doing feeding a cold one.

Orina and I were officially off the clock.

And as if to prove it, Orina downed her third shot of whiskey, finishing off with a grimace. I bit back a smile because hard liquor was so not her thing. She was a wine and cocktails kind of girl. But tonight was a hard liquor kinda night, and the fact she'd accepted the shot without any complaint told me she agreed.

She brushed tendrils of silver hair from her face before pulling out the tie and gathering it into a knot at the top of her head. The motion drew my attention to the flyer on the wall behind her.

Satan Dead. Ascension to come. How will this affect Morningstar territory? the flyer asked in bold, angry type.

Who gave a shit? Not me.

I reached for my own shot, but Orina beat me to it, downing it in one gulp.

I knew better than to ask her to slow down. "You want another?"

She squinched one eye closed, considering it, then belched. "Nah, I'm all good now."

This was my fault. I should have taken care of the sucker rat kid. "I'm sorry, babe."

She snorted. "It's all good. Needed to be done. I've done it before. That thing was wearing that child's body."

"I know. Doesn't make it easy, though."

"No, it doesn't."

Our food arrived. Two plates of beef stew and crusty buttered rolls. Perfection.

Orina rubbed her hands together and got stuck in. We ate in silence for several minutes until the edge had been taken off our hunger. Orina was the first to sit back. "Man, that's good stew."

"Told you. This place does the best food." I mopped up gravy with a hunk of bread and popped it into my mouth.

"Any news on Chase?" Orina asked.

The food turned to dust in my mouth. I shook my head, swallowing against the sudden lump in my throat.

"Hey." Orina sat forward and covered my hand with hers. "He'll be back."

I wasn't so sure. He'd been gone for almost a month now. The longest he'd ever left me.

"I'm worried something might have happened to him." I locked gazes with her. "I think he might be dead."

Orina exhaled slowly. "It's a possibility."

"Fuck." I pulled my hand free from hers. "You're supposed to say no, Nyx, he's fine. He can't be dead. Resourceful pooch like him. He's probably just gotten...distracted."

"We don't lie to each other."

"No. We don't." And my sidekick Chase, my huge hound buddy, had been gone for too long for it to mean anything but bad shit. "I just wish I knew what happened to him."

Chase had been with me since I was a kid. We'd found each other—both abandoned, unwanted creatures. And we'd become a family of two. He'd been my companion, my protector, my sidekick in the hunting business for years, and yeah, he'd go off from time to time for a couple of days, a week at the most, but he always returned. Except for this time.

This time I feared that Chase was gone for good, and my heart...My heart couldn't take it.

Orina glanced at a dirty flyer stuck to the floor. "Did you figure out who left the message on your phone?"

I shook my head. "Nope. And he hasn't called again, so fuck him."

She frowned. "But don't you think it's weird that someone would call to tell you that Satan was dead?"

Course I did, but I wasn't one for dwelling on stuff I couldn't affect. I'd tried to trace the call and come up blank. The dude, whoever he was, hadn't called again, so case closed.

"I think it's weird someone would think I gave a shit what happened to Satan."

Orina's frown deepened. "Nyx, Satan has ruled

Morningstar for...well, for as long as it's existed, even before the Mageri gave it a territory. He's the one who keeps the rest of the demon princes in check."

"Been brushing up on your demon lore?"

She pressed her lips together. "This is academy-level stuff, babe. We learned all this at the Magisterium."

I winced. "I might have skipped that lesson." I held up my hand to stall her when it was obvious she meant to recount the lesson. "Look. I might be a demon blood, but Morningstar isn't my home. I only ever go there if I absolutely have no other choice. So whatever happens now that Satan is dead isn't any concern of mine."

"He was killed, you know?" Orina said.

"Really, I thought he died of old age." I shot her a smirk.

"Cut the sarcasm. He didn't just die in a fight or some skirmish, he was assassinated." She sucked in her cheeks. "Now they're trying to fill his seat before any of the princes can gain a foothold."

Damn, she was a wealth of information, but then the Order always had its finger on the pulse when it came to politics. "And how do they intend to fill his seat?"

"Well, they—" Her phone buzzed angrily on the table. "One sec." She picked up the call. "Magnus, yeah? Uh-huh?" She closed her eyes, shoulders drooping. "Sure, I can cover. Be there in ten." She hung up and shot me an apologetic smile. "Rain check on the hangout sesh?"

"You mean I have to drink alone?" I pressed a hand to my chest and gave her a faux shocked look.

"Well, think of it this way, at least no one will steal your shots." She dropped me a wink as she pulled on her jacket. "Call you tomorrow?"

"Tomorrow."

She blew me a kiss and headed to the door, leaving me to my thoughts and the prospect of drinking solo.

Yeah, it didn't appeal to me tonight.

I downed my ale and motioned for the server to come over with the bill. She smiled and held up a finger, indicating for me to wait a moment.

I sat back, gaze traveling over the bar patrons to snag on the back of a dark head. Broad shoulders stretched a white T-shirt that hugged muscular biceps. My pulse jumped and then slowed as my mind registered the lack of tattoos and the height that fell a little short.

Damn, who knew it would be so hard getting over the first guy in forever who had made my pulse do the fucking tango.

Loke had come into my life like a whirlwind and exited just as quickly. No word, no contact. Nothing. I mean, I'd be pissed if I knew he had any other choice, but my almost lover had come from Tariffel, the afterlife for the supernatural, and he'd been pulled back there. Our story had been short and sweet and extremely unfinished. Did I think about him? Often. Dream about him? All the fucking time. And I was pretty sure it was because of a damned kiss. Kisses fucked with your head, which was why I, as a rule, didn't do them. But with Loke...Damn, that man...

Fuck, I needed that bill.

It was time to go home.

Home was my office above a jewelry store, cheap rent because the landlord felt that having a hunter in residence would reduce the chances of his store being robbed. So far, so good. My reputation preceded me. As one of the top hunters in the city, I was called upon for the jobs that others refused to take, not because they paid shit but because the chances of failure were high.

I took the risks.

I liked the risks.

Maybe there was something wrong with me, or maybe my psyche was simply trying to show me that there was worse shit than being dumped in the streets at the age of six with nothing but a backpack of tinned food, the clothes on my back, and a ratty blanket.

Taking risks made me appreciate that there were worse fates than being abandoned by your family.

I'd been lucky. Chase, a puppy back then, had found me. We'd kept warm on the streets for weeks, huddled together until Babs had found us both and taken us in.

The old woman had saved my life by giving me a home. Which reminded me, I should go visit her soon. Maybe tomorrow. Yeah, I'd go see her tomorrow for a nice cup of tea. The thought chased away the blues a little.

I tucked my hands into my pockets and strolled down the dark, empty streets that led to home.

Empty now without Chase to fill it. My heart ached.

Damn him for leaving me.

I sucked in a breath of fog.

Hey, when had the fog descended? My pace slowed as an icy finger trailed up my spine, waking up my senses and putting my body into high alert. An empty, nighttime-fog-drenched street equaled the scene from a horror movie.

Unfortunately, any beasties looking for a snack were gonna be in for a nasty shock. I dipped and pulled a dagger from my boot, barely breaking stride.

My skin buzzed with awareness of an otherworld

presence. Any alcohol I'd consumed had been long burned up by my demon blood metabolism.

I was alert and aware that I was about to be attacked.

As if on cue, three dark, beastly shapes loomed out of the fog.

Man, sometimes I hated it when I was right.

Chapter Four

A heavy silence settled on the world.

Okay, I hadn't seen creatures like these before. Their backs were about five feet off the ground, heads twice the size of my torso, and paws large enough to squash my upper body. Their eyes glowed red through the fog, finding me, zeroing in on me, lips pulling back in snarls that promised pain.

The dagger in my hand felt puny. I drew my short sword instead. "Easy, guys. We can talk about this. No need to get all growly."

My tone was light and even, but my heart slammed against my ribs, blood rushing to my head to leave me a little lightheaded.

What the fuck were these creatures?

One of them stepped forward and I resisted the urge to back away, locking my knees and bracing myself to counter an attack.

A symbol flared to life in the middle of its forehead and the back of my hand lit up with fiery pain. I glanced down to see the same symbol emblazoned on my skin.

Motherfuc—

The beast rushed me. I dove out of its path on instinct, rolling and coming to my feet, pulse racing because there was no way I could take down three of these things. The beast that had rushed me ground to a halt in the spot I'd been a moment ago and turned its huge head in my direction. I backed up, thighs bunching, ready to make a break for it as the other two beasts advanced.

Shit, shit, shit.

Thank gods this wasn't a residential area, just a market strip closed for the night. No one else could get hurt but me.

Ha, not the best thought, because it also meant no one would hear my cries for help.

The Order building wasn't far from here. "You guys don't mind if I make a quick call, do ya?"

The beasts snarled, moving closer and forcing me to back up.

"I didn't think so, but it was worth a try."

I'd learned to use my skill set to its advantage in any combative situation, but I'd also learned to recognize when I was outmatched. Like now. Three mega beasts on one demon blood left me undoubtedly outmatched, and when there was little hope of survival, the best course of action was retreat.

Lucky for me, I was damn fast.

I took one more step back, spun on my heel, and broke into a sprint.

Paws pounded the ground behind me, closer, closer, too fucking close. I pushed harder, feeling the burn as my muscles protested. My lungs screamed, desperate for a moment to draw a lungful of air, but all I could manage running flat out was shallow gasps. I couldn't keep this up. I couldn—

A weight slammed into my back, knocking me off my feet and sending me flying. I dropped my weapons and hit the ground with my palms, elbows buckling so my chest slapped cement. Fuck, I rolled in time to avoid the epic paw that smashed into the ground I'd occupied a split second before. My short sword was inches away from me. I grabbed it.

Up, Nyx, get up.

But my body was rubbery with shock, limbs doing their best impression of cooked noodles as the human aspect of me asserted itself. I scrambled forward, forcing my body to obey my brain's command. Move, dammit. Move.

Another beast smashed into me from the left. A sharp crack took my breath. A broken rib. Shit. The ground rushed up to meet me, resulting in a second crack. Blood coated the inside of my mouth. I rolled to my feet, sword still clasped in my bloody hand.

Running wasn't going to work with these guys.

Time to fight.

I lunged at the beast, slashing with my sword and catching air as the beast reared back to avoid the strike.

Rage bubbled up inside me, turning my vision red.

I ran at the beast and launched myself off the ground, blade coming up, ready to piston down and spear the creature. "Argh!"

I caught movement in the periphery of my vision a moment before I was knocked out of the air. Again.

I braced for impact and hit something soft and warm before smacking into the cold earth. I made to sit up, breath coming out in a wheeze, but a paw pressed to my chest, smaller than the beast's. Familiar.

Tears blurred my vision as I stared up at Chase's huge hound form. His warm brown eyes locked with mine and then he raised his head to fix his gaze on the beasts, a low, menacing growl rattling his chest.

He was back. My buddy was back.

He planted himself between me and the beasts, hackles up in warning to my attackers.

"Chase, don't." I grabbed hold of his haunch, using his sturdy form to pull myself up. "We can't take them on. We have to get away."

But Chase wasn't backing down. Instead, he advanced, head down, lethal growl vibrating the air.

Shit. "Chase, come on." I tugged at his fur, gaze flying from him to the beasts who weren't moving.

They weren't attacking.

Instead, they began to back away. The fog around them thickened before surging up to swallow them and then dissipated, taking them with it.

The tension drained out of Chase, and he turned his massive head to look at me as if to ask, *are you okay?*

I wanted to yell at him for leaving for so long and making me worry. I wanted to act all indifferent and annoyed and make him work for my affection, but he was back, and he'd saved my ass, and fuck it, I was too glad to see him, so I dropped to my knees and wrapped my arms around his neck.

He chuffed and then laid his chin on my shoulder in the hound equivalent of a hug.

He was back, and I was never losing him again.

THANK GOODNESS FOR DEMON HEALING. By the time I got home, my limp was all but gone and my chest was no longer on fire. It would probably be a few hours before I was completely healed, much slower than a regular demon, but that was fine.

There'd been a time when I'd dreamed about being full demon or full human; either would have been fine as long as I could find a place to belong. But then I'd remind myself how both sides had rejected me. My demonic sire hadn't wanted me, simply knocking up my human mother and then pissing off back to Morningstar territory, and I had no desire to find out who he was. My human mother had abandoned me too, not wanting me around when her pure human spawn had been born. She'd forced me away from my siblings and taken my family from me. Had I contemplated sneaking into her house at night and slitting her pretty throat? Sure, most nights growing up, but the love Babs gave me had soothed the raw edges of my heart.

Now all I felt for the gray, drab human who'd birthed me was pity. May she rot in peace.

Chase followed me up the steps of our apartment. I unlocked the door with stiff fingers and headed straight for the bedroom and the ensuite bathroom. I needed a shower.

"Don't you dare disappear again." I glanced over my shoulder from the bathroom door. "As soon as I'm washed, you and me, we're gonna have words."

Chase made a chuffing sound and then settled by my bedroom door, his habitual guard position when I was sleeping. The knots in my belly relaxed. Damn, it was good to have him back.

A quick scalding shower and fresh clothes did wonders post skirmish, and a couple of fingers of whiskey topped it off. I padded into my office, Chase at my heels, and lowered myself into my fabulously extravagant leather office chair. It was the most expensive item of furniture I owned, and yeah, it stuck out like a sore thumb in my drab office, but a woman's ass was sacred and the cushioning on this seat was heavenly.

I propped my stockinged feet on the desk and leaned back, sipping my drink. Chase watched me, waiting. Now was the time to chew him out for disappearing on me, but maybe I was going soft because I didn't have the heart to do it. Besides, we had bigger things to worry about.

"I could have died today, Chase. Those things wanted to kill me."

Chase growled low.

"I know, I know, you'd never let that happen, but honey, they were huge." But they'd backed off when Chase arrived. "Do you know what they were?" I locked gazes with him, and he held the eye lock steadily. "Damn, I wish you could talk. I bet you know what they are, don't you, and they fucked off when you showed up. Why?"

I looked at the back of my hand, no longer sporting a glowing mark. I needed to figure out what those creatures had been and why they'd attacked me. Chance or design, it made all the difference.

Time to call in the expert.

Orina picked up on the third ring. "Nyx? Is everything okay?"

Yeah, because we'd just seen each other, and I wasn't the clingy call-up-to-say-goodnight kinda friend. "I was just attacked by three massive creatures."

She was silent for several beats. "What did they look like."

I loved this aspect of Orina's personality, the way she acted on deductive reasoning. I was calling her, and therefore I was not dead. I was safe, so there was no need for coddling. "They looked like a cross between a hound and a lion. They had the hound face, but they had manes and huge paws. Oh, and glowing red eyes."

"Uh-huh, jotting this down. What else?"

"A mark glowed on one of their foreheads and then the same mark glowed on my hand."

"Wait...that sounds familiar. I'll call you back in ten." She hung up and I settled down to finish my whiskey.

If anyone could find information on these beasts it was Orina. Working for the Order gave her access to an extensive database of information on almost every supernatural creature in existence. They called it the Archive, and her access had saved my ass on more than one occasion. But there were things not even the Archive could tell us, restricted information that I could only get through my black-market contact-information dealers who ran a dark web of data accessible for a price. Usually a hefty one.

My phone rang and Orina's name flashed on the screen. I answered. "Hey."

"Nyx, this is bad."

"Okay, tell me."

"Those things that attacked you are helhunters. Not a huge amount is known about their origins, but we do know that they've been used in hits by demons. A mystical symbol is cast containing the identity of the mark, and once the helhunters find it the mark is transferred to the target and the hit commences."

Wait, was she saying what I thought she was saying. "A demon put a hit on me?"

"It looks that way. Nyx, you need to come into the Order. You can stay here with me until we figure out what's happening. You'll be safe here and—"

"No." I clutched the phone tighter. "There is no way I'm

running and hiding. If someone wants me dead, they can fucking say it to my face."

"Nyx...you're not considering—"

"Going to Morningstar territory to root out my attacker and kick their ass? You're damned straight I am."

Chapter Five

When the Mageri had split our vast city into territories, they'd made sure to put the ocean between the humans and the demons. Morningstar territory had its own island connected to the mainland by a golden bridge, home to the Shooting Star, an express train that carried passengers to and from demon territory.

I'd made this journey a handful of times in my life, each time to visit the same demon. My contact when it came to information, my supplier when it came to mystical artifacts, and my lover when desire called for it, which was every time we met.

Sin had that effect on my body. He awoke the hunger inside me, giving me an excuse to satisfy my carnal urges. Not that I needed an excuse. Sex was sex, recreational and healthy as long as emotions didn't get involved. I made sure of that.

Emotional connections had the potential to lead to heartache, and I only made them when I was confident the object of my affections wouldn't leave.

Right now, there were four people on that list: Babs, Chase, Orina, and Quinn. I'd lost touch with Quinn for a while, but there'd never been any doubt in my mind that if I'd called her, if I'd needed her, she'd have come. The three of us had a pact, the sisterhood pact, one we'd signed as teens up in the clock tower of the Magisterium the night the Accords had been signed. Ironic that as the world had been splitting into three parts, three young women from very different worlds had bound themselves to each other.

Yeah, I had my peeps, and I didn't need anyone else. Still, the thought of seeing Sin again after all this time made my thighs quiver.

The Shooting Star carried me across the angry gray sea toward Morningstar. Chase sat by my side, his head up, eyes watchful. He was on guard. I reached out and sank my fingers into the fur at his neck.

"It's okay, boy. We're gonna figure out who's responsible and deliver some pain."

Chase chuffed in agreement.

We landed in Morningstar a few minutes later, and stepped into the queue of demon bloods and other supernaturals disembarking. The market was close to the station and many supes came here to do business. Bartering was the currency here and anything could be on the table. Some demons wanted payment in sex, others in coin, goods, or favors. There was a market for it all. I'd never ventured further than the market. The only demons I'd come across were the imps and the demon bloods who lived and worked here—to be honest, my knowledge of the species and the hierarchy system was limited. Although I did know there were higher-level demons and lower-level ones. But then I'd never needed to understand it before.

But now someone was trying to kill me, and if I was

going to find out who, I needed to understand how the system of power worked in Morningstar and who'd have access to helhunters in the first place.

Sin was the only higher-level demon I knew. He had to be the one to help me, and luckily for me he lived and worked in the market district.

The streets were exceptionally busy today, filled with demon bodies of all shapes and sizes, and there was a buzz of excitement in the air. I caught snippets of conversation.

"Could be anyone really. You know what they say about him, right?"

"He got around."

"Could be me."

I had no idea what they were on about, but there was no mistaking the excitement in the cinnamon-sweet air. I mean, why did Morningstar have to smell so fucking good?

Sin's workshop came into view, and I veered toward it, cutting through the crowd to come to a halt in the shade of the shop awning. Chase lowered his huge body to the ground, well versed with the protocol for visiting Sin. He always kept watch.

I wanted to say I wouldn't be long, but depending on what price Sin exacted for the information I wanted, I could be a while. A shiver of expectant apprehension ran over my skin. It had been too long since I'd indulged in carnal exercise.

The inside of the workshop was separated into a storefront lined with shelves of machine parts and goods I had no understanding of, and the forge at the back where Sin could usually be found pounding metal, torso naked and sweaty. A damn treat for the eyes if there ever was one.

Except today the steady clang and thud of Sin working were absent. I made my way down the stacks toward the back of the store, which was more of a warehouse really. The storefront didn't give an accurate impression of how much space there was beyond the doors.

"Sin?" My voice echoed around me. "Hello?"

A strange sound drifted down the stacks to meet me. A slurping, suckling sound accompanied by a gentle vibration. I broke free of the towering units a moment later and froze, pulse kicking up at the sight before me.

Sin stood, ass propped on the workbench, legs planted wide, head tipped back as a demon female knelt before him, sucking on his cock noisily. Sin wasn't touching her. His hands were braced on the workbench behind him, chest vibrating as she worked him. What was she doing with her teeth? And that gobbling noise? That was *not* the best technique for sucking cock.

I tore my gaze from her, dragging it up Sin's washboard abs and hard pecs to find his midnight eyes fixed on me.

"Nyx." He said my name like an invitation, and I found myself fighting the urge to step forward, shove the useless cock-sucking woman out of the way, and take her place.

I didn't do any of that, though. Instead, I crossed my arms and arched an amused brow. "Hello, Sin, did I interrupt something fun?"

To give her credit, the demon hadn't stopped working him; if anything, her ministrations had become faster, almost desperate.

Sin placed his hand on her head. "Enough."

She disengaged with a pop, looking up at him. "But you said you had to come. You haven't come yet."

He looked down at her dispassionately. "I know."

"But that means I won't get what I want."

"Unfortunately, yes."

She stood slowly and turned to glare at me. "This is your fault. You interrupted us and ruined it."

"No," Sin said. "Your technique leaves much to be desired. Come back when you've perfected it and we can trade."

She opened and closed her mouth a couple of times and then pressed her lips together, pushing back her shoulders in determination. "I will be back, Sin. Mark my words."

"I don't doubt it." Sin smiled, but it didn't reach his eyes.

The woman brushed past me and dove into the stacks, eager to get away now, but her departure left me with an unobstructed view of Sin's demonhood, and damn...

Sin reached for himself, slowly, carefully tucking away his prize. I cleared my throat and pulled my gaze up to his face. Fuck, he had a beautiful face, hard planes and chiseled jaw, wide, flat cheekbones, and dark eyes that swam with flecks of silver. He would have been angelic in appearance if not for the slightly crimson hue to his smooth, velvety skin and the horns that curved up and back from his head.

"What do you want today, Nyx?" he asked in his deep, gravelly voice.

"Information."

"Hmmm." He patted the spot on the workbench beside him. "Come sit."

I crossed the room toward him, heart beating a little faster as our proximity increased. It didn't help that he was watching me as if I were a sumptuous snack.

I joined him at the bench and hoisted myself up. Sin was tall enough for his booted soles to sit flat on the ground while on the bench but mine dangled in the air.

"What do you want to know?" he asked.

"Someone in Morningstar has put a hit on me. I need to figure out who, and to do that I need to understand the hierarchy system here and why anyone would be interested in killing me."

"You've pissed off a lot of people in your time," Sin said.

"True, but I've never taken down a demon or worked for one."

"Hmmmm."

"Can you help me?"

"I don't concern myself with the workings of the courts, Nyx."

My heart sank.

"But I can see you have misconceptions about the creatures who reside in Morningstar. I can clear up those misconceptions."

Okay, that was something. Now for the price. "What will it cost?"

He'd already fucked me bent over this bench, and he'd also tasted me, making me come with his tongue under the proviso I made no sound. I was prepared for anything. An excited pulse beat between my thighs as he moved to stand before me, leaning in to cage me with his body.

His midnight eyes glowed with silver flecks as they raked over my face, settling on my lips.

"A kiss."

My pulse thudded hard. He'd been deep inside me with his cock and his tongue, but he'd never kissed me. Not once. A kiss was...intimate. Personal. Precious.

He locked gazes with me. "Will you pay the price?"

"Can't you just fuck me?"

His eyes narrowed. "I decide what the cost is, Nyx. Not you."

My mouth was dry. I licked my lips, and he tracked the movement, making my pulse jump. I didn't like this. Not at all. Sexual activity was one thing, but this...closeness, this heart-pounding, fluttery shit was a huge no.

"Well?" His breath kissed my mouth in an echo of what was to come.

I needed the information. I needed to find out who was gunning for me. One kiss wouldn't matter. It would probably be shit anyway, and yes, I was convincing myself to break a rule to get what I needed right now. I'd let him kiss me, but I'd stay detached. I'd think of something disgusting, like the cold one laying eggs in a human body. Yep, that would work.

I lifted my chin slightly, bringing our lips closer. "Deal."

His huge hand settled on my collarbones, sliding up to hug my neck and tilting my head back.

My pulse pounded against his fingers as he lowered his mouth to mine a hairbreadth from claiming my lips. My eyes fluttered closed in anticipation of first contact.

Long, aching seconds passed.

I opened my eyes to find him staring at me with a conflicted expression, nostrils flaring with each breath as if he was waging an inner battle. His grip on me tightened a fraction.

"Sin?"

"No." He released me and stepped back. "Not today."

"What?" Annoyance flared in my chest. I didn't have time for games. "I need that information, Sin. Just take the damn price and give me what I want."

"The price has changed." His eyes narrowed, jaw clenching. "Take off your pants."

My stomach flipped. "What's the price, Sin?"

"Your cunt. I want to claim it. I want to be deep inside you."

Oh, fuck. No. No, this was okay. This I could handle. I

shucked off my trousers and underwear, setting them to one side. He gripped my thighs and parted me.

"You keep your eyes on me," he ordered. "You don't touch. You don't make a sound. You just take it. That's the deal."

"What? Sin—"

"That's the fucking deal."

I nodded. "Fine."

He reached between us to free himself and I closed my eyes, centering myself, because damn I knew how good this would feel, and not crying out, not touching him, would be the biggest test of all.

I planted my palms on the bench either side of me and leaned back slightly. He pushed forward, chest heaving as his cock pressed against me.

"Look at me," he demanded.

I locked gazes with him, breath catching in my throat at the expression of ownership on his face. It was poignant and real but masked by carnal heat a moment later as he entered me. I bit back a cry, sucking in a sharp breath as he stretched me. Yes. I remembered this delicious moment, this feeling of being filled so completely that there was no room for anything more. I wanted to throw my head back and thrust my hips up to meet him, but I held still, keeping my eyes on his as he worked himself into me. My chest ached with an excess of emotion the sensation of him inside me evoked, and he hadn't even started to fuck me yet.

Oh, God. I didn't think I could do this.

He adjusted his grip on me, one hand on my hip, the other moving high on my thigh, rolling his hips as he settled as far as he could go.

I choked back a gasp. "Just get it over with."

His luscious lips curved in a slight smirk. He pulled out inch by inch and slammed into me.

My fingers curled, nails digging into wood.

"Good girl," he purred. "Real good."

He did it again and again, hitting that spot inside me that made me want to grab his shoulders, dig my nails into his skin, and scream his name. Instead I pressed my lips together, fighting the sobs of release clawing at my throat and swelling my chest. The slap of flesh, the burgeoning flood of heat, the tightening of my muscles as they prepared for release couldn't mean anything. Nothing. This was a business transaction, it didn't mean…Oh, God…Oh, fucking God.

I came hard, groin grinding against his as I milked the sensation through a sheen of tears.

He cupped my nape and pressed his forehead to mine, his breath hot on my face as he found his release inside me.

We came down together, increment by increment. Were his fingers massaging my nape?

His hand dropped from my body. He pulled out of me, turning his back on me. "You can use the washroom."

"Gee, thanks." My voice came out strong and sure even though my insides were still quivering.

It had never been like this with Sin before. Best to bury this moment, to forget it. Anything else would ruin our transactional dynamic. I grabbed my clothes and locked myself in the washroom.

Thank goodness there was no chance of transmitted infections for supernaturals. Our bodies were immune to most illnesses. Pregnancy was rare between supernaturals and humans, and a matter of biological compatibility and intent for most other supernatural pairings. Not that any of that applied to my kind. Demon bloods were barren. Yeah,

I'd discovered that nugget years ago and come to terms with the fact I'd never have spawn of my own.

I rejoined Sin in the workshop a few minutes later, composed and ready to claim what he owed me.

"Your turn, Sin. Tell me what I need to know."

"The demons who rule Morningstar aren't demons, they're angels."

Well, sucker punch me in the chops. I stared at him. "You're telling me that *angels* rule over *demons*?"

"Fallen angels, Nyx. They've been on the earthly plane for a long time. They were advocates of humanity, lovers of mortality. They came and settled here eons ago, residing in a dimension parallel to this one populated by creatures called demons." He leaned back against the workbench again. "They carved out order. Kingdoms rose and laws were laid. The demons fell into line. Back then this demonic realm was plagued by daimonic forces."

"Daimonic? Don't you mean demonic?"

"No."

"Okay..."

"These daimonic forces spilled from a place called the abyss. They rained chaos and carnage on the demons. The demons needed the fallen angels to protect them, to help them get organized against the threat. Thing is, demons are inherently self-serving, egotistical beings driven by id and ego. They make oral deals steeped in trickery and subterfuge to get what they want. But the fallen taught them the nature of lawful transaction by introducing written contracts and barter. Many demons adopted this ideology, raising them to the status of devil. Many demons dabble in minor contracts, but only those elevated to devil know the true art and intricacies of an ironclad deal."

"Okay, so the fallen promoted demons to devils and protected everyone from the abyss creatures."

He pushed away from the workbench and ambled toward the forge. "Yes, they recruited armies and fought the daimon threat, pushing it back into the abyss where it was controlled for centuries until one day when it broke free." He lit the fire in the forge. "On that day, the leader of the fallen, Lucifer Morningstar, went into the abyss to beat back the threat." Sin turned his head, offering me his profile and half a wicked smile. "The fool gave his celestial light to close the abyss and lock away the chaotic forces."

A shiver ran up my spine, because was it my imagination or did Sin's chin seem more pointed, his horns longer and thicker in that moment?

I blinked and he was just Sin again. "They named Morningstar territory after him, didn't they?"

He snorted. "A flimsy tribute."

"And Satan?"

He used bellows to crank up the fire. "A title bestowed to Lucifer's general, Beelzebub." He picked up his hammer. "Six of the nine kingdoms fell in the Chaos War. The three remaining princes have equal power. Satan's seat resolves disputes and maintains peace. Morningstar has the strongest army, and the courts are home to the most powerful devils. But now Satan is dead. Things are about to get messy."

Which reminded me of this ascension stuff. "What happens now? What is this ascension?"

Sin stoked the forge. "Not part of our deal, Nyx. You asked for an understanding of the hierarchy, and I gave that to you. We're done."

Shit. What had I learned from what he'd told me aside from the fact that I knew nothing? I was no one. "Why would a demon or a devil or whatever put a hit out on me? There has to be a mistake."

He tutted. "You haven't been listening, Nyx. A hit is a powerful *written* contract and demons don't make written contracts. Devils do."

A devil...I was looking for a devil, and those could only be found in the courts of Morningstar. It wasn't much, but it was more than I'd come here with.

"Thank you, Sin."

But the clang of hammer on metal told me he was already lost in his world of creation.

CHASE WAS on his feet and alert, head tipped up to the sky, when I joined him outside.

"What's going on, buddy?" I looked up to see a golden sheen in the air. "What is that?"

"It's happening," an imp to my left said.

"It's the final sweep, then it begins," a slender female demon said.

I stepped closer to them. "Hey, what's happening?"

The imp hawked and spat in my direction. "Get away from me, demon blood."

Yeah, my kind weren't exactly welcomed with open arms in Morningstar. We were scum to the pure bloods.

Chase growled at the imp, who backed up quickly.

"It doesn't concern your kind," the female said. "A demon blood won't be marked."

"Marked for what?"

She frowned. "Hush, it's happening."

And sure enough, the market had fallen into silence as

the world lit up with flecks of gold. They drifted over demons, kissing skin and then dissipating.

"Is it happening? Am I marked?" someone said.

"Am I one?" another asked.

This was bullshit and the demon was right, it had nothing to do with me, but for some reason my feet refused to budge. As the gold flecks fell and kissed upturned faces, groans of disappointment followed. Demons scanned each other.

"Should have known," the imp said. "He'd be fucking the devils, not the demons, not unless they be court bitches." He hawked and spat again.

"Who the fuck are you talking about?" My forehead tingled and I rubbed at it.

The imp glared at me, mouth parting, probably to tell me to fuck off, but then his gaze flew to my forehead and his eyes went round.

"Lucifer save us." He shook his head, his mouth breaking into an evil grin. "Ha, the fucker done fucked a mortal." But then his face paled as if he'd realized something. He sniffed. "It's changed. Your scent has changed."

Eyes were on me now, hot gazes, people closing in.

I held up my hands. "Whoa, chill out. Back up."

"We can't have this," the female demon said. "This is prohibited. She can't be permitted to exist."

Murmurs of agreement drifted over the crowd.

"Kill her," someone said.

Chase stepped in front of me, his body expanding to its full height and width, which was pretty epic, but not to this mob, who for some reason wanted to kill me.

What the hell was happening?

The imp flew at me, but Chase snapped, catching his arm and tearing it from his body.

That gave the crowd pause, enough for us to make a getaway. "Chase, run!"

My pooch looked torn, but when I ran, he joined me. I sprinted for the station, angry, murderous mob on my tail, confusion clouding my mind. The world had gone insane.

The station was in sight, arch gleaming, golden train waiting for its next load of passengers. Almost there.

The clatter of hooves and the whinny of horses rose over the bellows of the mob. A shadow fell in our path as two huge, equine creatures blocked our exit. Red eyes gleamed, smoke plumed from flared nostrils, and dark fog spilled off their backs, sliding past me and Chase to create a barrier between us and the mob who'd surprisingly come to a halt too.

The slam of a door drew my eye to the obsidian carriage attached to the beasts and the male stepping out of it.

I caught the flash of sapphire eyes beneath angry brows and the downturn of a displeased mouth before his gaze settled on me and his voice, filled with lethal authority, shattered the sudden silence.

"Satan spawn, you will come with me."

Chapter Six

"Satan spawn?" I stared at the demon in confusion. Wait, was he a demon or a devil? He didn't have any visible physical demon characteristics. Shit, was he one of the fallen Sin had told me about?

It didn't matter right now. "I think you have me confused with someone else."

"The mark on your forehead begs to differ." His tone was calm and cool now, but there was an urgency in his sapphire eyes as they flicked over my head toward the mob, held back by the dark fog. "Get in the carriage. I'm not sure how long my allure can hold off the mob."

So that's what the foggy stuff was.

"Now." This time there was a snap to his voice.

I didn't take well to being ordered about and my instinct was to argue and demand answers, but self-preservation reared its head.

Escape the mob and ask questions later.

Chase chuffed and nudged me, reinforcing my decision.

I made a beeline for the carriage, Chase on my tail. I expected the guy to kick up a fuss about my hound buddy tagging along, and I was ready to tell him to piss off if he did, but he didn't protest when Chase climbed into the carriage behind me.

The inside was dark wood and crimson velvet, like the inside of a plush coffin. I suppressed a shudder and took a window seat while Chase parked himself in the center of the floor, creating a barrier between me and the guy when he climbed in.

The demon, devil, whatever, closed the door and rapped his knuckles on the roof of the contraption.

The horses whinnied and the carriage lurched into motion. The fog outside my window parted briefly to give me a view of the thwarted mob, some shaking their fists at me in comic-book fashion, others spitting on the ground as if desperate to rid themselves of a bad taste.

It would have been funny if not for the very serious fact that they wanted to kill me, and they would have if this dude hadn't turned up.

Speaking of which...I raked my gaze over my savior. Yep, definitely no visible demonic features. His face was lean with high cheekbones, giving him an aristocratic air, but there was a dark glint in his eyes, a warning that if he was pushed too far he would snap back. Hard. I'd seen that glint in another man's eyes not too long ago, and I recognized it as power, reined in. Controlled. The kind of power that could burn someone up and spit them out. This time it was packaged neatly in expensively tailored clothes that fit his lean, broad-shouldered form perfectly.

"Have you finished your perusal?" he asked, the corner of his mouth lifting slightly in an action that would have denoted amusement if it had reached his eyes. But those peepers remained cold and assessing.

Yeah... He was giving me the once-over too. "What are you? Demon, devil, or fallen?"

He arched a brow, those cold eyes lighting up as if he was impressed that I knew the classifications. Thank goodness for Sin and his mini history lesson.

"Neither," he said finally. "I'm Nephalem and my name is Artimus."

"Artimus...Okay, and what's a Nephalem?"

The corner of his mouth lifted again. "A product of a demon and fallen angel pairing, like all of your siblings."

Siblings. My pulse quickened. I had siblings? I tamped down on the strange emotions surging in my chest and focused on the pertinent fact that he believed I was a spawn of Satan.

I touched my forehead and he tracked the action.

"Do you want to see it?" he asked. "It will only last for another twelve hours."

I swallowed the lump in my throat. "Yes."

He pulled a small compact from his pocket, flipped it open, and held it out to me.

I leaned forward and stared at the golden arcane symbol glowing in the center of my forehead.

There was no avoiding it now.

"Okay." I sat back in my seat. "That explains why my human mother wanted to be rid of me so badly. She didn't bang just any old demon, she banged Satan. Wait, I wonder if she even knew?" I frowned up at Artimus. "And why the hell would Satan come to the mortal realm to sleep with my mortal mother?" Because there was no way she'd have come to Morningstar territory. Humans didn't do crazy-ass shit like that.

He shrugged. "I can't account for Satan's actions. But I

can say that he was known for being generous with his seed."

Seed, urgh.

"All your siblings are Nephalem, and as you may already have surmised, as Satan's daughter, you are *not* a demon blood as you've probably been led to believe."

I hadn't surmised anything until he said it, but now I was surmising the crap out of things. "I'm the spawn of a fallen angel?"

"A Nephilim. The daughter of a fallen angel and a mortal."

"Wait, didn't you just say Nephilim were the spawn of fallen and demon pairings?"

"No. I said Ne*pha*lem were the product of fallen and demon procreation. You are Ne*phi*lim." His sapphire eyes darkened, and his mouth turned down slightly. "Unfortunately, all Nephilim were put to death centuries ago, and an edict woven into law stated that no more should be made."

"What? Why?"

"Nephilim inevitably devolve into insanity. They're powerful, and they're dangerous."

"Well, tendency to go insane aside, I have zero power, so there has to be some kind of mistake."

"There is no mistake. The mark on your head is definitive proof of your bloodline. However, evolution may have dulled a Nephilim's power, which will be an advantage *and* a disadvantage for you."

My mind raced to keep up. "In what way?"

"The advantage is you probably won't be executed for being a Nephilim."

I stared at him. "*Probably*?"

He shrugged. "Most certainly. Any creature with any

power can sense the lack of yours. You're not a threat." He said it in such a derisive manner that the urge to pull out my daggers and show him just how much of a threat I could be had my fists curling.

But I hadn't survived this long alone in the city by making dumb moves, and attacking a Nephalem seemed pretty high on the dumb moves list.

I let my agitation go on a breath and settled back in my seat. "Power isn't only about magical ability, you know."

He tipped his head to one side, as if considering it. "Maybe not in the world you're used to, but it is in Morningstar."

"Fair enough. If my advantage is *almost certainly* not getting executed, I dread to think what my *disadvantage* is."

"You'll be outmatched by your siblings in the ascension trials."

"Trials?" My mind spun, making connections. "You're bringing all the spawn together to face off against each other…for the throne? The throne has to go to one of his spawn, doesn't it?"

His eyes lit up again, as if he was pleased with my deductive reasoning. "Correct. You're lucky I found you when I did."

I ignored the pound of my pulse. "Lucky? Lucky is finding a four-leaf clover or winning the lottery or inheriting a huge sum of money. Finding out you're the spawn of Satan is *not* lucky. Especially when you might only *almost certainly* not be executed."

"*Not* being torn to shreds is lucky," he insisted. "And believe me, that's exactly what would have happened to you back there if I hadn't shown up."

I recalled the look of horrific revelation on the imp's face. He'd said my scent changed. Had the mark done that?

Altered my scent somehow. Had I somehow passed for demon blood all this time because of a false scent? Surely another supernatural would have realized I wasn't demon blood otherwise.

The imp had realized I was a Nephilim as soon as the mark appeared, they all had, so they'd banded together to kill me, risked getting blasted by whatever epic power I was supposed to have. That's how strongly they felt about not having a Nephilim ruler. And of course, if they believed I had power, they also believed I had a strong chance of winning these trials. More reason to end me.

It was all slotting into place. All except Artimus's timely appearance. "And how did you just happen to show up to save the day?" If he said he happened to be passing by, I'd punch him in the face and leg it, because I didn't believe in coincidences, not ones of this magnitude anyway.

He pressed his lips together. "I was tracking the revelation spell."

Okay, I could live with that response. "Why?"

His shoulders slumped slightly. "Satan was a close friend of mine. We have...history. I intend to ensure his progeny are taken care of, and that they all get a fair chance at winning the throne."

His words rang with sincerity, but I had no intention of trying out for the throne. "Look, I appreciate the assist back there, but I'm not interested in the throne, so if you can just turn the carriage around and drop me at the station, I'd be grateful."

He stared at me as if I'd started speaking in tongues.

I resisted the urge to cross my arms defensively. "What?"

"It's clear you don't understand how this works, and why should you, you've been raised outside of Morningstar." He leaned forward, bracing his forearms on his taut thighs and momentarily stealing the oxygen from the air because he was too close, so close I could see slivers of gold in his sapphire eyes, radiating outward like pretty little daggers. "The ascension isn't optional." His breath kissed my face, bringing the scent of honeysuckle into my nose. "It's compulsory." His attention dropped to my mouth, releasing me from his magnetic eye lock.

I exhaled and drew back, pressing myself into the plush velvet seat, because his presence was both intoxicating and alarming, heating the blood in my veins and sending it rushing faster through my limbs, demanding I act. Fuck, this guy was sending my fight-flight response into overdrive. I locked my muscles, tensing to keep myself in my seat and stop myself from launching my body at him.

"Back up." My tone was a growl.

His expression shuttered and he obliged, moving back into his seat in a fluid motion. With his aura out of my personal space, I was able to consider his actual words.

A band wrapped itself around my chest. "This is bullshit. I didn't sign up for anything and you can't make me take part if I don't want to." Okay, so I sounded like a petulant child, but fuck that. This was not part of my life plan.

He sighed. "*You* didn't sign up for anything, but your bloodline did. Satan made a pact and the Erinyes have it in blood. His spawn will compete for the throne upon his passing."

I had no idea who these Erinyes were and didn't give a damn. How could a father I'd never met, one who'd had no interest in me, dictate what I did with my future? He had no right.

"I'm not doing it."

Exasperation colored his features. "Then you will most

certainly be executed. If you run, the helhunters will be sent after you, and once they find you, they'll—"

"They already came for me and failed."

"What?" His brow creased in a frown. "Helhunters came after you?"

I sighed. "That's what I said."

He sucked his bottom lip into his mouth, brows coming down in concern. "This doesn't make sense. Why would someone want to kill you...Unless...Unless they knew of your existence *before* the revelation spell. But how?" he mused out loud. "It's obvious Satan kept you away for a reason. You were his mistake."

"Gee, thanks."

He continued as if I hadn't spoken. "I was his closest friend and he never told me." His brows shot up in sudden revelation.

"What? What are you thinking?"

"Vinal, Satan's advisor, is the only other person who could have known of your existence. He could have known that Satan broke the rules."

"You think he sent the helhunters after me to kill me and prevent the truth from coming out." My heart sank and the dark ache his words had evoked could no longer be ignored. "I really was unwanted, wasn't I?"

I hated how small my voice sounded and immediately wanted to take back the words because now he was looking at me with pity, and that pissed me off even more. Fuck them. Fuck them all. They'd thrown me away, tried to kill me to prevent my existence coming to light, and it was obvious from the way Artimus was looking at me that he didn't expect me to survive these trials.

I was the stain on Satan's character, the Nephilim who'd

been neutered by nature and was now the lame horse in an epic race for glory.

At least that's what they thought.

But they were wrong. I sat back in my seat and crossed my arms. "How long until we get there?"

Artimus's eyes narrowed speculatively, then his lips curved in a smile. "An hour. We'll be there in an hour."

I placed my hand on Chase's neck and the hound locked gazes with me as if to say, *are we really going to do this*?

I returned the question in his eyes with a determined look that said, *yes, boy, we totally are.*

Chapter Seven

The colorful market gave way to a town set on a rise with whitewashed three-story homes huddled together side by side. There was no pavement, just a winding road for both pedestrians and carriages, not that it slowed us down. I guess it was up to the pedestrians to get the hell out of the way. Before I knew it, we were out of the town and on a wide road flanked by rolling hills of green and gold. The sky was a swirl of pink and violet punctuated by poofy white clouds and the air had a zesty zing to it, but in mere seconds the colors bled away, leaving the world white and covered in glittering snow. Talk about a season change.

I sat back to allow my head to clear. The atmosphere here was different from the mainland. Potent and heady.

Artimus had taken off his tailored jacket, loosened the top button of his shirt, and rolled up his sleeves, taking him from imperious aristocrat to rakish rogue in a matter of seconds. He was dangerously attractive. How old was he? I was about to ask when I spotted a pillar in the distance. An inky black finger pointing up at the sky.

"What's that?"

He glanced out the window briefly. "A Monoport. A doorway to one of the nine demon realms. That one is inactive."

"It belongs to one of the six realms that fell in the Chaos War?"

His brows lifted in surprise. "You've done research. Not many outsiders know our history."

I shrugged a nonchalant shoulder. "I did a little."

His mouth twitched as if he was fighting a smile. "What did you learn?"

I rattled off what Sin had told me about the Chaos War, the daimons, and the abyss.

Artimus listened, nodding from time to time. "Good, you know the basics. But do you know about the courts that represent the three remaining realms?"

I shook my head. "Zilch."

"Would you like to know?"

"Knowledge is power."

He smiled, a close-lipped smile that almost reached his eyes. "There are three courts affiliated with the three remaining realms. The Court of Ivory, the Court of Flame, and the Court of Shadows. Ivory is affiliated to Superbia, which is ruled by Prince Ramiel, Shadow to Libidine and Prince Merihem, and flame to Iram and Prince Levistus."

"You don't happen to have a pen, do you?" Not that I needed one, I had an excellent memory.

He smiled thinly. "I suppose it is a lot of information. Think of it this way. The Court of Ivory is related to pride, the Court of Shadow to lust, and the Court of Flame to wrath, the emotions that best encapsulate their princes."

"Okay. Got it."

"But you won't be meeting the princes, not unless you

become the new Satan. They prefer to remain in their demon realms. Each has a mouthpiece here. A duke who rules over the court affiliated to them. You'll meet them soon enough. No doubt they'll be vetting the spawn to see who they should back in this race."

"What do you mean?"

He sighed. "Think about it, Nyx."

I did and the answer was obvious. "They want to be close to the new Satan."

"Having favor with Satan is a valuable commodity to the princes. It could allow them sway in future votes for… whatever." He looked out the window. "The princes are obsessed with power."

"And you? What about you? Do *you* want power?"

He snorted. "Trust me, if I was interested in power, I wouldn't be wasting my time educating you. I'd be back at the keep insinuating myself with one of the more promising candidates."

"Ouch."

He smiled with his eyes this time. "No hard feelings."

"None taken. So, what *is* your agenda?"

He chuckled. "Would you believe me if I said I had none?"

Like heck. "No."

"Clever girl."

Our gazes locked for a long beat and a kernel of warmth bloomed in my chest. He broke eye contact with a slight frown, and I turned my head to look out the window. Heightened emotions could flip my sex switch, and today had been a day of highs for sure, but getting into bed with a demon, devil, or a Nephalem was not on my agenda. Sin was an exception to my rule.

His face came to mind, the way he'd looked at me when

he'd asked for a kiss in payment, the conflict, his change of mind, then what he'd done to my body.

My neck grew warm.

Dammit. Stop thinking about it.

"Are you nervous?" Artimus asked. "Your pulse has quickened."

Fucking great, an emotion detector. "Yes." I looked back at him. "I'd be *insane* not to be, and considering my Nephilim nature..."

He smiled properly this time, showcasing even white teeth with pronounced canines. That smile transformed his face from handsome to stunning. What kind of demon was his mother? I wanted to ask, but maybe that was a question for another day, assuming he stuck around to keep an eye on me. It hit me then that I desperately wanted him to, which annoyed me because I didn't do the whole needing people unless those people were Orina, Quinn, or Chase.

I kept my circle small, and it had served me well. But here, in Morningstar territory, with a novel task ahead of me, I was out of my element. It would be stupid not to collect allies because I'd need someone to help me navigate this new world.

"So, Artimus, how do you feel about mentoring me?"

He arched a brow. "Is that a proposition?"

Why did he make it sound so intimate? "Only if you say yes."

He slow-blinked. "You'd put your trust in me?"

I shrugged. "I have to put it in someone, and you seem like a viable candidate." I bared my teeth in mock anger. "But if you fuck me over, I'll slit your throat."

He let out a bark of laughter. "You remind me of him. That is very much the kind of thing he would have said."

Him? Satan. The father who threw me away. The humor left me. "Yeah? Well, I wouldn't know."

I turned my attention to the view once more and spotted a dark line on the horizon. "What's that?"

"Lake Morbidus. It surrounds the keep. The water is considered to have healing properties, not that anyone would dare take a dip in it, because of the creatures that reside in it."

"What kind of creatures?"

"Creatures able to strip flesh from bone in a matter of seconds."

The lake drew closer, and the keep came into view beyond it, wreathed in mist and looking impressively spooky. It grew larger and vaster the closer we got. The place was the size of a small town.

I leaned into the window to catch sight of a bridge stretching across the lethal waters and a moment later we were clattering across it, over seething dark waves, where I caught sight of a jagged fin or two. The crossing took several minutes because the lake was that wide. Finally, we hit the cobbled streets of the keep.

Nerves fluttered to life in my chest as the carriage slowed to a gentle rocking gait and my stomach tightened as the full reality of what I was, where I was, and what was about to happen hit home.

I took a calming breath. "What happens when we get there?"

"We'll demand an audience with the Erinyes, get the matter of a possible execution out of the way, expose Vinal for trying to kill you and harboring Satan's mistake, and if all goes well, get you to the residential quarters with all the other spawn."

"That easy, huh?"

His expression hardened. "Oh, Nyx, if only it were."

These people had the power to end me, and as hard as I could fight, and as tough as I was, there would be no fighting off a full-blood demon, not with the measly arsenal I had on me.

I did *not* want to die.

My life was in Artimus's hands. "Get me through this, and I swear to you, I'll be the best fucking candidate for the throne you've ever seen."

The carriage came to a halt and Artimus's lips curved in a wicked smile. "I'll hold you to that."

Chapter Eight

Funny how emotions could oscillate between gung-ho and *fuck, I might just shit my pants*. But I wasn't a *shitting my pants* kind of gal, so this was a new feeling for me.

I'd give myself a pass, though, because if I didn't get flashes of fear and doubt in this situation, it would probably mean I was a psychopath, in which case, would I even be having this internal monologue with myself?

Shit, Artimus was waiting for me to get out of the carriage. He'd donned his jacket again and was cutting a regal, imperious figure once more. His face had settled into an almost bored, seen-it-all expression. Not the expression of someone who gave a damn what happened to me.

It was an act. It had to be, right?

"Nyx?" His eyes locked with mine and a flash of urgency lit them up. "We must make the meeting."

Yes, the meeting the Erinyes would be having that we hoped to crash.

I made to climb out of the carriage, but Chase beat me to it, coming to stand between Artimus and me. His breath plumed in the air, creating a misty barrier as he used his body to force the Nephalem back a step.

Artimus raked Chase over. "Courageous pup you have."

I climbed out, registering the intense cold for the first time. The ground crackled with frost beneath my boots and the air held the dead stillness of winter. How had it been so warm in the carriage?

I sank my fingers into the fur at Chase's neck. "Chase is my best friend and my business partner."

Chase chuffed in agreement.

Artimus's eyes narrowed slightly. "I should warn you, they might not allow you to keep him."

A flash of anger raced through my veins. "And I should warn you that he's not a fucking possession, and if anyone lays a hand on him, then I will hurt them. I might get my ass kicked doing it, but trust me, I'll leave my mark."

He inclined his head. "Let's hope it doesn't come to that. Follow me."

He set off across the frosted cobblestones of a huge courtyard filled with carriages similar to the one we'd traveled in. None had equine beasts hitched to them, though, and when I looked back, neither did ours. When had they been untethered and taken away?

Gray stone walls stretched out to my left and right, the outer keep walls, so high they reached for the sky. Artimus led us toward a stone arch set in a tower emblazoned with crests and dotted with iron balconies holding figures dressed in gray and black to blend with the stone. They were so silent and unmoving that I'd have mistaken them for statues if I hadn't caught the movement of their eyes as they latched onto me.

"Now that's creepy."

Artimus didn't glance up. "The Eyes protect the keep

from unwanted visitors. They're our alarm system, and our first defense."

"What are they?"

"Abyssbloods who owe fealty to Morningstar. And before you ask what an abyssblood is, the term refers to any breed of creature we liberated from the abyss when fighting the daimons."

"Getting fed up with my questions already?"

"Hardly," he drawled.

"Good, because you'd make a shitty mentor otherwise."

We passed under the arch and into a wide tunnel lit with blue flame sconces that sucked the chill from the air and pushed heat into my bones. The reprieve was momentary, and we were back out in the frosty air too soon.

This time it took everything I had not to suck in a chilly breath and stare at the vista before me. I'd expected an austere, forbidding castle of crumbling gray stone with maybe a gargoyle or two clinging to the eaves, but what I got was a shimmering tower made from silver stone, so high that it vanished into the churning violet sky. Silver birches lined the broad path leading up to the tower's wide stone steps where figures lounged about, chatting in clusters or sitting in groups. Some had crimson skin, some merely had a tinge of red. I spotted horns, red eyes, tails, and bat-like wings. Heat rose off some of their bodies, melting the air and leaving clear patches on stone around them.

Demons and devils no doubt, and they were all dressed similarly in gray, black, and silver.

I leaned closer to Artimus. "Who are they?"

"Some of the keep staff. It's repast time now. The hour when the staff are permitted to leave their posts to eat and rest. Shift changes happen now too."

They watched me as we approached. Most turned their

attention away when we began climbing the steps, but a couple continued to stare, their gazes more assessing than curious. Can't say I wasn't relieved when we reached the top of the steps. We stepped through a small door cut into the larger door and onto the black and silver marble floors of a circular space with an impressive staircase at its center. The bannisters were carved with intricate scale detail mimicking serpents that twined around twin balustrades at the bottom of the staircase.

The ceiling here was high-vaulted, the stone and wood carved with images of winged beings and horned demons in various poses of battle. But what drew my attention were the three bricked-up arches to my left. The stone that made each arch was a different color—white, red, and inky black.

"What are those?" I pointed at the closest arch.

"Gateways to the three courts," Artimus said. "Only accessible by members of the court or invited guests. You don't need to worry about them for now. You'll be introduced to the relevant members of each court at the opening of the ascension."

"If I don't get executed first."

"Yes."

I smiled wryly to hide my nerves. "I love the way you don't sugarcoat things."

I caught the slight curve of his mouth, an almost smile, before he began to climb the steps. "The courts may be connected to Morningstar but the creatures who reside there do not come here often."

"And why is that?"

"Many are pure demon, and the atmosphere of this world affects them negatively." We reached the top of the steps and passed through a set of double doors onto the first floor, where another flight of stairs sat to our right. We bypassed those and took the corridor to our left.

"Are you saying the atmosphere of the courts is different?"

"The courts exist in pockets of reality somewhere between here and the demonic realm. Here in Morningstar the atmosphere is attuned to mortals, as is the language."

"Wait, I'm not sure what you mean?"

"I mean not all creatures speak the mortal tongue; there is magic in the air that translates speech. A stipulation of the Accords."

"Wow, well, that explains a lot." Did Sin speak English or was he speaking a different language? I mean his mouth moved with the words. Did the magic make it look that way? Or did it alter the words as he spoke, shaping his mouth to make them?

"Don't think too hard on it," Artimus said. "It's a minor thing."

I let it go, instead taking in the landscape paintings covering the walls. Red skies and rocky hills.

He flicked a wrist toward the nearest painting. "Paintings of the demon realm. The forests of Erinyes, to be precise."

"You mentioned the Erinyes before. Who are they?"

"The law keepers of Morningstar. Powerful demons of the ancient bloodlines. Warriors in a past life. When the fallen came to the demon realm, it was the Erinyes who'd been fighting the daimonic threat from the abyss. They accepted the fallen as allies and eventually as their masters. But make no mistake, they are vicious with a keen eye for the truth. Whatever you do, do not lie to them. They will smell it."

"Great. Okay. No lies. I got it." I didn't need to lie. I was well versed in skirting the truth. In fact, if there'd been an

Olympic sport in truth dodging, I'd be champion. But he didn't need to know that.

The corridor opened into a creamy white entrance hall with red and black accents. Several closed doors lined the walls, and in the center of the hall sat a woman at a desk scratching words into a scroll with quill and ink. The pose was pure scholar, but her outfit screamed fighter: a chain mail vest, metal shoulder guards, and a silver helm with wings coming off it like tiny horns.

She glanced up and I got a good look at her. Her nose was slightly too big for her face, eyes too round, and her mouth was a little too thin to be feminine. She reminded me of a bird of prey in human form.

She glared at Artimus. "They're in a meeting. You know that."

"I do, and I also have a standing invitation from Erinea to join at any time."

She raked him over in obvious derision, lips thinning even further until they were a straight line, nostrils flaring. "Erinea always did have a soft spot for the pretty ones." She jerked her head toward the door to her left. "Go on. You might as well join them too."

"Too?" Artimus leaned in and pressed the tips of his fingers to the desk. "Who else is in there, Cerinea?"

She smirked up at him, her round eyes lighting up with wicked glee. "Oh, I wouldn't dream of spoiling the surprise. But I will say...you aren't the only pretty fool to grace Erinea's bed."

Her bed? Oh...right. I flicked a glance at Artimus in time to catch the tic of his jaw, the only indication he was put out by her comment, before his expression settled into a polite smile.

"Oh, I don't doubt it," Artimus said. "Erinea has

particular tastes when it comes to her bed partners. She likes them well endowed, so please, don't take her rejection too personally."

Wait...what? Was Cerinea interested in Erinea? And why the fuck did their names have to sound so similar?

Artimus straightened with a smug smile. "Always a pleasure, Cerinea." His tone dripped with insincerity.

I followed him to the door, glancing back in time to see the look of utter devastation on Cerinea's face a moment before she masked it with a snarl.

"I didn't say you could take the mongrel and the pup with you," she snapped.

Artimus's shoulders stiffened, and when he spoke his tone was the stab of icicles. "I don't need your permission, Cerinea, and you'd be well versed to remember your place."

She glared at his back for a long beat before dropping her gaze. "Yes, seneschal."

He pushed open the door into a plush-carpeted room bathed in the light of a setting sun. A fire roared in a stone hearth and figures sat in high-backed chairs around an impressively large table.

My gaze tripped over the figures, all female, dressed similarly to Cerinea in chainmail tunics with shoulder guards, but their helms were placed on the table in front of them. I skimmed past a figure near the head of the table and then did a double-take. Whoa, hello, you're not a woman.

Nope, this figure was very much a male. He held a silver goblet in his hand, and his tawny gaze was fixed on me in an assessing manner. I arched a brow and assessed him right back. Dark cropped hair, solid-looking build from what I could see of it. He was dressed in a dark, short-sleeve T-shirt that looked out of place amidst the medieval armor but totally at home on his body.

He set his goblet down and I noted the shimmer skate up his bare forearm and settle at his bicep. Silvery lines of an intricate tattoo that was barely visible.

He tracked my gaze, looking down at his arm then back to me with an unreadable expression.

Someone cleared their throat and my gaze whipped across the room to the man sitting by the wall at a small desk, scroll to hand. He had a wizened air about him, deep-set dark eyes, and a red tinge to his skin. His robes were black and edged with silver.

The same kind of robes the demons outside had been wearing.

"Artimus, what a pleasant surprise," the woman at the head of the table said. Navy lines made patterns across her forehead, pushing up into her hair where dark feathers grew out of her scalp, cascading down her back in place of hair. Her features were harsh and sharp, a slightly hooked nose and a pointy chin, but her lips were full and her eyes slightly slanted. "Come join us. We were just discussing the ascen…" Her gaze flicked to me. "You brought a guest."

"Satan spawn," Artimus said casually. "Picked her up in the market district when I was returning from doing some…business."

Erinea's eyes lit up for some reason. "Oh?"

Artimus smirked conspiratorially. "I'll share later."

Erinea's plumes fluffed up. "Indeed." Her gaze fell to me, the heat in them cooling. "And why do you bring her here?"

"What do you sense from her, Erinea?"

Erinea's eyes lit up as if Artimus had issued her a challenge, and for all I knew he had. She sat back in her seat, giving me a slow once-over. Her nostrils flared slightly, and her dark brown eyes lightened to a warm honey tone. Long seconds passed in which she just stared at me with those beacon-like eyes. "Practically powerless," she said finally. "Strange for a spawn of Satan, yet the mark confirms her status." She pouted, taking advantage of her full mouth. "Not demon or devil...too human-looking..." Her eyes widened. "No..." Her gaze flew to Artimus. "A Nephilim?"

The other Erinyes moved so fast I barely registered motion before I was surrounded by them.

Oh, crap.

Chapter Nine

A steady clicking filled the air as the Erinyes surrounded me. It was a warning, but where was it coming from? My gaze was drawn to their neck where a bulge had formed and was vibrating.

They were making the sound, and it was getting faster, leading up to a predatory attack.

My gut screamed danger. It screamed fight or flee.

Fight was my usual modus operandi, but right now, flee would have worked much better. Unfortunately, making a break for it wasn't an option. I needed to stay calm, stand my ground but not antagonize; still, my instincts had my thighs bunching and my body falling into a defensive stance.

Artimus sighed heavily. "Come now, there is no need for such measures. Like you said, she has no power."

"None that you can sense." The dark-haired man spoke for the first time. He set his goblet on the table and pushed back his seat, unfurling his frame to an epic height. Damn, how tall was this guy, definitely over six five for sure. The air behind him shimmered and wavered. Wait...were those wings? No. There was nothing, maybe just a trick of the light?

"Care to test her, Zepar?" Artimus said. "Your opinion is always valued." His tone suggested otherwise but Zepar didn't bite.

Instead, he made his way around the table and through the barrier of Erinyes to stand before me.

I craned my neck to look up at him. I was tall for a woman, five seven to be precise, but these guys made me feel minute. A novel feeling. Zepar's tawny gaze skimmed over my face, settling for a moment too long on my lips before traveling down to the pulse at my neck. "I assume you've completed a taste test, Artimus?"

"You know me too well, Zepar," Artimus said.

Once again, his tone clearly suggested otherwise, and once again Zepar didn't bite.

Also, I was confused. What did Zepar mean by taste test?

"Hello, Satan spawn, I'm going to test your power now. But I'll have to touch you to do that."

My pulse quickened. I didn't like being touched, not unless it was on my terms. "The name's Nyx, and what kind of touching are we talking about?"

Was that amusement in his eyes? "A simple laying of hands on your flesh. Your cheek will do."

I huffed. "Fine. Get it over with."

He tipped his head to the side slightly. "You don't like to be touched?"

"Not by random demons."

He smirked. "In that case, you're in luck. I'm no demon."

"What?" All thoughts fled from my mind as Zepar caressed my jaw with his fingers. A zing raced over my skin, and I pulled my head back instinctively. "What was that?"

His eyes flinched. "You shouldn't feel anything."

"Well, I did."

His fingers hovered mere inches from my cheek. "May I?"

I nodded. "Sure." I was ready for the zing, but this time it didn't come. His palm settled against my cheek for a moment, warmth seeping into my skin. It felt...nice. And it was over too soon.

Zepar dropped his hand and nodded in Erinea's direction. "Barely a sliver of power."

"Intriguing," she said.

"Evolution," Artimus said. "Nature neutering the threat."

"Indeed," Zepar agreed.

I was done being spoken about like I was some raggedy-ass mongrel they'd dragged in off the street.

I crossed my arms and tipped my hand to the side. "I'm far from neutered. I may not have magic at my fingertips, but I can turn pretty much anything in this room into a weapon."

"A Nephilim is a threat," the man in the corner of the room said. "The law is clear on that matter."

"Vinal." Artimus smiled. "How nice of you to chime in. I was wondering how long it would take for you to break your silence."

Vinal? Satan's advisor? This was the guy who'd probably sent the helhunters after me.

"We cannot suffer this mistake to stand," Vinal said.

Thank goodness I had a thick skin. "Fuck you, Vinal." The words were out before I could stop them.

Artimus made a sound of exasperation. "Excuse her. She was raised outside of Morningstar. Which you know, don't you, Vinal?"

Vinal paled. "What are you talking about. How would I know that?"

"Satan's beloved advisor. His confidant. You must have known of her existence."

"I knew no such thing," Vinal said.

"I can smell your fear, old man," Zepar said.

The Erinyes angled their bodies toward him.

"You'd do whatever it takes to protect the memory of your king, wouldn't you, Vinal?" Artimus said.

Vinal's chest rose and fell faster. He dropped his gaze. An admission of guilt if ever there was one.

"You sent helhunters to kill me."

"If they wanted you dead, you would be," he said softly.

"A scare tactic, then." Zepar sounded impressed. "Ah, Vinal, you should reconsider my offer to come work for me."

Erinea was watching me with a shrewd expression. "It would have been better if you'd stayed away, child. You may not have any power, but the law on the existence of Nephilim is clear. We execute."

My blood ran cold. I waited for Artimus to intervene and say something.

Finally, he shrugged. "It's the decision of the Erinyes, of course. As law keepers you know best which law to uphold, the protection of Satan spawn or the execution of Nephilim. I merely did my duty by protecting her from an angry mob and bringing her to you."

Erinea smiled warmly at Artimus. "And we appreciate your consideration, seneschal."

He inclined his head while holding her gaze and there was no mistaking the sexual tension in the air between those two.

"Kill her or let her join the trials, it's no concern of mine." He headed for the exit and the sting of betrayal lit up my chest.

The fucking bastard was throwing me to the wolves.

Chase growled, making his presence known as he came to stand beside me.

I placed my hand on his back. It looked like I'd have to fight for my own life. "You want to kill me, then you'll have a fight on your hands. I won't go down easy, and I guarantee I'll take a couple of you with me."

Zepar crossed his arms, biceps bulging. "She has backbone. No power, but a smart mouth, and we all know how the courts love to be entertained."

"The ascension isn't about entertainment," one of the Erinyes snapped.

"Oh, wake up, Rinea," Erinea drawled. "Everything is about entertainment when it comes to the courts, and the more visitors Morningstar has, the more chances we have of strengthening our alliances."

"All the contracts that must be updated and resworn..." Rinea's gaze flicked from side to side as she considered this.

"The dukes and lords do like to avoid their responsibilities." Erinea flicked a glance Zepar's way.

He shrugged one muscle-rounded shoulder. "Only devils love being tied in red tape."

"Red tape that the fallen gifted us." Her eyes gleamed. "But yes." She looked at me now. "I think on this occasion we can forgive the accident of your birth. Both laws are clear, and bearing in mind your lack of power, we can allow the scales to tip in favor of the protection law."

I released the breath I hadn't realized I'd been holding.

She waved me away. "Go now. Ask Cerinea to take you to Nugen."

That was it?

I was free to go?

I backed toward the door.

"Wait," Zepar said. "I'll take you. I need to speak to Nugen anyway."

"Oh?" Erinea's brows shot up. "Have you chosen a candidate to sponsor?"

He gave her a small smile. "I have indeed."

WHY WAS I disappointed not to find Artimus waiting for me outside the room? Oh, yeah, because the fucker had agreed to mentor me and then thrown me to the vultures. I mean, I should have known better; he was part demon, after all, even though he didn't look it, and demons served only their own agendas.

Assuming I mattered to him had been an oversight on my part, and now I had a new tag-along. One I knew literally nothing about, except that he could sense magic with a touch and that he had status enough to be hanging out with the Erinyes.

If I was going to survive these trials, I was going to need allies, and I may have miscalculated with Artimus, but I wouldn't make the same mistake again.

"You're thinking awfully hard, little Nephilim," Zepar said.

"I'm wondering who and what you are and why you're really accompanying me to see this Nugen."

"All very valid questions."

He led me up a flight of steps onto a flagstone corridor, and I was beginning to think he wasn't going to answer me when he finally spoke.

"I'm Duke Zepar of the Court of Ivory, and I'm one of the fallen. Not an original." He rolled his eyes. "But the progeny of two fallen, and before you ask, the white wings cannot procreate but the fallen can, with humans, with demons, and with each other." He looked down his nose at me, tawny eyes bright in the corridor's gloom. "They call my kind second generation."

"Are you less powerful?"

The corner of his mouth lifted. "The originals would like to think so." He leaned in, his tone dropping to something conspiratorial. "But they'd be wrong."

I caught a whiff of the distinct scent of an impending storm, electric and volatile. My pulse fluttered in my throat as my body reacted to his proximity. I stepped away, putting a little distance between us.

He chuckled low. "Don't worry, little Nephilim, I have no designs on your virtue."

I shot him a sharp look. "Good, because there's nothing virtuous to be had."

His eyes lit up and his gait slowed. "Oh really?" He studied me from his lofty height, gaze suddenly intense and probing. "In that case, I may have to reassess."

I ignored the rapid thud of my pulse and met his gaze levelly. "Please, don't bother. I'm not interested."

His eyebrow twitched slightly in surprise as if he wasn't used to women rejecting him. But then a smile bloomed across his face. "Your pulse says otherwise."

"My pulse doesn't control my actions. Like I said, I'm not interested."

I looked away. We were at a set of wooden doors reinforced by iron. "Is this the place?"

"Yes." Zepar knocked, three sharp raps.

The door swung open and a short, stocky man with a goatee and angry eyebrows glared up at us. He was wearing a vest over a hairy bare torso and his lower half was encased in loose-fitting pants cinched tight at his hooves.

"Again?" He placed his hands on his hips. "How many times are you going to vet them, Zepar?"

"That's Duke Zepar to you, Nugen," Zepar said, but his tone was light and tinged with humor.

"Lord smord, when you come to old Nugen, you're all the same. Don't forget who taught you to wield a blade, pup."

Zepar chuckled. "How could I? I still bear the scars."

"Scars pars, you were always too vain to get stuck in. So much potential on the battlefield."

"I prefer the court of the mind."

"Yeah, yeah, and who is this?" He raked me over, gaze darting from feature to feature. "Strong filly. Good muscle structure." His gaze dropped to Chase. "Well, hello." He reached out to pet him and Chase let him, his chest vibrating in that way that said he was pleased.

"Wow, he usually isn't so receptive to strangers."

Nugen shrugged. "I have a way with beasts, even off-realm ones, it seems." He scratched behind Chase's ears before dropping his hand to his side. "You fight?" he asked me. I opened my mouth to answer but he held up a hand. "No. I simply don't have the time to train anyone new. I have my hands full with Satan spawn." He tutted. "Such a handful."

"And I'm about to add to it," Zepar said. "Nyx is Satan spawn."

Nugen's gaze flew back to me, narrowing speculatively. "She is, is she? And what breed are we talking?"

Zepar leaned in, one hand bracketing his mouth conspiratorially. "Nephilim."

Nugen's eyes went round, and the color left his face.

"What?" His hand went to the hilt of his sword, but he didn't draw it, his instincts probably picking up on the fact I wasn't a threat.

Zepar let out a bark of laughter. "Oh, I never thought I'd see the day you looked scared, old man."

Nugen ignored him, focusing on me. "I don't sense power."

"Because there is none." I smiled wryly. "Doesn't mean I can't kick ass."

Nugen sighed. "The trials are about much more than fighting, child. But you'll learn that soon enough."

He was looking at me like Artimus had when he'd found out I had no power. With pity.

I didn't like it. I lifted my chin. "I've survived more than you can possibly imagine, old man. I've got this."

He huffed. "Yes, yes, all the bravado speeches. Get in here, and you"—he pointed at Zepar—"can wait till the Custodia to announce your sponsorship just like everyone else."

All humor left Zepar's face, and his eyes grew hard with determination. "No. I've made my decision."

Nugen balked. "You have?"

"Yes." His gaze settled on me. "I choose the little Nephilim."

Chapter Ten

"What does Zepar choosing me mean?" I followed Nugen away from the main doors and deep into a network of stone corridors.

Zepar had made his declaration, instructed Nugen to allow me to keep Chase, and left. Now the little hooved man was my only connection to what the heck was going on.

"It means he's staked a claim on you as a candidate for Satan. You'll wear Court of Ivory colors to show that you have Duke Zepar's backing. It also means that should you win, Duke Zepar will be granted a boon from you as Satan." He snorted. "I'm not sure what he's playing at, but you're far from the strongest candidate."

"Gee, thanks."

He stopped and turned to me. "Unless he sees something in you I don't." He frowned. "Only time will tell. What I do know is that Duke Zepar does *not* like to lose, so the pressure's on, girlie."

"Like it wasn't before?"

He gave a dry chuckle. "You have no idea what you're up against, and that's even before the trials begin."

"What do you mean?"

We'd come to a standstill in front of a tall, vaulted door made of dark wood with an iron latch and fleur-de-lis hinges.

"The creatures in that room may be your siblings but they were born and raised in Morningstar. They will chew you up and spit you out to get what they want."

"Why are you telling me this?"

He looked deep into my eyes. "It's my duty to ensure all of you get a fair chance at the seat. Letting you into a den of lions without a warning would be unsporting."

Great. "Thanks for the heads-up. I can handle myself."

"I hope that's true." He handed me a set of keys. "This door opens into a communal area, but these are keys to your personal quarters. Zinichi will show you where they are. We meet for training just after sunup. You've missed two weeks of preparation. I'm not sure how much you'll get out of the time left, but make sure you're well rested."

He turned on his hoof and clipped away, leaving me to make my entrance alone. Nerves bubbled to life in my belly. I took a deep breath to dispel the schoolyard feeling before clicking the latch and entering the room.

SIX FIGURES LOUNGED about the chamber in different poses of chill. Based on what I'd heard in the market about Satan being generous with his seed, I'd expected more spawn than this.

They all looked up as the door closed behind me, six pairs of curious eyes on the newcomer.

I raised a hand, taking in as much as I could in one sweep. There was a beautiful woman with a cascade of inky black hair and a sexy red smirk sitting beside a male with ochre skin and stunning blue eyes. Tiny horns protruded from his forehead and feathered wings rose behind him, too tiny to carry his weight. A male and female with crimson feathers for hair sat side by side on the floor oiling daggers—it didn't take a genius to figure out they were full-blooded siblings; were they Erinyes? A bulky male with bull horns and black wings folded tight against his back lounged on the window seat. The final occupant was a petite female with long dark hair and mournful eyes. She sat hunched in a corner clutching what looked like an embroidery wheel.

No one spoke for several long beats as the blood pounded in my head with the acknowledgement that these were my kin.

"Oh fucking great," the feather-haired female finally drawled. "Another one."

"Don't mind her," the woman with the cascades of hair said. "Mallini is a natural-born bitch."

"Watch it, Tristeene," the feather-haired guy said.

"Oh hush, you know you love it when I talk dirty." She winked at him.

He balked. "Stop that."

"Didn't bother you before, did it, Charod?" She blew him a kiss.

His alabaster cheeks turned red. "I didn't know," he snapped. "None of us did."

"What are you?" the bulky guy sitting in the window seat asked. His voice was gravelly and deep, sending a shiver of foreboding through me.

I shrugged casually. "Tired mostly. It's been a long day."

"I told you the revelation would bring more," the demon with the small wings said.

"No one asked your opinion, imp," Mallini said. "The fact that the likes of you is even here makes me sick."

His wings drooped and he tucked in his chin.

"There you go again," Tristeene said. "Being a bitch."

"Watch your tone," Charod warned. "Abyssbloods should know their place."

"Satan blood to you." Tristeene's eyes flashed red.

I caught movement in the corner of the room where the small demon with the embroidery was seated. Or had been seated. She was gone now.

"You frightened Veena," the guy with the tiny wings said.

"Forget Veena, we need to focus on the fresh competition," Tristeene said with a smile. She left her seat in a fluid motion and glided toward me. My skin tightened at her proximity, but I kept my posture relaxed as she circled me.

Up close she was even more beautiful than first impression gave credit for. The skin on her face was pale and smooth but it developed a slight red tinge at the base of her throat. Her waist-length hair was so black it shimmered blue where the light hit it. She moved with a sinuous grace that was almost serpentine.

"I don't sense power," she said. "What demon are you?"

Mallini had joined the circling. "If I didn't know better, I'd have pegged her for a demon blood, but she smells...off."

"She has the mark," the small-winged demon said.

"I know that, Gus," Mallini snapped.

Gus's wings drooped.

I was done with the assessment. "I'm part human."

The room stilled.

The door opening and closing was the only sound and then someone clapped their hands.

"Okay, back up. Back up," a female voice said. "She's harmless. A dud. A mistake the Erinyes have permitted to suffer."

Dud? "Excuse me?"

My siblings moved away to make room for a rotund demon with sparkling hazel eyes and a wide smile.

"Well, let's take a look at you. Hmmm, yes. I can work with this." She nodded curtly. "Come with me and I'll show you to your room. The rest of you get washed up. Supper will be here shortly."

My siblings dispersed, padding out of the lounge in different directions. I followed the demon out of the lounge and down a hallway lined with several doors. She stopped at the third on the left.

"This is you."

I unlocked it and pushed the door open to reveal a modest-sized room with a single bed, dresser, and washbasin with a small mirror above it.

"Bathroom is across the hall," she said. "One to each corridor." Her hazel eyes dimmed. "You won't have any competition for yours, though. This wing is empty now."

Wait a second. "Were there more spawn living here?"

She nodded slowly. "We had eighteen to begin with."

Dare I ask? "What happened to them?"

"They died."

"What? I thought the trials didn't start for another week."

She sighed. "They don't."

"Then how? I thought spawn were protected."

"They are. But accidents happen. Food poisoning...sleep walking..." She sighed again. "It's just the seven of you now."

"Twelve accidents in two weeks?" I arched a skeptical brow.

She pressed her lips together. "It is what it is. Just…watch your back, and if you're worried about anything, come to me." She placed her hand on my arm. "Lord Zepar has chosen you to wear his colors but I would advise not to speak of this to the others. Not until you have to. Not until it's too late."

I didn't need to ask, and she didn't need to spell it out for me to draw the conclusion that although spawn were protected from outsiders, there was no one to protect them from each other. Someone in these residential quarters was a murderer, and if they found out that I'd been chosen by Zepar, I'd be next on their hit list.

The bed was small but surprisingly comfortable and it was tempting to skip supper and go to sleep, but if I was going to win the Satan seat, I needed to understand my opponents. The way they thought, their strengths and their weaknesses so I could use the information against them.

My stomach felt hollow.

Chase stepped closer and nudged me with his nose.

"Yeah, I know. It doesn't feel good, but what can I do? We can't all win this."

Chase chuffed in agreement.

I pulled my phone from my pocket and stared at the blank spot where the reception bars should have been. "Orina's going to worry." But there was nothing I could do about that right now. I had to hope I got a chance to send her a message soon. "Let's get washed and grab a bite to eat. I'm fucking starving."

I splashed water on my face and stared at my reflection. I looked exhausted. Movement in the mirror caught my eye, but when I looked over my shoulder there was only Chase, sitting on his haunches, waiting for me.

Yeah, I needed some rest and soon. But first, I needed food.

I joined the others in the lounge where a huge table had taken up residence in the center of the room, along with several silver plates loaded with food. The other Satan spawn had already claimed seats, but no one had loaded up their plate yet.

I took an empty spot between Veena and Gus with a space either side of me. Chase settled on the floor at my feet, huge head on his paws.

"He has beautiful fur," Veena said. "May I pet him?" She peered at me through her curtain of hair, huge, brown, almond eyes filled with hope.

"That's up to Chase."

Chase raised his head and sniffed the air around Veena before shifting close and lowering his nose in invitation.

Veena sucked in a sharp breath and then tentatively reached out to stroke the spot between his eyes.

Chase's chest vibrated and she pulled back quickly.

"It's okay." I smiled reassuringly. "It means he likes it."

"Oh." Her eyes lit up and she stroked him again with a look of marvel on her face as if she'd never petted a hound before.

Wait... "Is this your first time petting a hound?"

The bull-horned guy snorted from across the table. "That beast isn't a hound. Hounds are huge with claws and teeth and red eyes."

The helhunters came to mind.

"That's a pup of some unknown human world breed," he continued. "We don't have them here."

Chase slowly turned his head to fix his dark eyes on the bull-horned demon.

The demon's eyes narrowed. "Why is it looking at me like that?"

"Probably because you're an asshole, Keelan," Tristeene said. "He can smell it."

Charod snickered and shook his head, ruffling his crimson feathers.

Mallini elbowed him and he snapped his mouth closed.

There was obviously no love lost between those two females. "Are we going to eat?"

"Go ahead." Tristeene smirked.

"Don't," Veena said. "We have to wait until it's tested...in case."

Realization dawned. They thought the food could be poisoned.

"You could do it," Keelan sneered in Veena's direction. "That is what your kind are good for."

Veena tucked in her chin, her embarrassment and fear palpable.

"Hey." I snapped my fingers to get his attention. "Do you know what we call people like you where I come from?"

His lip curled cruelly. "No. And I don't care."

"We call your kind bullies. Cowards who hide behind their physical stature or positions of power to intimidate and terrorize people they consider weaker than themselves."

He snorted. "Like I said, I don't care what you think."

I ignored him and addressed the rest of the table. "You know what's interesting about bullies?"

"What?" Gus asked. "Tell us."

"They usually have tiny dicks."

Keelan's chest vibrated. "I do *not* have a tiny dick."

"Uh-huh, if you say so."

"Fuck you," he snapped.

"Tut, tut." I wagged my finger from side to side. "That would be incest."

Veena giggled.

Keelan's crimson-tinged cheeks went red.

"There, there." Tristeene stroked his bicep. "She doesn't know how well hung your kind are. But I do." Her eyes twinkled. "Your kind definitely don't have small dicks. But you do have teeny brains."

Charod let out a guffaw, which earned him a glare from his sister.

Keelan's response was interrupted by the arrival of two small demons wearing gray clothes edged in black and silver.

"Finally!" He threw up his hands. "Are you zuni ever on time."

Veena tensed as the creatures rounded the table. I caught one of them staring at her but she kept her head down. The zuni proceeded to sample each dish using a different spoon for each.

They were testing for poison. They even sampled the water. Once done, they inclined their heads.

"There are no toxin traces," they said in unison before exiting the room.

"Thank fuck." Keelan began piling his plate with food.

I held back. "What about slow-acting poison?"

"The little devils will detect anything," Tristeene said. "Won't they, Veena?"

Veena continued to add food to her plate, ignoring the

question. Veena was a zuni like the poison tasters. A devil. A worker here at Morningstar. If they were working here, it meant they were Nephalem. They had to have some fallen blood to be able to withstand the Morningstar atmosphere.

Everyone was already eating. I was the last to load my plate. I made up one for Chase too and placed it on the floor beside him. Conversation buzzed around me, things I didn't understand but wanted to. Maybe even needed to.

Then I caught a name I recognized.

"Zepar will be back to announce his choice," Keelan said.

"You wish he'd choose you, Keelan," Mallini said. "Just because your ancestors fought Beelzebub's battalion."

"And thereafter." He raised his chin and bared his teeth. "We're warriors and the seat needs a warrior."

"He might wait and announce his choice at the Custodia like everyone else," Gus said tentatively.

"And risk getting the drop on the other dukes and lords?" Mallini snorted. "Hardly."

"If I can't have Zepar I'll take Ignatius," Charod said.

"I don't care as long as I don't get Umbrane." Tristeene shuddered, her bright eyes darkening.

"Is what they say about him true?" Gus asked her.

But it was Veena who answered. "Yes," she said softly.

Everyone turned to look at her and she ducked her head, allowing her hair to shield her face.

Silence reigned for several seconds but Charod broke it. "If he comes near my sister, I'll rip out his throat."

Mallini lifted her chin proudly. "I'll rip it out myself, brother."

They grinned at each other, their resemblance intensifying, and it hit me. These two were twins. They had to be.

"Not unless you get the Satan seat you won't," Tristeene said. "Umbrane isn't someone to mess with."

I needed to understand this obsession with sponsorship. "Why does it matter who sponsors us? I mean, what's the benefit to us during the trials?"

Mallini sat back in her seat with a smile. "You really are clueless, aren't you?"

"It's not her fault," Gus said. "She wasn't raised here." He smiled tentatively at me. "It must be quite a shock to you."

I returned his smile, about to respond, but Mallini cut me off.

"Oh, look, Gus is trying to make friends. Afraid the killer will pick you off next, hmmm?" There was a cruel glint in her emerald eyes.

"Unless he is the killer and wants to get close to his new mark," Charod added.

"You best watch your back," Keelan growled.

The same words Zinichi had said to me, except when she'd said it, it had sounded less like a threat and more like a warning.

"You suspect someone in this room is a killer and yet here you are, breaking bread together." I shook my head. "I love it."

Tristeene shrugged. "You know what they say..."

"Keep your friends close and your enemies closer?"

She grinned, showcasing sharp canines like Artimus's. "Exactly."

"I want to know about you." Gus propped his chin on his hands and blinked at me. He looked like a fucked-up cupid, if cupid were orange with no round belly. His wings fluttered delicately behind him. "What was your life like out there?"

Silence fell. They were all focused on me. Waiting for

my origin story. I set my bread down and wiped my mouth with a napkin. "Well, I was abandoned by my human mother at the age of six or seven and then I found Chase." I looked down at my buddy, who was stretched out by the table at my feet. "We were homeless for a year until a woman found us and took us in. She gave us a home. I grew up thinking I was a demon blood, became a bounty hunter, kicked ass, made a life for myself, and then...well, now, I'm here."

"You just happened to be in Morningstar territory for the revelation?" Gus asked.

"I had business here." No need to tell them about the helhunter attack. "Artimus found me and saved me from a mob attack." I gave them a wry smile. "I guess they didn't stop to do a proper sniff test and discover I wasn't a danger. They put two and two together, came up with Nephilim, and attacked."

"You can't blame them," Mallini said. "Nephilim are responsible for too many demon deaths. When the fallen first arrived, they chose humans over demons to procreate with, attracted to their fragile beauty. The result was powerful, mentally unstable beings hellbent on taking down the fallen, and they trampled over the demons to get to them. The purge was a blessing, ridding us of the Nephilim threat in time for us to focus on the Chaos War."

"She doesn't need a history lesson," Tristeene said.

"I beg to differ," Mallini said. "She associated with Artimus."

"So does your mother," Tristeene said. "Often, from what I hear."

Whoa, they needed to back it up a little. "What's wrong with associating with Artimus?"

"Nothing's wrong," Tristeene said.

"I beg to differ again," Mallini countered. "Everyone knows Satan distanced himself from the seneschal the last two decades. After being Satan's right-hand man forever, Artimus was relegated to the outer circles." She licked her lips and leaned in, drawing us to do the same. "Everyone knows he's a suspect."

"A suspect?"

"In the assassination of Satan."

My blood ran cold. Artimus was a suspect? He'd given the impression that he'd been tight with Satan till the end. He'd made me want to trust him. I guess the way he'd abandoned me to the Erinyes should have been a clue.

"That's bull," Keelan growled. "If you want to base suspects on a list of people who lost favor with Satan, then you'd need to put every duke on it. Toward the end of his life, he pretty much antagonized everyone with his blasé attitude to running Morningstar. Zepar stepped in often, liaising with the Erinyes on his behalf when he should have been in Ivory managing his own court."

"I heard about the uprising at Ivory," Tristeene said.

Keelan snorted. "Didn't last long. Peeran, his army general, knocked it on the head. He held the seat for Zepar until he returned and re-established order, which is why he'll want to back the strongest candidate for Satan. His hold on the Court of Ivory depends on it."

There was so much to absorb and unpack here. Too much. And Zepar's interest in me made less sense than ever now. I was under no illusions that I was the strongest candidate, despite my determination and drive.

"All he did the last decade is sit on his throne and mope," Charod said. "Mother said he lost all interest in matters of state. Trade agreements, fuel export and import, they all had to be signed off on by Satan and he refused to cooperate. It was only a matter of time before someone put an end to him."

"Wasn't he out of realm when it happened?" Gus asked.

"No, it was the throne room," Charod said.

"Bullshit," Tristeene said. "The Court of Shadow was buzzing with the news. He was definitely off realm when it happened."

I turned to Tristeene. "You're from the Court of Shadow?"

"An abyssblood," Mallini sneered before sipping from her goblet.

Artimus had mentioned them. Creatures who'd been liberated from the abyss. "I thought the atmosphere in Morningstar wasn't suitable for your kind."

"You thought correctly, but I'm also Nephalem."

Of course. "Like the seneschal."

"He told you he was abyssblood?" She looked surprised.

But not as surprised as I was.

"Ah, he didn't reveal that part." She licked her lips. "Tell me, did you feel a little tingle down there when with him?" She smiled wickedly. "Did you get horny?"

I met her gaze levelly, unabashed. "Yeah. A little. He's a sexy guy."

She let out a sultry laugh. "Honey, you have no idea."

"He's an incubus," Mallini said, shooting Tristeene a glance that said she wasn't impressed with her theatrical flair. "And Tristeene is a succubus."

"Not related," Tristeene said. "Artimus is the last of his bloodline. The Basr bloodline was wiped out in the Chaos War. Satan took Artimus in and raised him like a son."

"Basically, what they're saying is that you can't trust anyone," Gus said.

"There is only one Satan seat," Mallini said. "Only one of us can ascend."

Everyone took a moment to side eye each other.

Veena pushed her chair back. "Goodnight." She drifted away from the table and into the shadows.

"She'll die in the first trial." Keelan shoveled stew into his mouth. He looked up at me. "You'll be next."

No one bothered to contradict him. But then they didn't know me the way I did, and I had no intention of dying anytime soon.

Chapter Eleven

I didn't think I'd be able to sleep, but my body had other ideas. I woke to the gray light of dawn, Chase nudging me in the face, and a soft knocking on the door.

Urgh, I was not a morning person. I rolled off the bed and shoved my feet into my boots before padding to the door to answer it. Yeah, I'd slept fully clothed, what of it?

I yanked open the door to empty space. Chase chuffed and nudged me.

I looked down to find Veena standing with her face tipped up, huge, dark eyes drinking me in.

I dragged my hand through my hair. "Hey...morning."

She pulled a bundle from her pocket. "You missed breakfast." I went to take the package, but she pulled away slightly, unwrapped the hunk of bread, and pinched off a bite with her fingers. She popped the piece in her mouth, chewed and swallowed, then blinked up at me.

We stood face to face for several seconds and then she handed me the bread.

She'd just poison checked it for me. I mean, it had

probably been checked at the table, but she'd just given me peace of mind by checking it again.

I took the bread. "Thank you."

She bobbed her head. "We meet at the door in fifteen. Nugen gets mad if we're late." She pointed to the ground where another package sat. "Zinichi left you clothes."

"Thanks." I picked up the bundle. "I'll see you in a bit."

She glided off down the corridor and I retreated into my room and closed the door. It looked like I'd made a friend.

I wasn't sure how I felt about that considering what I had to do.

I split the hunk of bread in two and handed one to Chase. "Eat up, boy. I have a feeling we're going to need our strength."

THERE WAS no time for a shower, but I washed as best as I could in the sink in my room and donned the change of clothes Zinichi had left for me. Soft jogger pants and a long-sleeve lightweight polo shirt. There was no fresh underwear in the package, but there was a pair of sneaker-type footwear without any laces. They molded to my feet like gloves, and damn, they were comfortable.

I joined the others by the door in the main lounge. They were dressed in clothes like mine. We looked like we were about to go on a team run.

The door opened and Nugen appeared, legs encased in joggers, chest puffed out in a black, long-sleeve sports shirt.

I mean, I wasn't sure what I'd expected, but it wasn't sportswear. I guess Morningstar imported from across the golden bridge.

"I hope you're ready for some strenuous activity," he said.

Everyone groaned.

Nugen cackled. "You think just because you've been training every day for the last two weeks I'm gonna go easy on you, huh? The Custodia is in two days. If you want a decent sponsor, you need to look the part. We're hitting the gym."

"Yes!" Keelan fist-pumped the air.

"Typical," Tristeene said.

"Stamina training," Nugen added.

"What?" Keelan's face fell. "I want to do weights."

"Trust me," Nugen said.

"Why can't you just tell us what the trials involve?" Gus asked. "All the hand-to-hand, the puzzles, the gym sessions, the cross-country runs."

Shit, it looked like I'd missed a ton of stuff.

"To prepare you for anything," Nugen said. "The trials test more than your body; they test your mind and your emotions. They test your worth to be Satan, and if we told you what exactly was being tested, you'd fake it. We can't have that."

"Fake it? Me?" Tristeene fluttered her eyelashes. "Never."

"Let's just get this over with," Mallini said.

Nugen led us down the corridor and up a flight of stairs that opened out into a huge gym area. Once again, the equipment was familiar and modern and totally at odds with the keep's medieval décor.

The others got to work straight away, hitting the treadmills and rowing machines. Chase padded over to the wall and lay down, while I headed toward a cross trainer machine and hopped on. Time to work up a sweat.

When your day job involved running to and from

danger, then you kinda built up your stamina, so it was about twenty minutes before I got my sweat on, armpits mainly, and only because Morningstar didn't provide deodorant.

I kept pushing, my favorite track blaring in my head. My cheek itched so I reached up to scratch it. My skin felt hot. In fact, my chest felt tight too.

Chase barked a short warning as he rushed toward me.

"What is it, boy?" My voice sounded breathless not just because of the exertion but because my windpipe felt constricted.

Chase barked and growled as if urging me to act.

I looked down at my hand, covered in red blotches. What the—

A wave of heat rushed from my toes to my head, and the world tilted. Chase's huge body cushioned my fall.

"What the feck?" Nugen's face hovered over me.

"Poison..."

"Toxin..."

The world was fuzzy.

"Take off her clothes." Veena appeared above me. "It's on the clothes, I can smell it now."

Hands clawed at me, desperately tugging off my clothes until I was down to my underwear. My two-day-old undies. Urgh.

"Can we wash it off?" Gus asked.

"Too late, it's in her bloodstream," Tristeene replied.

"What..." I tried to sit up, but the world spun.

"What's happening?" I recognized the voice. Male, authoritative, and arrogant.

Zepar.

The other spawn backed up as he fell to a crouch beside me. His tawny gaze grew dark with anger, jaw tightening.

"Morningbrew." He snarled the word. "Amateur, but effective." He scooped me up into his arms and hauled me to his chest. Chase growled. "Down, beast, unless you want your mistress dead."

Chase cut off his next growl.

"Can you heal her?" Veena cried. "Please, can you heal her?"

"Out of my way, zuni," he ordered.

I wanted to protest, to tell him not to speak to Veena like that, but my tongue refused to work. Shit, the world was getting dark.

"Where are you taking her?" Nugen asked.

"To Lake Morbidus."

The world shattered, then an icy breeze kissed my cheeks. If I'd been more in control of my body I'd have thrown up.

My body was floppy, head lolling, gaze tipped to the sky as Zepar carried me. How had we gotten outside so quickly?

"Hold on, little Nephilim. Hold on."

Slivers of icy air made it into my lungs as the band around my chest tightened further and my vision tunneled. The sky surged toward me, then my stomach dropped. A splash was followed by the shock of icy water against my skin. If I could have screamed, I would have, but water was pushing against my mouth and nose. I couldn't breathe. I couldn't—

Warm lips covered mine. My eyes snapped open in the murky depths of the lake to lock onto Zepar's glowing gaze. He held me tight, keeping us just below the surface while his mouth channeled heat into my body. Wait, he was breathing for me. How was this possible?

My limbs tingled and pinched, and heat spread through

me, giving me back control of my upper body. Dark movement behind Zepar caught my eye.

Something was headed toward us.

I pushed at his shoulders, eyes darting to the side in warning. He spun us in the water, adjusting his grip on me to free one of his arms. White light radiated outward, and a muffled shriek vibrated against my water-clogged eardrums.

The creatures were coming for us. Too many and too fast.

This was insane. Zepar was insane, so why was there a bubble of euphoria expanding in my chest?

We spun again and another vibration of light and sound rocked my frame.

My legs tingled. I could feel them again, but more legs would mean nothing if they got eaten off by the hungry monster fishies surrounding us.

Did he know? Of course, he knew.

He gripped me tighter and shot to the surface, tearing his mouth from mine.

I sucked in cold air, chest heaving. "We have to get out. Now!"

He canted his head. "Really? I was thinking we should stay and pet the aquatic life."

Fins raced toward us. The bubble of euphoria grew, forcing a squeal of excitement up my throat. I bit it back and wrapped my arms around Zepar's neck. His chest vibrated in a chuckle and in the next moment we were airborne. Huge, beautiful, inky wings snapped open at his back, catching the air to hold us suspended over the lethal lake for an achingly long second. A second in which I was acutely aware of the hard planes of his body molded to mine, and his hot breath at the spot just beneath my ear. Then we were making an arch toward the bridge. To safety.

He landed in a crouch with me cradled in his arms.

Fuck, I was practically naked in my two-day-old underwear, which, thanks to the lake, had just gotten a wash.

I stared up at his wet face, at the hair plastered to his beautiful fucking skull, as the adrenaline from almost being eaten, the joy at being alive, rushed through me, nudging me into impulse mode.

I kissed him hard on the mouth. A smacker of a kiss, then grinned up at him. "Now that was fucking awesome. Want to do it again?"

He stared at me, stunned, water skating down his chiseled cheeks and hanging from inky lashes much too long for a male.

His tawny eyes were bright against his tanned skin, and as they raked me over, his pupils dilated and his lips curved in a smile. "You're insane." He said it as if it was a compliment.

"Maybe. Or maybe I just live for the thrill, and that, my friend, was a thrill."

I released him, but my knees buckled, and he snatched me up against him again.

"How do you feel? Physically?" he asked.

Shit, focus, Nyx. I'd been poisoned. The lake and the whole thrill thing had only been necessary because someone had tried to kill me.

"I feel fine. Pissed off, but fine." And he'd saved my life. Damn it. I was beholden to him now.

He must have read my thoughts on my face because a smile tipped his lips. "Yes, Nyx, you owe me, and you can pay me back by winning these trials. Now let's get you back to the keep so you can dry off."

Teleportation, or body displacement, was a thing the fallen could do, but boy did it leave me with an unsettled tummy. Or maybe that was the after-effect of the poison someone had tried to kill me with.

The spawn were protected so no one outside of our group could hurt us, not unless they wanted to risk being executed, but within the group and trials, all bets were off.

Dry and dressed in fresh clothes tested in front of Nugen by the resident zuni, I stood in the lounge glaring at the other spawn. The murderer was in this room. One of them. It made my stomach hurt because despite my best efforts, I was beginning to like them.

"That was a bitch move. But it shows me that whoever you are, you think I'm a threat. Good. I am. I'm a big threat."

"I'm not even gonna protest," Tristeene said. "It's pointless. But I'm glad you're okay. Things got interesting when you arrived. These lot are so predictable."

"It was on the clothes," Keelan pointed out.

"We know that." Charod rolled his eyes.

But he was right. The clothes given to me by Zinichi.

The door opened and Nugen entered with a red-eyed Zinichi. She made a beeline for me and grabbed my hands. "Oh, thank the earth you're alive."

Nugen stood with his hands on his hips. "The clothes arrived pre-packed from the market and Zinichi merely delivered the package."

"So they could have been tampered with before," Tristeene said.

"Or after." Keelan's gaze settled on Veena. "I saw you go

into her corridor after breakfast with something under your robe."

Veena shrank from the accusation.

I moved to stand beside her. "She brought me some bread."

"And could have tampered with your package at the same time," Mallini pointed out.

I looked down at Veena, not wanting to believe the sweet zuni could hurt me or anyone, but this world was new to me and these people strangers. Everyone was a suspect.

Nugen strode toward Veena. "Come with me. We will search your rooms."

Veena peered up at me, eyes glistening with tears. "I didn't do it, Nyx. I swear it."

"I believe you, but the search still has to happen, for your sake as much as mine."

She nodded and dropped her chin, allowing her hair to shield her face as she followed Nugen to her quarters.

"I fucking hate this," Charod said.

Silence reigned for long seconds.

"So... is anyone going to address the helhunter in the room?" Tristeene said. "Zepar came for you. He saved you."

"He went into Lake Morbidus for you." Gus's tone was saturated with awe.

"One of the wall guards saw it all," Charod said excitedly. "He dove in with you in his arms, then there were streams of celestial power under the dark waves, then he shot out into the sky with you." He shook his head. "Zepar risked his life for you."

Hardly. He'd looked completely relaxed in the water, blasting the creatures with ease. "He's a fallen, I doubt those creatures could hurt him."

"One bite and he would be dead," Mallini snapped,

feathers puffing up in indignation. "Don't you know anything?" She shook her head. "Why you?" She looked me over as if searching for something, anything that made me worthy. "Why would he risk his life for you?"

I didn't know, but I was going to find out. One way or another.

Chapter Twelve

"What the hell are we doing here, Chase?" I lay in bed staring at the ceiling, waiting for sleep to claim me. "One more day until the Custodia and then this whole ascension thing kicks off. Can I do this? I've missed all the training. Someone obviously wants me dead, and it'll only get worse once the group finds out that Zepar's sponsoring me."

Chase lifted his head and rested his nose on my shoulder, as if to say, *it's a bitch of a situation, but you've got this. You can do it.*

"Thanks, buddy. You always know just what to say to make me feel better." I turned my head to look into his intelligent dark eyes. "Where did you go for so long, huh?"

There was a whirlwind of emotion in his eyes, so many unsaid words. I knew some people thought I was being fanciful, but I was sure Chase understood everything I said. He was smarter than smart. He was more than a hound. He was my person.

"It's okay. You don't have to tell me. I'm just glad you're okay and that you're back with me again. I missed you so fucking much." I stroked his ear. "Don't leave me again, okay?"

He chuffed softly in promise.

There was a soft knock at the door. He sat up, alert, sniffing the air, then his muscles relaxed.

Not a perceived threat, then?

I swung my legs off the bed and crossed the room to open the door.

Tristeene stood in the corridor, a silver shawl that was more decorative than warm wrapped around her slender shoulders. "Good, you're awake."

I arched a brow. "What do you want, Tristeene?"

"Look, I didn't try and kill you, okay. Let's just get that out of the way first. Also, I have no idea who did. Up until now everyone's been a suspect, until you."

"Oh?"

"You came after. You were almost killed. You're not a suspect."

Her dark eyes gleamed with relief, and it hit me how tense, how frightening, how exhausting being here must be for them. All of them except the killer, of course. To be on your guard all the time, around everyone you're thrown into proximity with. To watch them be picked off one by one from eighteen down to six.

I couldn't imagine the last few weeks.

The cynical voice that also served as my self-preservation reminded me that she could still be the killer, here to lull me into a false sense of security before making her move to end me.

If she was, then she was a fabulous actress. "Look, you might be okay to trust me, but I can't trust any of you."

She pressed her lips together and nodded. "Okay, I get it.

Bring your hound. If I try anything, he can tear out my throat."

Chase's chest vibrated in agreement with that plan.

"Fine."

"And grab a shawl," she instructed.

"I don't have a shawl."

"A blanket will do."

I pulled one off my bed and followed her down the corridor. "Where are we going?"

"You'll see."

"That statement would be fine if you weren't a potential killer, but in light of our current situation, it's not."

She chuckled, low and sexy. "Point taken. I did some exploring when we got here. I found a hidden tower with a breathtaking view. I go there often, just to think. I found it the second day we were here. I haven't told anyone about it."

We crossed the lounge and through the doors into the network of corridors beyond.

"But you trust me."

She smiled over her shoulder. "I do. We're sisters, after all."

Oh, shit, did she just play the sibling card? "Don't do that."

"What?" She gave me a sidelong glance before taking a right at the next intersection.

"The sibling thing. Sharing the same bloodline does *not* make us family."

Her smile was sad. "No, it doesn't. Family is so much more than that. But...wouldn't it be nice...if things were different..." She trailed off and turned away, picking up pace down the narrow corridor until we came to a tapestry hanging on the wall. She pushed it aside to reveal a flight of steps.

Nice.

I followed with Chase's hot breath on my heels and the blanket clutched to my chest like a weapon to ward off Tristeene's warm familial advances.

I should turn back now. Tell her I'd changed my mind. Getting close to any one of them was a bad idea.

But the lure of a view, of fresh air in my lungs, kept me moving forward. Okay, so it was more than that; maybe a part of me wanted a taste of this family thing? Of getting to know this succubus who happened to be my half sibling.

We reached the top of the stairs and she pushed open a door. Cool air rushed into the passage, brushing my cheeks and rifling through my hair.

I followed her into a circular room with a high domed ceiling and huge arched windows all around us. The room had a hearth, but it was dark and unlit. There was some dusty-looking furniture covered in sheets and one small purple chaise pushed up against the far window.

Tristeene made a beeline for it now. "Come on."

I joined her on the padded seat and wrapped the blanket around my shoulders. It *was* a little chilly up here, but the view made up for it.

Acres of land stretched out below us, snow-covered rolling hills and plains that sparkled beneath the moonlight. Clusters of buildings snuggled here and there, lit up with twinkling lights and punctuated by steepled towers. The world was a winter wonderland, crisp and beautiful.

"I used to wonder what Morningstar was like," Tristeene said. "As a child I'd heard the elders speak of it. The glittering beauty and the glorious hours of sunlight. The colors and the people, so many people. But this was before the Accords, before Morningstar was pulled into the mortal plane fully and gifted mortal soil to meld with. I heard there was a golden bridge that leads to the mortal lands. I wanted to see it for myself. And then my wish was granted in the worst possible way." Her mouth turned down. "You know, I was always the oddity amongst my siblings. Succubi have tails, they said, where's yours? Why can't you shift, they asked."

"Shift?"

She smiled sadly. "A pure blood succubus has two forms, a humanoid form and a demonic one. As a Nephalem, I'm unable to access my demonic form. It made me an outcast among my people when I wanted desperately to be accepted."

This was too much disclosure, too soon. "Why are you telling me this?"

Her smile was wry. "Maybe because I see myself reflected in you." She gave me a knowing smile. "You and I share the same wounds."

"I doubt that very much. You had a mother who loved you. Mine threw me away."

She let out a bark of laughter. "If you call selling your daughter to the highest bidder as soon as she reaches maturity love, then yes, she loved me."

I stared at her in horror. "No..."

"Oh, don't look so shocked. Succubi are sex demons. It's what we do. We need sex to survive. We crave it. I would have found a duke or lord to serve and to feed off eventually, the choice was merely taken from me."

"But why? Your mother must have known you were Satan's spawn. Wouldn't that make her want to take care of you more?"

She let out an incredulous laugh. "Succubi aren't maternal. If she'd realized that Satan might die and I could be in line for the title, then maybe she would have treated me better. But that edict wasn't revealed until his death."

"I'm sorry you had to go through that."

"It made me strong, and when the lord I was sold to died, I inherited his estate." She grinned. "Now I can fuck whomever I want."

I couldn't imagine being forced to be with someone, to give them my body. "Good for you."

She blinked at me in surprise. "You really mean that, don't you?"

"Yeah, I do." I studied her heart-shaped face in the moonlight. "I'm glad you're free."

She swallowed and then fixed a bright smile on her face. "If you're going to survive Morningstar, you need to learn about its inhabitants. Abyssbloods aren't a threat. The bloodlines have sworn featly to one of the surviving princes. They either reside in the demon realm they're sworn to or in its affiliated court. Incubi, succubi, and nightmares are the main class of abyssblood." Her mouth turned down. "Although nightmares are less citizen and more cattle. From what I've heard, Duke Umbrane treats them awfully. Luckily for me, the lord I was sold to kept me far away from the duke." Her eyes grew dark. "The stories I've heard about him...You'd think he was a daimon, not fallen."

"The daimons are in the abyss, right?"

"Yes. How much do you know?"

"Not enough."

"Okay, let me see. Daimons are powerful, ancient beings who rule the abyss. They used to capture demons and drag them into the abyss to procreate with them. The product was abyssbloods. The fallen liberated many of my kind. Then you have the efreet. Not many of them left. They're something different. They came from another world entirely and took refuge in the demon world. They allied with the Erinyes in helping to push back the daimon forces. But something happened, an affliction or a curse, I'm not sure which. The efreet have struggled to procreate ever since. Their numbers are close to extinction. Ignatius, the duke of the Court of Flame, is an efreet. He was given the court and the title by Prince Levistus because it was rumored he saved the prince's life in the Chaos War."

"Everyone is ancient."

"Which is why most of them are slightly unhinged."

"Which explains why this ascension thing is so crazy. I mean, why go to such lengths? Why not just pick based on who's the eldest like they do in the mortal world?"

"Satan isn't just a title, Nyx, it's an active responsibility, and age doesn't always equate to wisdom."

"Point taken." We exchanged smiles. "I wish I didn't like you."

Her smile fell and that same sadness filled her eyes. "Me too. I wish the ascension didn't pit us against each other."

We sighed in unison and settled to watch the view. Chase lay at our feet and closed his eyes and another time came to mind, another tower, another view when three young, idealistic women had watched the world change.

It was changing again. For me. And for the first time in a long time, I wasn't sure what the future held.

Chapter Thirteen

"How old are you?" Gus stared at me in horror.

I rolled my eyes. "Mid-twenties." I'd already told him three times. "You heard right the first two times, Gus."

"As in just over two decades?" Charod's eyes were wide. "You're a baby. A squalling little infant."

Ouch. "In demon years maybe. But up here." I tapped the side of my head. "I'm wiser than all of you put together."

Keelan stopped sharpening his horns with a file and snorted, blowing actual smoke out of his nostrils. "You'll break. You'll snap and you'll lose. Satan is a title of power destined for a spawn with power." He pressed his fist to his chest and raised his chin. "Someone like me."

"Yeah, we get it," Mallini said. "You Minorax are all the same. Brawn first, brains second."

He glared at her, his mahogany irises gleaming with violent intent.

"Try it," Mallini sneered.

He huffed and tossed his head before continuing with his horn filing.

"Not so dumb after all, then," Mallini said.

We were waiting for Nugen to come get us for whatever he had planned. It was the day before the Custodia and everyone seemed antsy. I had no idea how the subject of age had come up, but I now knew that most of the spawn were around a century old, which was young in demon years. To them I was a fetus. But when it came to life experience, I'd learned that many hadn't even begun to live yet; most of them still existed under the wing of their sire, preparing for what demons deemed adulthood. Veena was an exception. Zuni started working as soon as they could walk. The lowest of the demon classes, they were grunts who never got a break.

She stood silently, hands clasped in front of her, head bowed, waiting with us but apart from us. My heart went out to her. She was as much of an outcast here as I was; the only difference was she didn't have the balls to assert herself.

I made a note to chat with her and give her a pep talk, then mentally kicked myself. This was a competition, for fucksake, and the last thing I needed to be doing was injecting confidence into my competitors.

The door opened and Nugen appeared. His gaze skipped over us all, counting heads. "No pup today?" he asked me.

"He's asleep, I didn't want to wake him." Chase went through a cycle where every few weeks he went into hibernation mode, not complete hibernation but just sleeping between eighteen to twenty hours a day. I called it his recharge mode.

Nugen nodded. "Good to see you all made it through another night alive. Today there is no training."

"Thank you!" Gus's shoulders sagged in relief. "I still ache from yesterday."

"Ache smache. You're Satan blood, spawn, you'll live. Today we'll be visiting Satan's seat."

Silence fell.

I had to ask. "What's Satan's seat?"

"The pinnacle of the keep where the throne is kept," Nugen said. "It's time you saw what it is you're fighting for and learn what it represents."

Up until now we'd been kept within the residences, a network of rooms and corridors that seemed to house whatever we needed. But this time Nugen led us out of the main doors Zepar had dropped me off at three nights ago and into the keep proper.

No one spoke as we followed the stocky devil through the silent, opulent corridors to an ornate golden door. Nugen reached into the front of his tunic and pulled at the thick chain around his neck to reveal a heavy iron key.

He slotted it into a keyhole set into the wall beside the golden door and twisted.

The door rumbled and slid open to reveal a ten-by-ten space.

"In you go." He ushered us inside.

"What is this?" Mallini resisted. "A cage?"

"It's an elevator." I pushed past her and into the lift. "We have them where I come from. Humans use them in almost all the buildings with more than three floors."

Veena shuffled in beside me and Tristeene followed, shooting me a smile. Keelan was next, his huge, bull-like frame eating up space, and Charod and Mallini entered next followed by Nugen and Gus.

The doors closed and my stomach dipped, telling me we were in motion.

Veena gripped my wrist. I looked down at her and she released me quickly, her eyes widening in horror at what she'd done.

"It's okay." I took her hand in mine.

The door slid open and warm sunlight filled the elevator. We spilled out into the vast room beyond, Veena still clutching my hand like a lifeline.

The floor was smooth obsidian marble sprinkled with specks of silver like a starlit night. Balconied seating rose on either side of us; the barriers and balustrades were made from silver wood, and the cushioned seats were covered in dark velvet. But the main feature of the room, the pièce de résistance, was the stately throne set on a wide platform. It looked as if it was carved from obsidian and etched with silver patterns. The backrest was the same shape as an upside-down kite shield, the tip jutting up to separate two epic black wings that curved inward as if protecting the throne, or whoever chose to sit on it.

"Earth and stars," Mallini said. "I've seen renderings, paintings, sketches, but this...this defies all my expectations."

She was right, the throne was something out of a fairy tale, even more so with the winter sky, visible through the many windows behind it, providing a backdrop. The shimmering silver drapes pooling on the marble like waterfalls completed the picture. Yep, the throne made a solid statement.

Nugen gave us all a moment to take in the view before ushering us forward. "Take a look," he said. "Have a seat. Your blood permits it. But remember, only the chosen one, the initiated one, will be permitted to call the seat their own."

Mallini was the first to park her ass. She looked small and delicate, feet several inches off the ground. "I'll need a footstool."

"You'll get whatever you need if you win the trials," Nugen said.

"*When* I win," she corrected. She caressed the arm of the throne. "It feels right."

Nugen studied her, narrow-eyed. "Does it?"

"But we may have to get it padded," she added.

"Move," Keelan growled. "My turn."

Mallini slipped off the throne. "I'll never know what Satan saw in your bull-faced mother."

Keelan puffed smoke from his nose and lowered his head, his eyes bleeding to scarlet, but Charod stepped between the bull demon and his sister.

"Enough!" Nugen snapped. "Have some respect."

Everyone fell into silence.

One by one they tried out the throne.

Charod only sat for a moment, almost eager to get off. Tristeene crossed her legs and leaned back, perfectly at ease on the seat of power.

It came to Gus's turn, and Keelan and Charod guffawed at his attempts to climb up. The demon was part imp, barely five feet tall, and the throne seat was high, built to house a fallen. His wings fluttered uselessly, unable to lift him off the ground.

"Oh for fucksake." I stepped forward and gave him a boost.

His deep ochre skin darkened high on his cheekbones, and he blinked his stunning blue eyes at me. "Thank you."

"No worries, dude." I stepped back. "It suits you. Contrasts well with your skin tone."

He smiled. "It does."

"It really does," Tristeene agreed.

I caught Nugen watching me with an odd expression. Oh, yeah, we were supposed to be in competition. I guess helping Gus might be considered a sign of weakness. If so, fuck it. If being Satan meant being a huge dick, then they could go suck it. I didn't want it that badly.

Yes, you do, my inner voice of no bullshit spoke up. *You want it so you can show them you're as worthy as them.* Damn you, inner voice.

Veena was next but she shook her head. "I'm fine."

I touched her lightly on the shoulder. "You sure? I can help you up."

She smiled up at me, a close-lipped smile that filled her dark eyes with warmth. "I'm sure."

"You're up, Nephilim," Keelan said. "I, for one, can't wait for you to burn."

"What the hell is that supposed to mean, Mabel?"

"What?" He stared at me in confusion.

Mallini giggled. "I believe humans name their cows. Mabel is a common cow name."

Keelan's face went redder than his usual red, but he held his temper, probably trying to impress Nugen. "Only a Satan blood can sit on the throne." He grinned, showcasing his blunt white teeth. "Let's see if your mark was real, shall we."

"Why wouldn't it be? Fuck it, I'm not arguing with you, Clarabel."

Mallini snickered again.

I headed for the throne, ignoring the voice of doubt in my mind. I may not have chosen to be here, but I had as much right to this seat as any of these fuckers. I parked my ass and glared at Keelan defiantly.

His smirk fell from his lips, and then he nodded curtly once.

A ripple of awareness skimmed over my skin, a questing caress, and then a sigh filtered in my ears. Like a welcome. Like a hello. My muscles relaxed as I settled into the seat that felt as if it had been made for me.

Is it you?

The voice was a whisper, familiar yet alien.

Could it be?

Either I was going nuts, or the throne was speaking to me. My gaze flicked about the room, from face to face. Had any of the others heard the voice?

"Nyx? Nyx?"

I blinked and focused on Nugen. "Sorry?"

"How does it feel?"

I spoke without thinking. "Like coming home."

A strange expression flitted across Nugen's face, one I didn't know him well enough to decipher.

He turned away and clapped his hands. "All right. The Custodia is tomorrow, so this afternoon you'll be fitted with your ascension wardrobe and briefed on what's expected of you by your personal attendants."

"Finally!" Mallini said. "I requested my own attendant, was she approved?"

"Yes," Nugen said wearily. "The rest of you will be getting vetted attendants. They will be your intermediaries, at your beck and call during the next few weeks as the trials progress."

Weeks? "How many trials are there?"

"Your attendant will explain everything." Nugen strode toward the elevator. "Back to residences now."

We crammed into the elevator and rode down in silence, each of us deep in our own thoughts. Mine lingered on the voice I'd heard while sitting on the throne, not the inner voice that forced me to cut the bullshit but a different one. Deep but feminine. I was either going nuts or the throne had spoken to me. I needed to think on this one.

To tell the others, or not to tell them? That was the question.

The doors opened and Nugen hurried us out.

We were almost back at the residences when my hunter sense picked up a familiar presence.

It was Artimus, and he was striding straight toward us.

Chapter Fourteen

I hated that my pulse decided to do a little skip at the sight of his tall, broad-shouldered frame and hated it even more that he looked so fucking delicious in the fitted navy waistcoat and thigh-hugging slacks he was wearing. His dark hair was brushed off his forehead in a windswept style and his sapphire eyes were locked on me with a fiery intensity that was undeniably possessive.

Nugen brought us to a halt. "Seneschal." He inclined his head.

"Weapons master," Artimus said. "I need to speak with the Nephilim."

I could feel the other spawns' eyes on me, and it didn't take a genius to figure out what they were thinking. First the duke of the Court of Ivory and now the seneschal. Thank goodness the ascension wasn't about making friends.

"Of course," Nugen said. "If you could return her to the residences when you're done, the attendants will be arriving soon."

"Indeed." Artimus nodded.

Wow, who knew Nugen could be so polite. I guess he didn't have history with Artimus like he did with Zepar.

Nugen and the others continued toward the residences, leaving me alone with Artimus. He approached, coming to stand a couple of feet from me, but even then, his presence was a powerful force pressing in on my personal space. I resisted the urge to hug myself and allowed my anger to surface instead. He'd promised me support and he'd dumped me at the first hurdle.

I placed my hands on my hips. "Well? What do you have to say for yourself, *mentor*?"

He pressed his lips together as if choosing his words. "You think I abandoned you."

"I *know* you did. I was there when you did it, remember?"

"And yet here you are. Unscathed. With an offer of sponsorship from the Ivory Court."

I narrowed my eyes. "And let me guess, that was your plan all along."

He smiled.

Like hell was I going to let him weasel out of his betrayal so easily. "Bullshit. Do you know what I think? I think you're a has-been advisor who Satan replaced, and when you found out he was dead, you thought, hmmm, how can I climb back up the ladder, and so you came to the market to look for a candidate, a nobody, someone oblivious to what and who you are. Someone you thought you could manipulate into being your champion. But when it came to the crunch, to a point where you had to stand up for me, you flaked."

He let out a soft whistle. "Impressive theory, so good that I could almost believe it. But no. You're wrong."

"Whatever, I don't have time for this, or you." I made to

brush past him, but he grabbed my arm and hauled me close.

I sucked in a breath, ready to tell him to piss off, but his honeysuckle scent filled my head and washed away my ire.

"Listen to me, Nyx, I'm not the enemy. I just can't be seen as your friend. If I'd fought for you against the Erinyes, it would have pushed Erinea to execute you. She's the jealous type. She can't know I'm actively helping you."

"You're *not* helping me. You haven't been there. I almost died and you didn't come to see me. Not that I care. I'm just stating a fact. If you wanted to help, you'd have been there, but you weren't. Zepar was."

His jaw tightened. "When I heard what happened, I rushed to the river. I saw you two on the bridge. The way he looked at you..."

Yeah, that look. The spark, the interest, and then his words. "He thinks I'm insane."

"He's intrigued and that's good. He's attracted to unique things. He likes to own them. Zepar protects what belongs to him."

Hell no. "I don't belong to anyone." He smiled at me like he was humoring me, like he thought I was delusional. "No one owns me, Artimus."

"Being owned doesn't have to be ugly, or bad." He leaned in, his sweet breath like nectar to my senses. "It can be like letting someone scratch an itch that you didn't know was there." His eyes were deep and filled with promise... dark, inky pupils... "It can be freeing to let someone else take control and give you all the things you never allowed yourself to admit you craved."

My pulse hammered in my throat, and a matching throb flared to life between my thighs. I was suddenly acutely aware of his hand on my arm, his fingers like powerful brands holding me together. What would they feel like on other parts of my body?

I lifted my chin, mouth parting in invitation before I could check myself. His eyes snapped in a sharp blink, and he released me abruptly.

"I…I'm sorry." He dropped his gaze.

My head was suddenly clear, the throb between my thighs an echo of what it had been a moment ago. Fuck. He was an abyssblood, an incubus.

"Did you just use your sex mojo on me?"

He clenched his jaw. "Not intentionally."

"No? Cos it felt pretty intentional, and all the stuff you were saying…" Fuck, he had the words to back up his mojo for sure. "And you want me to trust you?"

He made a sound of exasperation. "I can't change what I am, but your father was like a father to me. I loved him and I will do whatever it takes to ensure his legacy survives."

My anger ebbed, unable to burn when faced with the sincerity in his tone.

"So why me?" I canted my head. "Why not one of the others, hmmm?"

He exhaled through his nose. "Because out of all the spawn, you remind me of him the most."

Once again, like in the carriage, his words reeked of authenticity. "I don't like games, Artimus. If you want to help, then you can do so by giving me a heads-up of what to expect next time."

"If I'd done that, then your reactions and responses in that room with the Erinyes wouldn't have been as authentic as they were, and it would have gotten you killed. I need you to trust that I'll act in your best interests. I will not abandon you."

Abandon. That fucking word. "Don't try and use my

wound against me." I'd read enough psychology books to understand my issues and how my weakness could be taken for granted.

He took a step toward me. "I would never—" His head jerked up and then his expression smoothed out to something haughty and cool. "I see you survived your meeting with the Erinyes."

What the fuck?

I registered the clip of boots on stone a moment later. Ah, okay. We were in play-acting mode now, were we?

I gave him a small smile. "No thanks to you."

The bootfalls slowed slightly.

"It isn't my place to advocate for you. It was enough that I saved you from the mob."

"Only to leave me to potential execution." I crossed my arms.

"I hear Duke Zepar has agreed to sponsor you." He smiled coolly. "You do have options, you know?"

"Oh?" What was he playing at? I thought he didn't want anyone to know he was helping me.

"Other powerful figures who'd be happy to step in as mentor and—"

"Artimus." Zepar appeared by my side. "What are you doing in this part of the keep?"

There was no doubt in my mind that Zepar had heard the play-acted part of our conversation, so he knew exactly what Artimus was doing...or what Artimus wanted him to think.

"I was checking up on our little Nephilim," Artimus said, flashing elongated canines.

I flinched in surprise when Zepar's arm closed around my shoulders. "*My* little Nephilim, not *ours*. I've staked my claim."

His tone had my hackles rising, but I grit my teeth and resisted the impulse to shove him away. I needed to see this play out.

"Your claim is in sponsorship, yes," Artimus said. "But what harm is there in her having two mentors."

"No harm," Zepar said. "Unless one of those mentors happens to be an out-of-favor faux son who's forgotten his true lineage and place."

Burn.

Zepar went straight for the jugular, no messing about.

"I forget nothing." Artimus's gaze fell on me, heat and longing blooming in his eyes.

Whoa, how had he gone from cool as a cucumber to *give me your body now* in a matter of seconds?

Zepar's grip on me tightened, drawing me against him so I had no choice but to place a hand on his chest to maintain a little distance. Damn, his pecs were hard beneath his shirt. Steel beneath silk. He grazed my shoulder with his fingertips and a shiver ran up my spine to hug my nape.

"If you're longing for another taste of her blood, then you can forget it," Zepar said. "One taste, to test her power, is all you'll get."

My gaze flew to meet Artimus's. Test my power? *Taste* my power. When we'd been with the Erinyes, Zepar had asked him if he'd tested my power and Artimus had said yes. I hadn't thought much of it at the time, assuming he'd tested me somehow without my knowing, but now...now it made sense.

Artimus tested power through blood, but he most certainly hadn't tested mine.

If he read my thoughts on my face, he didn't give any indication of it, drawing inward instead, composing himself as if with effort. If I didn't know he was faking it, I'd have been sold. He was a fabulous actor. Note to self, don't take him at face value.

The incubus was dangerous.

"A shame," he said. "Her blood may not be saturated with power, but the human aspect is sweet."

Zepar snorted. "Your kind and their taste for human blood sickens me. Thank the earth for Satan's edict preventing you from feeding on pure humans."

Artimus smiled coldly. "And yet the fallen continue to prey on them in human guise. You may not procreate with them, but you continue to enjoy bedding them."

He turned on his heel and sauntered away.

Zepar's grip on me tightened. "Stay away from my custodia."

"She's not officially yours until tomorrow," Artimus threw over his shoulder. "Much can occur between then and now."

He rounded the corner and was gone.

Zepar released me and turned me to face him, his tawny gaze dark with anger or concern, I wasn't too sure. "Stay away from him, little Nephilim. He's dangerous."

I wasn't about to make a promise I wasn't sure I was prepared to keep. "I have to get back to the residences."

He nodded. "I'll take you. I can remind Nugen of my sponsorship request while I'm there."

There was an edge to his tone, possessive and hard, and Artimus's attitude and actions suddenly made complete sense.

He wanted Zepar to continue to be interested in me, to be protective and possessive, and now that Zepar knew Artimus was sniffing about, he'd certainly be that.

Question was, why the fuck were they both *really*

interested in me? Because so far, nothing either of them had said to me in response to that question felt adequate.

There was only one person I could trust in this place. And that was me. Everyone else was a steppingstone to my goal.

Now all I had to do was remember that.

Chapter Fifteen

Zinichi let us into the residences, bowing profusely to Zepar before Nugen appeared.

"You again." Nugen grinned at Zepar, then frowned at me. "I left you with the seneschal."

"Don't do that again," Zepar said. "She belongs to me."

Nugen's hairy eyebrows snapped down. "Now, now, Zepar, you know the rules. You can't monopolize the spawn. She's your custodia as long as she accepts you tomorrow, but she can speak to whomever she chooses."

"I know the rules, Nugen, and I don't care for them. You'll keep her safe or you'll answer to my blade," he snapped.

Nugen pressed his lips together as if holding back a choice curse or two. When he spoke, his tone was even and calm. "It would do you well to recall who taught you to wield that blade."

Zepar's shoulders sagged. "You are and always will be my magister, Nugen, but on this I must stand firm. My custodia, my rules."

"I will not prevent her from seeking out mentorship elsewhere should she wish to," Nugen said.

Zepar made a sound of exasperation. "In that case it will be up to me to keep the seneschal at bay."

"Take Nyx to the dressing room, Zinichi," Nugen ordered.

Zinichi lightly touched my elbow to steer me away from the door.

"I'll see you tomorrow night," Zepar said. "You'll join me in my chambers for a meal after the Custodia ceremony."

I looked up, locking gazes with him, catching the flare of heat I'd seen on the bridge. The physical attraction. He wanted me sexually, and under regular circumstances I wouldn't have been opposed to a dalliance, but I didn't fuck guys whose intentions weren't clear. My legs were staying firmly closed until I knew what his true agenda was.

I smiled and inclined my head. "Until tomorrow night."

ZINICHI HURRIED me down a wide corridor, up a short flight of steps, and through an open set of double doors into a huge room filled with clothes racks and conversation.

Full-length mirrors lined one wall and dressers lined another. Charod and Keelan were seated on leather recliners while two imps fitted them with boots.

Gus was having his long, dark hair braided, Mallini stood in front of a full-length mirror, turning side to side to study the lines of the shimmering blue halter neck dress she was wearing. Her crimson feathers spilled down her back, contrasting beautifully with the deep blue, and her emerald eyes sparkled with pleasure at the sight of her reflection.

"Dresses?"

"The Custodia is a showy event," Zinichi said. "A chance for the spawn to attract sponsors and mentorship."

Tristeene was a couple of mirrors down, being poured into a gold, fitted number perfect for her voluptuous figure. The color sat beautifully against her tanned skin and dark eyes. Her hair had been brushed to one side and braided. A shadow in the mirror caught my eye, a figure. I blinked and it was gone.

What the hell?

A soft yelp snapped my attention to Veena, who was being forced into a plain white tunic and dark slacks. Her attendant, a zuni like her, worked with quick, abrupt motions.

"Why isn't Veena getting a dress?"

Zinichi sighed. "The family provides the outfits. Zuni aren't wealthy."

"That hardly seems fair. Surely all spawn should be treated equal."

"Fairness doesn't come into it, child." She patted my arm. "But bless you for caring. Come." She led me across the room to a dresser where a stocky woman with gazelle-like horns sat.

"Chesra, this is Nyx, Duke Zepar's custodia-to-be."

I felt rather than saw the other spawn pay attention. There would be questions later no doubt, but for now they remained in their designated lanes.

Chesra raked me over and pursed her lips. "Well, let's get a look at you. Let's see what Duke Zepar sees in you, shall we? Strong physique, pretty in your own way. Mouthy?" She narrowed her eyes and pushed her head forward, waiting for a response.

"I call it having an opinion."

Her face broke into a smile. "Yes, yes, I suppose it can be called that. Well then, let's get to work and find you the perfect outfit."

"Does it matter what outfit I wear? I already have a sponsor?"

"Of course it matters. You must wear the Court of Ivory colors and the dress must be magnificent. The other dukes will need to see what Duke Zepar sees in you and they must feel as if they've lost out when you accept Duke Zepar's offer."

Nugen had mentioned me accepting Zepar earlier too but it finally clicked what he'd meant. "I have a choice?"

She frowned and looked uncomfortable. "I was told you'd made your choice."

"Not strictly true."

Zinichi interjected, "You're Satan spawn so you get a choice, but from what I understand you have an agreement with the duke." She looked worried. "Lord Zepar is a powerful fallen."

It was a warning. "I'm sure he is, and I'm grateful for his interest in me."

That seemed to appease them both.

Chesra bustled over to a covered rack and trundled it over before whipping off the covering to reveal several outfits in ivory and gold. A few more dresses in various other colors hung at the back of the rack.

"We have these five to choose from." Chesra fingered the delicate ivory and gold material. "I made them myself to the stately specifications fit for the Court of Ivory."

They looked nice enough but an emerald number at the back was drawing my eye.

"What about the others?"

Her cheeks pinkened. "Oh, these are some personal

pieces I've been working on in my own time. I should have unloaded them before coming, but I didn't have time."

My mind whirred. I had options. Zepar didn't own me, even though he thought he did and wanted me to believe it too. But nothing was official yet, and frankly I was fed up with being pushed about like a pawn on a board. It was time to take the reins.

I wasn't planning to reject him. I believed it when they said he was my best option. Duke Umbrane sounded like a wanker, and I had very little information on Ignatius. Artimus was team Zepar too, despite coming across as contrary when faced with the duke himself.

I'd accept Duke Zepar's offer, but I'd make him work for it. I needed to show him who was in charge. I needed to show him that I wasn't a pushover, because my gut told me a woman who rolled over and gave him what he wanted wasn't someone who'd hold his interest.

I pushed aside the ivory dresses. "Show me your creations."

Zinichi made a squeaky noise of distress, but Chesra merely studied me for a long beat as if she was trying to determine what the heck was going on inside my head. Finally, she smiled and spun the rack so that her designs were visible.

I plucked at the emerald one with my fingertips. "This one. I want to try on this one."

I'D NEVER BEEN one for dressing up, my line of work didn't call for it. But as I slipped on the emerald beauty, my inner princess sat up and roared. The material was lightweight and silken, settling against my toned body like a second skin. The plunging neckline stopped above my belly button. If my tits had been bigger the dress would have looked obscene, but as luck would have it they were the perfect size to go without a bra. The skirt hugged my hips, then flared at the bottom in a myriad of peacock colors that swished and swayed when I walked. I twisted at the waist and studied the backless design. It was sexy as hell.

"This one."

Zinichi began to hyperventilate but Chesra merely grinned. "If you're certain?"

"Positive."

She nodded. "As you wish."

I turned back to the mirror to take another look and spotted Veena watching me. Her hair had been brushed but still fell forward to cover her sweet face, and she was back in her regular clothes.

I turned to Chesra. "Do you have anything small?"

She frowned. "Smaller than what you're wearing?"

"Not for me." I turned and waved Veena over. "For her."

Chesra took a deep breath, the kind of breath that precedes a speech about why they can't do something, but I cut her off.

"Please." I smiled. "She deserves something nice. She's Satan's daughter too."

Chesra and Zinichi exchanged glances.

"This isn't how it's done." Zinichi looked down at Veena. "As much as I'd like it to be."

"Is there a rule against it?"

"None at all." Tristeene joined us, back in her sweats. She turned to her attendant. "Bring the rack."

Her succubus attendant hurried over with the offerings on her rail.

I glanced across the room at Mallini, who was chewing her cheeks. She looked away quickly.

For a moment there, I'd thought...Never mind.

Chesra looked the dresses over. "They're all much too large."

Veena was staring at Tristeene's rail of clothes. I followed her gaze to a ruby red dress with full sleeves and a cinched waist.

"Can we alter this one?" I tugged it off the rack and passed it to Chesra.

Chesra rubbed the fabric between her fingers and turned it over. "Beautiful stitching, delicate and perfect."

"I have excellent seamstresses," Tristeene said.

"I can tell. And yes, I can alter it if I work through the night."

"Would you? Please?" I flashed her my sweetest smile.

She returned it with a bob of her head and a twinkle in her eye.

Veena sucked in a sharp breath. "You mean..."

I placed a hand on her shoulder. "You'll have a dress for the Custodia."

She looked from me to Tristeene, her huge, dark eyes glistening with tears. "Thank you."

"Don't thank them yet," Chesra said. "If I'm going to adjust this, I'll need you as a model. You won't get much sleep."

"I don't need much."

"Good. You'll have to come to my workshop once we're done here." She looked to Zinichi. "You'll want to send a guard."

"I'll arrange it."

I frowned. "I thought that Satan spawn weren't to be harmed."

Tristeene smiled bitterly. "Not everyone follows the rules."

Well of course they didn't, because where would the fun be in that?

It was late by the time we got back to our shared lounge. Supper was a silent affair, and I was surprised no one asked me about Zepar and the sponsorship. Maybe they'd heard enough to draw their own conclusions. All would be settled tomorrow regardless.

I headed to bed to find Chase sprawled on the floor snoring softly. He'd be hungry when he finally awakened, but I'd asked Zinichi to pack me some food for him and I placed it on the small dresser now for him.

I parked my butt on the bed, ready to kick off my boots, when someone knocked on my door.

It had to be Tristeene, but I wasn't in the mood for a midnight trip to the tower tonight. I opened the door, intending to tell her that, and then stared dumbly at Mallini.

She sighed and rolled her eyes. "Don't look so shocked. I thought I'd go for a walk. Wanted to know if you'd like to come with me."

Oh man, there were so many ways I could respond to this one. But I recognized her type. They didn't do stuff unless that had to or wanted to. I needed to know which one it was.

"Why are you asking me?"

She sighed. "I've spent the past few weeks with my brother. I could do with some refreshing conversation and

I'm sure I don't have to point out that you're the only safe option right now."

Ah, yes. "I'm the lesser of all evils."

She bit back a smile. "Something like that."

I didn't want to go for a walk, but a chance to get to know Mallini wasn't something I wanted to pass on. It was prudent to know your enemy, after all. She was the competition, and you could glean a lot about someone from one conversation if you steered it right.

The gleam in her eyes told me she was thinking the same thing.

Bring it.

"Sure." I raked her over, noting the calf-length coat she'd donned. It looked like leather, fur-trimmed and snug so it fit her frame as if it was tailor-made for her, which it probably was. I bet it even had weapon holsters hidden inside. "Let me grab a jacket."

MALLINI TOOK us out of the residences and into the keep proper. It did occur to me that I could be walking out with a murderer, but I'd slipped a dagger into my boot and there was another inside the holster in my not-so-fancy jacket. If she attacked me, I'd kill her.

The keep was silent, the darkness punctuated by shafts of moonlight that lanced in through a series of gothic windows high on the walls.

"Is it always this quiet and...empty?"

"I suppose you're used to the hustle and bustle of the mortal territories," she said.

"Something like that."

"The keep is home to Satan's retinue, the Erinyes and various staff. It's a vast place and yes, relatively empty. But tomorrow night the halls will be filled with devils, demons, and fallen."

"The demons and devils can't stay long on this side, though, right?"

"Some can withstand the atmosphere for days, others mere hours, but believe me, they'll come for as long as they can. The Custodia, the trials...They're the most exciting thing to happen in the demon realms for centuries."

We meandered down a breezy corridor with mosaic floors, and I slowed my pace even further to read the stories pictured in the intricate weave of the tapestries hanging on the walls. I caught fragments of them here and there: nine thrones beneath a star, winged males hovering above a horde of smaller figures, an army standing above a chasm, and rising above them was a figure wreathed in a silver glow, dark wings stretched wide.

"The Chaos War," Mallini said. "This corridor depicts what happened." She joined me by the tapestry. "They say Lucifer was the true king. He kept the other princes in line. Kept the peace. He gave his life to save us all." She reached out to touch the tapestry reverently. "We'd all be dead without his sacrifice. The Arch Daimon would have razed the demonic realm to ash and then marched into the mortal world."

"What do daimons want?"

"Power. And they take it using chaos and destruction. It's all they know or understand." Her lips turned down slightly. "And now with Satan gone, the balance could tip. When that happens, chaos always follows. The seat needs a firm hand. A strong leader." She turned her head to look at me.

"Someone who understands the demon world, the laws, the creatures. Someone raised to rule."

Oh, right, I saw where this was going. "Or it could do with a fresh perspective. Someone who understands how the world around this territory works. Someone who isn't stuck in a box but can think outside of it."

She angled her body toward me. "You don't belong here, Nyx, and deep down you know it." There was no fire in her words, she was merely stating her view. "You were lucky Zepar was there to save you from the poison in those clothes."

My pulse quickened. "Did you put the poison there, Mallini?"

She snorted. "I wish I was the killer. Then maybe I'd get one good night's sleep." She set off down the corridor again. "Charod claims he keeps watch over us, but he's snoring within an hour and then I'm watching the door."

"There are things called locks, you know."

"Which can be picked." She slid a glance my way. "Not all of us have pets to protect us. Which brings me to another bone of contention. Why do you get to keep a pet and none of us do?"

"Do demons even have pets?"

"Not the point."

"It's very much the point, but to clarify, Chase isn't a pet. Pet implies ownership and I don't own him. He's my friend, my hunting partner, and my family."

We came to a set of steps, and she set off down them. This was familiar. The steps led to a foyer and a wider set of stairs. I knew where I was now. Artimus had brought me into the keep this way.

A moment later we were in the circular chamber with the high, vaulted ceiling and renderings of beasts and winged creatures in battle. The three bricked-up arches sat to our left.

Mallini wandered closer to the nearest arch. "You know, if we get through the first two trials we get to go to the courts."

"How many trials are there?"

"Three, as far as I know." She placed her hand on the bricked-off gateway beneath the black arch.

A prickle of unease ran up my spine. "Should you be doing that?"

She grinned at me over her shoulder. "Aw, are you worried about me?"

"I don't care enough about you to worry, just curious."

"It's fine. Only the court members can pass in or out without an invitation. I've heard that court members can enter at any location in the court that they visualize. There isn't just one entrance."

"Sounds complicated."

"Not for these sentient wards, but Morningstar is my home. I don't belong to any of the courts." She ran her fingers over the brick. "Still, I can feel the power of the wards vibrating in the walls." She closed her eyes. "It's invigorating."

I joined her, curious to feel this power too, and placed my palm on the brick. A tingle ran up my arm.

"Do you feel it?" Mallini asked. "Close your eyes and focus."

I followed her instruction, gasping as the buzz traveled to my chest and settled there. "I feel it. I—"

The buzz expanded, sudden and violent. A hand landed on my back and shoved. Mallini cried out and the world tipped and shattered.

Chapter Sixteen

I'd been on a rollercoaster exactly once in my life. I'd thrown up afterward and decided being turned upside down and then right-side up only to be flipped again wasn't for me.

This felt just like that.

But worse.

I crouched on all fours, dry-heaving, eyes watering, as I waited for the nausea to subside and my brain to make sense of what the hell had just happened. It was dark here and it smelled like mold and dead things.

My inner voice spoke up. *Nyx, I don't think we're in Morningstar any longer.*

Ya think? I sat up on my knees, ignoring the cramp in my stomach that warned of another bout of heaving, and focused on my surroundings. Stone floors, stone ceiling, two small windows high above filtering moonlight onto a bundle of hay on the floor. There was a doorway behind me but no door.

Good. An exit.

I moved toward it stealthily and peered out into the

corridor that looked like it had been literally hewn from rock. To my left was a dead end. The only option was to go right. I stepped out, heart hammering against my ribs, because if my assessment was correct, I'd somehow been shoved through the gateway into the Court of Shadows, and I could be literally fucking anywhere in this realm.

If not for the windows and moonlight I'd have pegged this spot to be underground. Thank goodness it wasn't. I needed to scope it out, get my bearings, and then come up with a plan.

If my being here was Mallini's doing, then I doubted anyone was coming to my rescue. Lucky for me, I was adept at rescuing myself. At least I had been, but Morningstar was new ground, new dangers, and powerful creatures, and to a Nephilim with no power, that was a lethal combination.

Stealth and wit would be my friends, and my wit told me that all I had to do was find an official entity, a guard or something, explain who I was and what had happened, and they'd get me back to Morningstar pronto.

Easy.

My stomach quivered, warning me not to be naive.

I had my daggers. I could defend myself. I was partway down the corridor, approaching a patch of moonlight that indicated a doorway up ahead, when a lashing sound echoed on the walls followed by a grunt. I froze and listened. The sound came again, and again.

It was coming from the room.

I skulked forward, then pressed my back to the wall, inching along the corridor, crablike, until I got to the door.

The lashes were loud and stinging, slapping against something with a fleshy sound.

Someone was being whipped.

I dropped low and risked a peek into the room. Benches

lined with wickedly sharp silver implements lined one wall, and shackles and strange metallic devices were bolted to another.

This was a torture chamber, and taking pride of place in the center of it was a dark figure on his knees being whipped by two imps.

They babbled in tongues, leaping and taking it in turns to lash at their captor with their whips. I caught glimpses of a broad, bloody back, but the demon being whipped barely flinched.

They continued to babble, but suddenly the babbling morphed into something I could understand.

"This no fun," one of the imps said. "Me likes the ones that scream."

Fuck, they weren't speaking English, but I could fucking understand them. How was this possible?

"Got to be done," the other replied. "Umbrane's orders."

"Scream, nightmare, scream!" The first imp grabbed the nightmare's silver hair and tugged his head back. "Scream for us."

"Fuck you, Amnu." The voice was smooth, the tone almost lazy, as if he'd just woken from a restful nap. "And fuck your boar-faced mother too."

The imp let go with a cry of frustration. "You don't talk about my mother."

"No, I just stick my cock in her mouth and cum. She likes it."

"Argh!" The imp shook with rage and then released the nightmare. "Go. Get out. Useless, worthless scum. You not rile me. Not today."

"He'll die soon anyway," the other one said.

The nightmare stood slowly, unfurling his lithe frame to its full height. His back was wide, tapering to a narrow waist where a long, thick tail began and ended in an arrowhead. His legs were encased in black slacks and his feet were bare. He rolled his muscle-rounded shoulders and tilted his head from side to side as if loosening kinks caused by the whiplashing. The imps backed away, then hopped forward, then backed up again as if unsure what to do next.

Was he a prisoner or not? I mean, he wasn't shackled. He'd just knelt there and taken the beating.

Shit, shit, shit. There was no way I was dashing past this doorway without being seen. As the nightmare began to turn, I ducked out of view and ran back toward the room I'd started in.

I pressed myself into the shadows and waited. Crap. Maybe I should have shown myself and spoken to the imps. But it wasn't obvious that they were in charge here. I needed more information. I needed a moment to gather my thoughts and make sense of what I'd seen.

Nightmares...They were the cattle of the Shadow Court, right? Except *that* nightmare hadn't looked like cattle.

A shadow slipped through the doorway.

I shrank back into the gloom and held my breath as the nightmare entered the room. He wasn't as tall as Zepar and Artimus, maybe just over six feet, less bulky too, but there was lethal promise to the fluid way he moved. He had the wiry, powerful physique of a sprinter or a martial artist. Powerful thigh muscles and calves spoke of lower body strength and stamina.

If I ran from him, odds were I wouldn't make it far. My hand itched to go for the dagger in my jacket, but any movement could alert him to my presence. I held still.

The nightmare's chin was tucked in, silver locks falling about his face so that it was impossible to see his features. I caught the cruel curve of a mouth and the sharp angle of his jaw as he walked over to the pile of hay. His tail trailed against the floor, arrowhead scraping against the stone softly, as if too weary to do anything else.

He lowered his body onto the hay with a soft groan. Bathed in moonlight, his skin was an Aegean blue unlike anything I'd ever seen.

"Who are you?" he asked.

I tensed. Was he talking to me?

"I can smell you. Did you enjoy the show?"

Damn it, my shitty cover was blown. It looked like everyone in Morningstar had extra sharp senses.

I stepped out of the shadows. "No, I didn't enjoy watching them whip you. Did you enjoy getting whipped?" I genuinely wanted to know. He'd seemed so unfazed by the beating.

He raised his head and his silver locks slid back to reveal a face that was criss-crossed with slender scars. Defiance blazed in his silver eyes, burning a path into my soul.

Fuck, he was beautiful.

"You like scars?" He canted his head, tongue peeking out to touch the corner of his mouth. "What do you owe him? What could be worth your sanity?"

"I have no idea what you're talking about."

He moved so fast there was no time to evade before he had me pushed against the stone, his fists punching the wall either side of me. "Do you know what it does to me?" He exhaled and my head swam. "Did he tell you what you're in for?" His tone was thicker now, saturated with need. "When I feed, I fuck, and when I fuck, the person beneath me gets hurt."

"What?" My lungs felt tight and the air too thin.

"You shouldn't have accepted his offer." He dropped one hand and shoved it between my legs to cup my pussy.

What the everloving fuck? I brought my knee up and twisted my body, knocking his hand away and shoving my back into his chest to create distance between us. But it barely moved him, and the next moment I was squished against the wall with his chest crushing my back and his breath hot in my ear.

"What is this?" he crooned. "A fighter? He's never sent me a fighter before." His breathing quickened. "Oh...this might be worth it after all. A final treat and a worthy farewell."

I pressed my palms to the wall and pushed with all my might, but he was immovable. Cruel laughter rang in my ears and panic began to edge in.

"I like this," he said. "I like this game. I'll enjoy hurting you and you'll enjoy letting me."

My mind raced, absorbing his words and drawing conclusions. "Listen to me. I wasn't sent here for you. I fell through the gateway from Morningstar. It brought me here. No one sent me. I'm Satan spawn."

He stilled and then let out a low, menacing growl.

Had I just made things worse?

His chest heaved against my back, then he grabbed my hair and yanked my head to the side.

I bit back a cry and grit my teeth as his tongue cut a hot path up the side of my neck. My stomach tightened, heat blooming between my thighs. He licked me again and nuzzled the spot below my ear, inhaling my scent. My body reacted like a wanton hussy.

I clenched my jaw and breathed through my nose to fight the feelings his attentions were evoking. "I'm not here for you."

Something pressed against my ass, hard, large, and

insistent. "What are you?" He swept his tongue along my jaw. "Like home..."

He had a boner. Great. Focus, Nyx. "Nephilim. Satan spawn, and *not* for you. So get the fuck off me now." My voice echoed off the walls in undeniable command.

He released me immediately and put distance between us. "Not for me."

I turned to face him, breathing through the anger burning up my lungs. But one look at his horrified expression and the rage melted.

His silver gaze sharpened, cutting through the gloom to rake over me, as if seeing me for the first time. "You're not safe here."

I let out a bark of laughter. "Gee, thanks for the heads-up."

His chest vibrated in a growl that was more admonishment than warning. "You are not mine. The others cannot claim what is gifted to another by the master. But you are not a gift." His gaze darted to the door. "They will smell you and they will come."

"Who?"

He muttered something I couldn't catch, took a step toward me, then stopped, hands balling into fists. "They're hungry. We're always hungry."

There was no stemming my panic now. "Hungry for what?" Why had I asked that?

He licked his lips. "Blood, pain, sensation, emotion... They'll come unless I mask your scent with mine." He moved a step closer, then turned his head to the side. "I have your taste in my mouth, your scent in my nose. It will be enough." His hand went to the bulge in his pants, and I realized there were no pants. He was naked, but the skin of his lower body was inky black and leathery dark. The bulge was a pocket of skin; it parted, and an impressive cock pushed out to rest on his palm. He curled his long fingers around his arousal and began to work it.

"Yes, enough." He groaned, then sucked air through his teeth as he masturbated in front of me.

I'd like to say I wanted to look away, but that would be a lie. I was mesmerized by the beauty of this act, the play of muscle up his arm and across his abs as he chased his release. He kept his gaze averted, and I took advantage of that to drink him in.

They didn't make porn like this in the real world.

Heat hugged my neck and peaked my nipples, trailing a path down my abdomen to my pussy, where it settled in a throb that echoed the motion of his hand.

I was depraved. Horny as fuck, and I didn't give a shit.

He came with a grunt, hips jerking as he released his seed on the flagstones. The air was suddenly saturated with a sweet scent that made my knees weak.

His arousal retracted and he bowed his head, shoulders rising and falling as he composed himself.

"The scent won't last long," he said finally. "We need to get you to the guard room. They'll make sure you get to a gateway."

There was conflict in his eyes, as if he wasn't sure he was doing the right thing, but then his jaw set. "Come with me. Stay close so the others don't catch your scent."

He crossed to the exit, and I followed, stepping close so that his sweet scent enveloped me too. He moved fast down the corridor, and I kept to his shadow, within the radius of his scent. The wounds on his back were already healing, raised welts now crusted with blood.

We passed the blood-spattered torture room and

continued past several doorways. I caught movement, the flash of glowing eyes, and shivers of shadow.

"Fuck," the nightmare said. "Your scent is too strong." He grabbed my arm and yanked me forward, placing me in front of him. "Move."

I picked up speed toward an intersection. "Which way?"

"Left."

"What is that?" someone called out.

"What are you hoarding, Sev?" another called out.

"Back off, Greeves," my nightmare ordered. "She's not for us."

"Not for *you*, but if it entered the stables, it's fair game. Umbrane's rules."

We were running now, sprinting across the flagstones toward a wooden door. It was the only way out. I skidded to a halt and grabbed the handle, twisting and yanking to no avail.

"It's locked."

"I scent her!"

"Mine."

"Mine!"

"Stay back!" Sev's bellow had the hairs on my neck standing to attention. I turned away from the locked door and peered around the nightmare's bicep at the crowded corridor beyond.

More nightmares, creatures similar to Sev but varying in stature and shade of blue, filled the corridor.

"She's not for us," Sev repeated.

"Umbrane's pet," someone said. "The favored. The pampered."

"Out of favor now," another said.

"Gone soon."

What? I looked up at Sev, catching his profile and the hard edge of his jaw.

"I'm still here. Right now. You will obey me."

Some of them cowered, but one pushed forward and stood tall. His hair was bone white, irises inky black against stone-gray skin.

"You hold no power over us," he said. "Not here. Not now."

They surged toward us. Sev pushed me toward the door, then fell into a crouch, hissing and growling. The action and sound acted like a warning, causing some of them to falter. Not the white-haired one, though; he kept coming.

I drew my dagger from my jacket, ready to defend myself, when a gust of cold air hit the back of my head.

Arms wrapped around me, and I was hauled away from the nightmares and through the door, losing my grip on my dagger.

It clattered to the floor as I fought on instinct against this new threat.

"It's okay, Nyx. It's me, Artimus. I've got you."

The last thing I saw before the door closed on the corridor were Sev's silver eyes filled with triumph.

Artimus hugged me to his chest, his honeysuckle scent acting as a calming balm to my frazzled nerves.

I let him hold me for a moment because there was no doubt in my mind that if he hadn't shown up when he had, I'd have literally been fucked.

Sev and I would have fought, of course, but against all

those nightmares, stuck in a network of stone corridors with no escape to hand, we would have failed.

I allowed myself to work through the close call, shut it down, and then shoved at Artimus's chest to let him know I was good.

He released me but used the crook of his finger to force me to look up at him. "Did they hurt you?" His tone was laced with a suppressed emotion I was too frazzled to identify.

"No. Sev protected me."

"Sev?" His eyes narrowed. "Umbrane's pet."

"You know him?"

"I know of him. He's Umbrane's favorite toy, or he was. I hear the duke has chosen a new plaything and Sev has been demoted from the position." A dark look crossed his face.

"What? What are you not telling me?"

"Nothing that you need to worry about. We need to get to the gateway before Umbrane discovers you're here. I don't trust what he'll do."

We were in a small entranceway with two stools and a table set against the wall. An empty weapons rack was bolted to the wall and an iron door stood ajar behind us.

"How did you find me?"

"One of the spawn alerted Nugen to what had happened. He summoned me because my affiliation to the Court of Shadows allows me access."

Mallini? Had she called for help? If she did, it meant she hadn't tried to murder me, unless she hoped I'd be dead by the time they found me.

"I tracked your essence and it led me here." He took my hand and led me through the iron door into a room filled with sleeping imps.

They lay across tables, hung off stools, sat up against the

walls. Some had food dribbling out of their mouths, others clutched tankards of ale that had partially spilled.

Artimus led me across the room. "Hurry, before the effects of the spell wear off."

"Spell?"

"I have a conji on retainer who provides me with a few minor potions and cantrips. My abyssblood allows me to use them, but they don't last long."

I had no idea what a conji was, but I was more than happy to get out of here. We made it past the sleeping imps and through another door that opened onto a starlit courtyard with the view of a field rich with a swaying harvest.

"This way." Artimus dragged me toward the wall, where an arch of black stone stood starkly against the gray rock.

"Stop!"

"Get them!"

Voices lit up the night behind us.

The gateway began to glow as we approached.

Something whizzed through the air, a sound I recognized. I ducked, yanking on Artimus's arm to force him to do the same. An arrow buried itself in the stone above the arch with a *thunk*.

Another one whizzed past my head.

Artimus wrapped an arm around my waist and propelled me across the courtyard at double speed. The wind rushed through my hair and the gateway swelled to meet us. The imps' cries grew distant, and the world tipped and shattered.

THE WORLD REASSIMILATED, this time with less nausea and a warm body to cushion my fall, although I wasn't sure how much cushion there was in the layer of muscle and sinew beneath me.

Artimus and I lay entwined, bodies flush against each other, touching in places they had no business touching. How had my fingers slipped into his silken hair? How had my mouth gotten so close to his jugular that I could feel his pulse pound against my lips? I could kiss him there if I shifted my chin just so, and for some inexplicable reason, in that moment I wanted to.

Maybe it was the fact that I'd just escaped being fucked to death by a bunch of nightmares, then being impaled by imp arrows. Adrenaline coursed through my veins, making me reckless. I took a deep breath to ground myself. The inhalation pushed my breast against his chest, reminding me of the power that lay beneath me.

He didn't move, didn't speak, all tension and harsh planes, one arm around my waist, the other at my nape, cradling me to his chest.

We breathed in unison for several seconds longer as I oscillated between reveling in the contact and wresting my emotions into control.

I finally lifted my head, cheek grazing his stubbled jaw to look into his stunning sapphire eyes. His pupils expanded, inky and compelling, drinking me in. My body forgot how to produce saliva.

His nostrils flared, sniffing the air. "You're bleeding."

The pain registered then, a fiery gnawing sensation on my thigh. "Fuck." I scrambled off him, ass hitting marble as I twisted to examine the wound.

A flesh wound, the graze of an arrow, but damn, it hurt like a motherfucker.

Artimus gripped my thigh and dragged me toward him. Was he panting?

What the hell?

His eyes were red with bloodlust, lips pulled back, canines pronounced as he stared at the wound.

"Um...Artimus, you might want to put those away." I'd dropped my dagger when Artimus had yanked me out of the corridor and away from the nightmares, but I had another in my boot. Not that I'd be able to get to it before he attacked, because there was no doubt in my mind that was exactly what he intended to do. "Don't make me hurt you."

His grip was so tight it was painful, his face a mere foot from my thigh. "Hit me." He growled out the words. "Hit me now."

I slapped him hard enough to rock his head on his shoulders. He released me quickly enough, blinking and backing away from me. "Get that seen to. I'll find you at the residences in an hour." He turned and ran, leaving me with the strong impression that I'd just dodged another bullet.

I pulled myself to my feet and headed for the stairs. I had an Erinyes to find and question, and if I didn't like her responses, punch in the face.

Repeatedly.

"How could this happen?" Nugen asked again. "You've no invitation and you don't belong to the Court of Shadow."

I sat on a chair with my leg stretched out. Zinichi had cleaned up the wound, but she'd had to tear my trousers to do it. She'd promised to procure me a new pair. The wound, however, was already healing.

"Someone pushed me." I glared at Mallini.

Mallini rolled her eyes. "I did not. I tried to grab you. You just...you fell through."

"Bullshit," Keelan said. "I always knew you and your twin were the murderers."

The room broke into a cacophony of sound as the spawn began to argue.

"Enough!" Artimus strode into the lounge.

He'd changed out of the cream shirt and black slacks he'd been wearing when he'd rescued me and into something more formal. The tailored silver waistcoat contrasted well with his black silk shirt and pants.

His dark hair was damp and brushed back from his forehead.

He'd run away to shower. Artimus in the shower. Naked.

Stop it.

"It's been confirmed that the wards were tampered with," Artimus said. "Someone knew you would be there."

"She knew." Keelan pointed a dramatic finger at Mallini, like an actor in a soap pointing out the bad guy. "She took her there."

Mallini made a sound of exasperation. "I go there all the time. It's my thinking spot."

She'd shared her thinking spot with me? Just like Tristeene had shared hers with me. "Wait...if you go there all the time, then the trap must have been set for you?"

Mallini's eyes flew wide. "Oh..."

"But she never fell through, *you* did," Gus said.

"And I touched the wall," Mallini said.

"You didn't get a chance to touch the right spot," Artimus explained. "The ward was weakened in a specific spot."

I watched him speak, explain it, and my gut twinged. He was lying. Explaining this away. But why?

"I can't believe it dropped you at the nightmare stables," Keelan said. "You're lucky to be alive. Those creatures are vicious. Umbrane is the only one who can keep them in line."

Yes, they'd had the potential for violence, but now that I was safe and able to reflect, I couldn't help but wonder how much of that violence was manufactured by Umbrane himself. If you withheld a creature's basic needs, was it the creature's fault if it turned rabid?

"It's late," Nugen said. "It'll be dawn soon and you have a big day tomorrow, so get some sleep."

He lifted his chin in Artimus's direction. "You need to go now."

Artimus looked toward me, his expression torn, but then he nodded and followed the demon out the door.

"Zepar and Artimus..." Mallini let the sentence hang, no need to elaborate.

I shrugged. "I can't help it if I'm irresistible."

"It begins tomorrow," Veena said softly.

A solemn atmosphere settled over us. The excitement of the earlier dress-up session was gone.

"It'll be fine." I smiled at her. "Three trials and we'll have a Satan."

Veena looked at me with dark, soulful eyes. "You don't understand, do you?"

"Understand what?"

Tristeene cleared her throat. "Nugen told us at the start. You weren't here. Once the trials start, all bets are off."

"I don't understand?"

"The spawn protection is withdrawn," Mallini said. "If we don't kill each other during the trials, then someone else might kill us outside of them."

The importance of sponsorship made perfect sense now.

After the ascension opened tomorrow, we were going to need protection.

Sleep, which had sounded like a fabulous idea a few moments ago, now seemed like an impossibility.

Tomorrow the circus would begin, and once we stepped on the ascension tightrope, the only way off would be through death.

Chapter Seventeen

The food I'd left for Chase had been eaten and he was awake but dozy. I shucked off my boots and climbed into bed, and he shuffled closer so he could lay his head on my belly.

I stroked his head. "Want to hear about my insane day and night?"

He rolled his hazel eyes my way as if to say, *don't I always*?

I smiled and scratched behind his ears, then proceeded to tell him about the throne room, the weird voice in my head, the awesome dress I'd be wearing tomorrow, and my dark encounter with the nightmares followed by the narrow escape.

He listened, chuffing here or there, and somewhere along the way my eyelids drooped, and I dropped into the arms of the sandman.

I WAS BACK in the Shadow Court realm. Back in Sev's stone room. He sat on his pallet of hay, arms wrapped around his knees, staring up at the square of moonlight high up on the wall.

His silver hair flowed away from his face to reveal his sharp profile. His eyes were at half-mast as if he was reveling in the kiss of moonlight, and maybe he was, because his Aegean skin shimmered here and there where the silver rays touched him.

"I was wondering if you'd come," he said softly.

There was an aching quality to his tone that made my breath catch and twist in my throat.

This wasn't real. I was back in Morningstar in my narrow bed. "This is a dream."

"It is?" The corner of his mouth lifted. "Then you're at no risk of coming closer, are you?"

It wasn't a challenge or a taunt, merely a statement of logic.

I took a step, and the chill from the stone floor seeped into my bare feet. "It feels so real."

"Yes," he said. "Even dreams are their own kind of reality." He turned his head toward me slightly and I caught the flare of his nostrils. "Come, sit."

This was a dream. I was certain of that much and so there was no real danger here. I crossed the room and lowered myself onto the hay beside him. It pricked at my thighs beneath the hem of my shorts, and when my bare arm brushed his, a shiver passed through me.

He sighed at the contact and tucked in his chin. "It's been too long."

"Too long? Since what?"

"This."

There it was again, that aching throb in his voice. "I'm not sure what you mean."

He looked down into my face. "So innocent and new." I

flinched when his fingers caressed my cheek. "When I had you here, pressed to the wall, my body flush against yours, I felt your desire. You wanted me to fuck you. You would have reveled in the pain, wringing a twisted pleasure from it."

I pulled my head back. "That wasn't desire. I was confused. Scared."

"Liar. You weren't scared. Not for a moment."

I cast my mind back to our encounter, running it through my memory, scene by scene. His scent, the weight of him, and the heat that had bloomed in my belly at the threat he'd posed. A threat that my body had read as more of a promise.

"What is this? Some kind of nightmare mojo?" Oh man, I was such an idiot. "You're in my dream, aren't you? I'm not sure how, but you found a way into my head."

His moon-drenched eyes kissed my cheek, lingering on my mouth before locking with my gaze.

"Still a dream. Still not *real*. But you owe me."

I wanted to tell him to piss off, but his words were a weight settling over me. A debt.

Fuck it. "What do you want."

"A taste." He licked his lips and my stomach flipped.

"A taste of what?"

"A painful memory."

"Yeah, I don't think so." I made to get up, but he grabbed my arm, halting me. "Let go."

"*You* let go." His breath was warm and enticing. "This is a dream. You can do whatever you want, without consequence. Give me a memory and I'll give you pleasure."

My gaze dropped to his mouth, then down to sweep over the hard planes of a body honed to perfection. I lingered at his Adonis belt, then dropped further to his bulging groin.

"Touch it." He leaned back and stretched out his legs. "You can do what you want in a dream."

Heart pounding like a jackhammer, I reached down to run my fingers over the bulge that hid his arousal. His skin was leathery but soft, warm, alive. I liked sex. A lot. It was my favorite recreational activity, and this *was* a dream, a gloriously vivid one conjured by my subconscious because I needed this.

Why shouldn't I have it?

I pressed my palm to his hidden arousal, and he sucked in a sharp breath.

"Take it." I looked up, gaze snagging with his. "Take what I owe you."

He twisted and pinned me beneath him, stretching my hands above my head and pinning them there with one of his own. His slender hips settled between my thighs, groin to groin.

I let him arrange me, staring up into his beautiful, scarred face twisted with an indescribable hunger.

"It's been so long since I fed, truly fed." He ground himself against me and I gasped at the heady sensation. "Oh, there'll be more, so much more, but first I need you to pay." He leaned in so his mouth hovered above mine.

I turned my head to the side. "No kisses."

I'd broken that rule once, taken what I'd vowed would be a fun romp into intimate territory that could have broken my heart.

I didn't do broken hearts.

"Not a kiss," he clarified, "but a seal. You owe me."

I turned my face to his and he lowered his mouth to graze mine. His lips were soft and warm, his breath fresh like a starlit night. A tingle passed through my mouth, over my cheeks, and then claws dug into my head. I cried out in shock and pain.

My vision went dark, and when the world reformed, I was holding my mother's hand as she led me through an unfamiliar town. I had my best shoes on, the boots that kept out the wet, and my yellow raincoat. Mummy had packed my red backpack for me. I'd asked where we were going. A surprise, she'd said.

The surprise trip was long. Two buses and lots of walking, and my legs were tired now.

"Are we there yet?" I hated to whine, I was a big girl now, but I was getting hungry.

She didn't answer, just tugged me along faster. We passed through busy streets, past the colorful stalls and through delicious smells. So many people. Too many. I gripped Mummy's hand tighter. I didn't want to get lost.

We rounded a corner into an alley, dirty walls rising either side of us, and finally Mummy stopped.

I looked about in confusion. "Is this the surprise?"

She made a strange choking sound.

"Mummy?"

She crouched down and placed her hands on my shoulders. Her face was a blur. Why was her face a blur?

"Mummy, what's wrong?"

"You are," she said. "You're all wrong, Nyx, and I have to let you go."

Panic squeezed my chest. "Go? Go where?"

"Anywhere but with me." Her fingers tightened on my bony shoulders, and I winced in pain. "There's food in the pack, some money too. Someone will find you and take care of you. This place...This place is filled with creatures like you. Someone will take you in."

She sounded like she was talking to herself. Like she was trying to make herself believe a lie.

My stomach hurt. "I don't understand."

She shook me once. Hard. "You'll stay here. Don't follow me. Don't try to find your way home. Do you understand me?"

"No..." I tried to grab hold of her, to put my arms around her neck and hold on to her the way she used to let me before Oscar and Jen.

But she shoved me away. I fell to the ground.

"Mummy!" I got up and rushed toward her. She grabbed me and this time she shook me so hard my teeth rattled.

"Stay away, you hear me. I don't want you. I don't want you anymore."

This time when she walked away, I let her.

I stood in the rain, watching her retreat, my heart shattering into a million pieces. As the heavens opened properly, I crawled beneath the metal staircase and curled up with my pack, closing my eyes and allowing sleep to take me because this was a dream. A bad, bad dream.

I sucked in a breath and stared at Sev through a sheen of tears, the weight of forgotten sorrow heavy on my chest. "You bastard."

His eyes were bright, pupils dilated, mouth parted as he panted. "Oh...that was...delicious."

I shoved at his shoulder. "Get off me. Now."

He obliged, rolling to the side so I could sit up. The memory was like a fresh wound in my heart. As if I were five again. Being abandoned again. Alone again. My chest swelled and then a sob broke from my lips, followed by another and another. Grief tore through me, my body too weak and drained to fight it.

Beside me Sev groaned softly. A sound of pleasure.

Something warm trailed up my arm. I turned my head to find him licking me.

"What the fuck?" My voice was thick with tears. "What is wrong with you?"

He wrapped his arm around me and pulled me close before pressing his mouth to my neck and lapping at my skin.

"Get off!" I punched his shoulder, but he held me tighter, moving his mouth against my skin, lips and tongue and the scrape of teeth until a fresh heat bloomed low in my belly, chasing away the weight of sorrow and replacing it with need and desire.

"Yes." He pushed me to the ground and rolled on top of me. "Take the pleasure."

He ran his hand down my side, over my clothes, and when he trailed it up again, he caressed bare flesh.

My clothes were gone.

I was naked, vulnerable, hot, and ready for him.

He reared up and looked down at me with carnal hunger in his silver eyes. "A feast for my cock."

I looked down in time to see his arousal surface, glistening at the tip. Ready for me.

My pussy throbbed, eager and wanting, the awful memory forgotten.

He gripped my thighs and pressed himself against me. I was ready, so fucking—

He stopped and pulled away.

"What?"

He looked down at me with a conflicted expression, his mouth turning down in regret. "Our time's up. Shame...such a fucking shame."

. . .

I woke to knocking on my door.

"Final fitting's in an hour," Zinichi called through the door. "If you want breakfast, you best get out here."

I rolled onto my side and looked down at a sleeping Chase, then flopped back onto the bed and stared at the ceiling. My heart was still beating too fast, and I was wet from the dream. A pretty messed-up one that made me realize my abandonment issues would probably never go away completely.

An image of Sev filled my mind. An echo of the memory of his cock pushing against me. Just a dream, but now I needed a shower and some alone time with my hand.

I'd need a clear head for the day to come, because by the end of it, we'd all be fair game.

Chapter Eighteen

The emerald dress clung to my body in all the right places, brought out the green flecks in my hazel eyes, and accentuated the ink running up my arm. Chesra had brushed my dark hair until it gleamed, then put it up into an intricate style, leaving tendrils to fall against my cheeks.

I looked almost regal.

Ha.

Just went to show how looks could be deceptive. My hand went to my thigh, the spot where a small dagger was strapped. A gift from Zepar, intricately carved with the Court of Ivory crest: two wings with a sword between them. It was his gift of ownership. How pissed would he be when he saw I wasn't wearing his colors?

Doubt stabbed at me for a moment, because taunting him, especially now that I knew the spawn protection would be lifted after the Custodia, was probably not a great idea, but I pushed it away. If he was serious about having me under his protection, then a dress wouldn't change that. If anything, it would demonstrate his conviction.

Around me the others were making the final checks to their reflections. Tristeene looked stunning in the gold, fitted number. Her dark hair was pulled into a chic long braid that draped over one shoulder and rested on her chest. Mallini's shimmery blue halter neck dress had been modified to add slits to the skirt so you caught a flash of slender thigh every time she took a step. Her plumes lay against her back like a crimson waterfall. Her eyes were heavily made up with kohl, giving her a battle-ready look that provided a powerful contrast to her feminine attire.

She flashed me a grin when she caught me looking, and I returned it with a thumbs up.

Charod joined her, looking dashing in a matching gold shirt. He'd paired it with a crimson waistcoat to match his plumes.

Across the room Keelan polished his horns, looking lethal and barbarian in a black studded waistcoat, sans shirt, and loose-fitted slacks, a customary ceremonial outfit for Minorax, it seemed.

Gus wore a deep purple shirt and slacks to match. His wings were adorned with tiny glittering gems. He smiled nervously and lifted a hand in greeting before going back to adjusting his waistcoat.

We were all here, all ready, except one.

I turned to the fitting room in time to see Veena emerge. The drab figure had been transformed into a fairy princess. Chesra had altered the ruby red dress that had been too long for her into a miniature gown with a sweetheart neckline, cinched waist, and ruffled skirt that came to just above the knee. She wore black stockings and black ballet shoes, and her hair was pulled up into a high ponytail that cascaded down her back in inky sheets.

Her dark eyes looked huge in her pale, oval face as she waited for our judgment.

I shook my head, grinning from ear to ear. "Well, I think I know who's going to be the belle of the Custodia."

"You look beautiful," Tristeene said.

"Gorgeous," Mallini added.

Veena's face crumpled, and she burst into tears.

Ah, shit, we'd overwhelmed her.

"Now, now!" Chesra fussed around her, dabbing at her face with a handkerchief. "You'll make yourself all blotchy if you cry."

Veena nodded. "I'm sorry. I'm just so...happy." She said the word as if it was new to her, as if she'd never had cause to use it before.

That pissed me off. Everyone had a right to happiness, no matter their breed or race or fucking social standing.

I crossed the room and carefully crouched in front of her. "You're allowed to be happy, Veena. We all are."

She pressed her lips together and nodded, but there was no hiding the conflict in her dark eyes. "Not for long now, though," she whispered softly. "Soon we'll all be targets."

"Way to bring down the mood," Charod drawled.

"She's right, though," Keelan said. "After tonight we'll be fair game to anyone who wants to tip the scales in favor of their custodia."

I straightened and stood. "Then we make a pact. Here and now, that we don't let that happen. We don't let any outsider determine our fate. We protect one another."

"Are you forgetting there's a killer in our midst?" Tristeene said.

"No. But that killer will be just another target soon. A target just like us. So we draw a line in the sand, and we vow to protect each other."

The room fell into a hush as everyone exchanged glances.

"There can only be one Satan," Keelan growled.

"I know." I smiled. "So let the trials pick who that is. Whoever performs best overall will win, right?"

"She has a point," Mallini said. "If we watch each other's backs outside of the trials we can all have a fair shot inside them."

"I'm not agreeing to anything." Keelan narrowed his eyes at me. "You could be planning something." He glared at me. "A trick."

I rolled my eyes. "What trick, Keelan? How could this possibly be a trick?"

"Minorax are naturally paranoid and suspicious," Gus explained.

"Shut up, you walking encyclopedia," Keelan snapped.

"I'm surprised you know the word encyclopedia," Tristeene drawled.

"Enough!" Nugen entered the room. "Your bickering will have to wait. It's time."

My stomach dropped, but I fixed a smile on my face and gathered my skirts. "Let's do this."

I was expecting us to be taken out of the main doors into the keep proper, but Nugen took us in a new direction. He unlocked a narrow wooden door and led us into a large study lined with books and racks piled with scrolls.

"Is this your study?" Tristeene asked.

"No." He crossed the room and tugged on a sconce fixed to the wall. A mechanism?

One of the bookcases slid open to reveal a dimly lit corridor beyond.

"A secret passage, nice," Mallini said.

"And there are plenty more," Nugen said. "As Satan spawn you will be made privy to some of them once the Custodia is over, but only Satan will be made aware of the full network."

"So we can escape from potential killers?" Charod said.

Nugen ducked into the passage. "Exactly. Come now. We need to hurry. You'll be announced soon."

We slipped through the hidden passages, past several sets of steps and doors. I noted symbols etched to the walls, some kind of map for whoever used these passages.

We came to a flight of steps wider than the rest and Nugen stopped and turned to us.

"These steps lead to the Conventus Locus."

"Assembly room," Tristeene whispered. "Satan had a thing for Latin."

"We'll exit into a backroom," Nugen said. "From there we'll take a short corridor to the balconies where you will be seated. The drapes to the main Locus will be closed. Once you are announced, they'll open and you'll be asked to step forward for all to see. The dukes and lords will then make their bids for sponsorship and you will be asked to accept or reject their offers. Once that business is complete, you can relax, drink and eat, and enjoy the entertainment."

"Entertainment?" Mallini frowned. "What kind of entertainment?"

Nugen looked away. "The bloody kind." He climbed the steps. "Hurry now."

I lifted my skirts and followed, thankful for the comfortable footwear. Demons didn't do high heels, their footwear was all soft velvet and leather. Chesra had found me ballet flats with diamantes pressed into them.

Nugen shoved open the doors at the top of the stairs and ushered us into the room beyond. It looked like a storage space filled with baskets of fabrics and shelves lined with odds and ends I couldn't identify. A dressmaker's model stood in a corner, stuck with gleaming pins, and a pair of boots lay abandoned at its feet.

"What is this room?" Mallini asked.

"One of the many dumping spots around the keep," Nugen said. "It gets cleaned out once or twice a decade." He closed the door we'd come through. The side that faced the room was a cabinet, hiding the existence of the exit to anyone who didn't know it was there.

Nugen hurried past us and opened the main door, letting in the distant sound of music and chatter.

"It's almost time. Quick." He picked up the pace down a short corridor and pulled back a set of thick drapes hanging from a high arch. "In you go and grab a seat."

Seven high-back silver seats were arranged on the balcony's marble floor. Thick black drapes speckled with silver dust blocked our view to the Locus beyond. Keelan took the seat furthest from us, then Gus, then Charod, Mallini, me, and Tristeene, then Veena.

We'd barely settled ourselves when the drapes began to move.

"Good luck." Nugen ducked out of the balcony, leaving us to it.

The drapes drifted open and the full force of the assembly beyond hit me in a wave of sounds and smells. We were on a balcony with a circular chamber below us and three balconies directly opposite.

The one in the center, facing us head-on, was decorated

in ivory and gold hues. Sitting amidst the demon dignitaries, male and female, and standing out like a diamond in the sand, was Zepar himself, his tawny eyes bright in his chiseled face as he locked gazes with me. His smile dipped as he looked me over, noting my emerald dress, but then his lips tipped back up in a crooked smile that said he accepted my challenge. I inclined my head with a small smile of my own.

"Looks like Duke Zepar isn't too upset you refused to wear his colors," Tristeene said. "He'd be worried if he could see how Duke Ignatius is watching you right now, though."

My gaze flicked from Zepar to the balcony to his right. It was decorated in shades of red and orange and stood out starkly against the calm hues of the Ivory Court.

There were no females here, just males, all huge, bulky creatures. And in the center, set like a jewel in a crown, sat a golden man. My breath snagged in my throat as I raked him over. His skin was literally golden, like all over. It gleamed in the light from the chandeliers high above. His hair was spun gold and his eyes embers.

He sat with one leg propped up on a pedestal, the other stretched out, elbow resting on the arm of his chair, head tipped to one side, regarding me through narrowed, speculative eyes. I caught movement across his skin: gold tattoos that seemed to move like flickering flames.

He sat forward slowly, his gaze growing intense.

My stomach tightened and warmth spread through my limbs. Why was he looking at me like that?

"Fuck," Tristeene whispered. "I've never seen him show so much interest in anything. The efreet is a psychopath, cold as ice, despite his fiery nature. Nothing fazes him. This isn't good."

"Why?"

"Because Duke Ignatius may not want for much. He may not demand much, but when he sets his sights on something, he gets it."

A shiver ran up my spine. "Just as well *I* have the choice and not him, isn't it?" I tipped my chin up and arched an imperious brow in Ignatius's direction before deliberately turning away to focus on Zepar.

Zepar was the known entity. He'd saved my life. He had the most power here, and Artimus, my secret mentor, approved.

Ignatius could want, but he wasn't going to get.

Zepar smiled, confidence seeping from his pores. Okay, so it annoyed me a little that he was so sure of himself, so secure that I'd pick him, but he *was* the smart choice, so I'd have to deal with his smug ass for a while.

I scanned the many faces, horned and scaled, some more humanoid than others, some with bat wings, others with feathers. "How do you tell demon from devil?"

"Well, most of the creatures here are devils," Tristeene said. "Willing to enter into a sponsorship contract. The demons are usually the lower classes, the ones in the market who do business in physical trade. The zuni are demons and so are the imps. You'll get used to identifying them. Devil is more a way of life, not a breed."

Movement in the balcony to Zepar's left drew my attention.

"Urgh," Mallini said. "Lord dark and dirty just arrived. He makes me sick."

"You're not the only one," Tristeene said with a shudder.

"Oh, have you met him?" Mallini asked.

"No, and I hope to keep it that way."

Lord Umbrane was a tall, wiry male with a shock of dark

hair, a cruel mouth, and... were those horns poking out of his forehead? "Are those horns?"

"Yep," Mallini confirmed.

"But...isn't he fallen?"

"Yes, he is," Tristeene said. "The fact he's developed horns is telling. Horns are an inherently demonic trait that people often associate with chaos and evil alignment. Fallen self-actualize when it comes to their form."

"Wait...so you're saying he's made himself have horns by being...evil?"

"It's the only conclusion," Mallini said. "And trust me, there's enough evidence of his awful acts to back it up."

My mind went to the nightmare stables, to Sev being whipped on Umbrane's orders, and my grip on my armrest tightened. Umbrane needed a smack in the mouth, preferably one that would knock out his teeth. Teeth he was showcasing in a smarmy smile while he ran his gaze over us one by one.

"I feel violated," Gus said.

"Why hasn't the prince of whatever realm he's aligned to stopped him?" The prince would be one of the original fallen, so surely he wouldn't want an evil wanker ruling the court affiliated to him.

"Prince Merihem?" Tristeene asked.

"Yeah."

"I doubt he's aware of what happens in his court. After all, it's Umbrane who sends updates."

That hardly seemed fair. But I was beginning to realize that fair didn't factor into much here in Morningstar, not unless it was written in some rule or contract and signed in blood.

"The lords are eager too," Mallini pointed out. "They get to make their offers once the dukes have made theirs."

Another row of balconies lined the wall below the dukes. Devils in fancy clothing sat or stood looking up at us. The counts and their countesses, the marquises and the barons, no doubt. They chatted amongst themselves and pointed toward us. Probably calling dibs.

The ambient music died and Tristeene gripped my hand.

"It's about to begin."

Chapter Nineteen

Silence fell across the room, then a voice filled the chamber.

A voice I recognized.

"Lords and ladies, dukes and duchesses, welcome to the Custodia." A platform appeared out of the far-left wall. It jutted out, hanging over the circular space below, and standing at a lectern was Artimus. Erinea and Cerinea, the head of the Erinyes and her assistant, sat at a desk behind him, quills and paper to hand. A pedestal holding a bowl of blue flames was placed at the back of the platform.

Intriguing.

"Tonight, our Satan spawn will be offered sponsorship and protection," Artimus continued. "Tonight, you will choose who you wish to see on the seat. The candidates will step forward one by one and be introduced. Then, as befits their station, the dukes of the courts of Ivory, Flame, and Shadow will make their offers for the spawn to accept or reject. The lords will make their offers next."

"Counts mainly," Tristeene whispered. "The marquises

and the barons don't have the kind of clout to offer sponsorship."

Artimus looked toward us. "To clarify, Satan spawn are not obligated to accept an offer, or *any* offer for that matter, however once the Custodia is closed, the Spawn Protection Law will be abolished."

He glanced over his shoulder at the Erinyes. Cerinea held up a scroll for all to see.

"They'll burn it," Mallini said. "In the Svarog flame."

Leaving us vulnerable. Great.

"Keelan of the Minorax, Satan blood, step forward."

Shit, it was starting.

Keelan stood tall, his powerful frame intimidating in the studded vest that left his bulging biceps bare.

"Keelan of the Minorax, son of Briatzu, general in the Morningstar army. He has been raised to comprehend the complexity of war. A trained warrior with a keen sense of justice."

Well, that about summed up Keelan.

I studied the dukes. Zepar sipped from a goblet, seemingly uninterested. Umbrane was busy listening to some guy who was whispering in his ear, but Ignatius studied Keelan with keen interest.

The lords' balcony buzzed with excitement. Keelan was a strong contender, probably the strongest out of us all based on his heritage and history, so why weren't any of the dukes offering sponsorship?

Finally, Duke Ignatius raised a finger.

"Duke Ignatius of the Court of Flame offers sponsorship to Keelan of the Minorax. Satan spawn, do you accept?"

Keelan blew smoke out of his nostrils, then boomed, "I accept."

On the platform behind Artimus, Cerinea bent over a scroll, scribbling furiously with her quill.

"You may be seated," Artimus said to Keelan.

"Gustus of House Solar, please step forward."

Gus stood slowly and shuffled forward. He stood with his shoulders rounded, as if he wanted to hide, to disappear.

"Gustus of House Solar, one of the oldest, most prestigious imp bloodlines. House Solar was instrumental in providing fodder in the Chaos War. Renowned for their thirst for knowledge, their keen minds and sharp wit, Gustus would make a wise Satan."

Gus's shoulders rolled back, spine straightening beneath the reminder of his worth. I bit back a smile. Good for him.

Lord Umbrane raised his finger, a wicked smile spreading across his face. Gus's wings fluttered in agitation.

"The duke of the Court of Shadows offers to sponsor you. Do you accept?"

"Don't," Tristeene said softly.

Gus glanced our way, his face contorted in indecision. On the one hand we were going to need protection, but on the other was it really protection if it put you in debt to the Shadow Court duke?

"We have each other." I smiled.

He nodded and turned back. "I do not accept." His voice trembled.

Umbrane sneered and made a cutting of the throat motion, blatant and obvious for all to see.

Gus's shoulders curved inward again.

"The lords may make their offers," Artimus said.

Silence reigned.

"No one's going to offer protection against Umbrane," Mallini whispered. "Poor Gus just made himself a target no one will want to defend."

Fuck.

Gus clasped his hands together and stood firm. Man, I was so proud of him in that moment.

Just as I thought Mallini was right, and no one had the balls to step up and claim Gus, a female devil appeared on the balcony below. Delicate horns extended from her forehead, sweeping back to disappear into her voluminous mahogany hair. Her skin was a pale gray and her slanted violet eyes smiled up at Gus. She raised a slender finger and inclined her head.

Gus sucked in a sharp breath.

"Lady Minera of the great House Lunar offers sponsorship. Gustus of House Solar, do you accept."

Gus made a soft sound, part sob, part laugh.

I leaned in toward Mallini. "What's going on?"

"House Lunar hasn't paid attention to any political shit in centuries. When the Chaos War happened, they barricaded themselves in their underground city and waited it out. Solar stepped up, and because of it the House of Solar is now almost extinct, weakened and small. Minera being here tonight, offering to sponsor Gus, is a huge deal. A hand of friendship to Solar, an act that asks for forgiveness."

"Do you accept?" Artimus asked again.

"I accept," Gus said.

Lady Minera inclined her head once more while behind Artimus Cerinea scratched away at the scroll.

"You may be seated," Artimus said. His gaze flicked to me, locking briefly and lighting up before dropping to his lectern. "Charod al Erineas and Mallini el Erineas of House Furorem of the Erinyes, please step forward as you have requested to be sponsored as one entity."

The twins stepped forward and stood side by side, heads held high.

The dukes didn't move.

What? "I don't get it? They're Erinyes? I thought the Erinyes were powerful?"

"Some might say too powerful." Tristeene arched a brow.

"Fuck..."

Mallini and Charod held hands, seemingly unfazed by the overt rejection. I slid a glance toward the platform to find Erinea staring straight ahead with a stony expression. Cerinea had her head bowed.

"Their mother is not happy," Tristeene whispered.

"Wait... Erinea is their mother?"

"You didn't know?"

"How could I?"

"Oh, honey, we have so much to educate you on."

"Trust me, I know. The learning curve is steep."

"Lords, you may cast your sponsors," Artimus said.

Once again no one offered to sponsor. The two second strongest candidates, children of the Erinyes, were being left defenseless. This had to be a political move. If the Erinyes were already considered too powerful, having one as Satan would give them full control.

It sucked for Charod and Mallini, but I understood it.

"No sponsors have been cast. You may be seated."

Mallini and Charod sat down.

Mallini's jaw was tight, her eyes bright with anger. I knew that look, and I knew better than to offer platitudes. Platitudes meant shit at a time like this.

"Nyx of no family name, you may stand."

Shit, he was calling my name.

I stood quickly, adjusting my emerald skirts and nodding toward the seneschal.

His lips tightened and dropped to my gown. Yeah, he

was probably wondering what the hell I was playing at. I gave him a cheeky kitten grin and set my gaze on Zepar.

"Nyx is an unknown, a Nephilim with no power. Hunter by trade, raised outside of the demon realms and Morningstar with no real knowledge of our world."

Way to make me sound appealing.

"But this means she has no preconceptions and no outside allegiances. Nyx presents a blank slate ready to absorb what it means to be Satan."

Ooo, nicely done. With one sentence he'd turned me, a nobody, into an ambitious man's treat.

Zepar caught his bottom lip between his teeth, tawny eyes gleaming, before slowly raising a finger.

"Lord Zepar of the Court of Ivory offers sponsorship," Artimus said. "Nyx of no family name, do you ac—" He broke off, blinking in surprise, his attention on the balcony next to Zepar's.

I tracked his gaze to find Ignatius holding up a finger.

What the fuck? I turned to Tristeene. "Can he do that? Can he have two sponsors?"

She looked as confused as I did. "I don't know."

"Lord Ignatius," Artimus said. "May I remind you that you have already secured a custodia."

Ignatius slow-blinked. "My memory is perfectly intact, seneschal. Maybe it's you who should test yours. There is no edict in the Custodia laws that states a duke may not sponsor more than one candidate. I believe the limit is two."

Artimus's expression shuttered and he turned to look at Cerinea, who was already busy scanning a fresh scroll. Finally, she looked up and nodded.

Artimus turned back to the room. "Lord Ignatius is indeed correct. His offer stands. Nyx of no family name, which offer do you accept?"

"She need not choose simply one." Ignatius's eyes lit up. "She may choose both, as is her right."

Once again Artimus looked to the Erinyes for confirmation, and once again they gave it.

"Mother of daimons," Tristeene hissed. "Take them both, dammit. You'd be a fool not to."

"Agreed," Mallini said softly. "It's the smart choice."

But I doubted Zepar agreed. His tawny gaze gleamed with rage and his knuckles were white where they gripped his armrest.

His posture told me that he was definitely not up for sharing, but this wasn't about him. It was about me. About my life and protection. I hadn't known my siblings long, but if both Mallini and Tristeene were advising me to accept Ignatius, then so be it.

"Nyx of no family name, what is your decision." Artimus's tone was tight. There was no way to tell what he wanted me to do here. This was up to me. My choice.

Finally.

"I accept both offers."

The twitch at the corner of Artimus's mouth told me I'd made the right choice, but the storm raging in Zepar's eyes made me nervous. The fallen was pissed.

Not my problem.

Heck, I was Satan spawn.

The reminder chased away my doubt.

"You may be seated," Artimus said.

I parked my ass, exhaling in relief.

Tristeene was called next, and she sashayed to the balcony edge, looking resplendent in her golden, figure-hugging number.

The lords' balconies buzzed with appreciation and even the dukes took notice. How could they not? Tristeene was gorgeous *and* a succubus who oozed charisma and sex appeal; heck if she wasn't my sibling and I swung that way I'd totally do her.

"Lady Tristeene of House Moray, consort to the late Count Moray, a succubus held in high esteem with her own wealth and standing. Lady Tristeene has charm, wit, and beauty, and she would make a persuasive Satan."

Umbrane was practically salivating. Fuck, if she'd avoided his attentions thus far, she was certainly making up for it now. He sat forward in his seat, which couldn't be comfortable because I had no doubt that he had a raging boner right now.

His finger went up, probably mimicking his cock.

Tristeene's fists clenched at her side. I scanned the faces of the other two dukes to find Ignatius watching me with a shrewd expression. I was practically sitting on the edge of my seat, holding my breath for my...friend... Shit. When had that happened?

Maybe he could sponsor her. Shit, no, he couldn't, he'd already sponsored me and Keelan, which was the Custodia limit, but Zepar had a spot. I tore my gaze from Ignatius and fixed it on the fallen angel, pouring my request into one look.

He sighed and closed his eyes in resignation before raising a finger.

Tristeene exhaled sharply.

"Lady Tristeene, what do you decide?" Artimus said.

"I accept Duke Zepar's offer."

Umbrane smiled thinly, seemingly unfazed, and it took a moment to realize why. Tristeene was Shadow Court, a succubus. If she didn't make Satan, she was at his mercy.

Shit.

"You may be seated," Artimus said.

Tristeene slipped back into her chair. “Thank you.”

“What for?”

“He wasn’t going to offer for me,” she said. “I saw you pleading with your eyes. Thank you.”

“Just putting off the inevitable,” Mallini said bitterly. “Once this is over, you’ll be back at Shadow Court and Umbrane will make you pay for rejecting him.”

“*If* she goes back.” I glared at Mallini.

“You forget that if she stays it’s because she won and you lost.” Her smile was a jagged thing. “I doubt you want that, do you?”

I had no response because I’d be lying if I said I didn’t want the win.

“Thought as much.” Mallini crossed her arms.

Veena got to her feet.

I’d missed her being summoned.

She stood like a beautiful waif, her head barely cresting the balcony. I spotted a pedestal in the corner of the balcony, quickly grabbed it, and popped it beside her.

She smiled shyly at me, then climbed up.

I reclaimed my seat as Artimus announced her.

“Veena, zuni. The cogs that keep the wheels turning. Veena is of the class that we rely on. On hand to always get the job done. Humble and kind. As a zuni, Veena would make a compassionate Satan. Please cast your sponsorships.”

My heart skipped a beat, stomach dropping as Duke Umbrane raised a finger.

“No…”

“Shit.” Tristeene sat forward. “Not good.”

I implored Zepar with my eyes once more, but he set his jaw and shook his head slightly. Of course, he’d already stepped in and sponsored Tristeene to thwart Umbrane. He'd used up his spots as had Ignatius.

But Veena didn't need Umbrane; a lord would sponsor her. If not, then she had us.

"Veena, don't," I whisper-hissed.

Her small frame tensed and she looked over her shoulder at me, her huge, dark eyes filled with fear.

"You don't have to. You'll be fine." I smiled and nodded at her encouragingly.

She turned away, spine straightening.

Good girl, tell him where to shove it.

When she spoke, her usually soft voice came out strong and sure for the first time.

"I accept the offer."

Chapter Twenty

I stared at Veena as she reclaimed her seat, waiting for her to look my way so I could ask her why she'd accepted Umbrane's sponsorship. But she kept her head down and her gaze averted.

"Well..." Tristeene shuddered. "Well, well..."

"The sponsorships have been made," Artimus said. "Contracts drawn up and witnessed by all. The Custodia will close after the following entertainment provided courtesy of Duke Umbrane."

Bloody entertainment is how Nugen had described it. A soft rumbling sound drifted up from below. Keelan stood and dragged his seat toward the balcony rail.

"You won't get a view from back there," he said.

I looked to Tristeene and she shrugged.

Fuck it. I grabbed my seat and carried it to the rail.

The floor below us was gone, retracted to reveal a hollow chamber made of smooth stone. From where I sat, I could see that a barred arch was built into one of the walls. The bars rolled up and a figure stepped into the chamber. His silver hair glinted in the light shining down from above.

My heart leapt into my throat.

"Sev?" I sat forward in my seat.

"You know him?" Mallini asked.

"He's the nightmare who protected me from the others in the stable. He held them back and gave Artimus time to find me."

"He's also Umbrane's favored," Tristeene said. "Has been for...forever. I wonder what he did to make him angry enough to make a spectacle of him like this."

Sev was defenseless. No weapons, no armor. They'd even bound his tail. "Why have they tied his tail?"

"A disadvantage," Tristeene said. "They use their tails for balance and as a weapon. He really is in some shit."

I looked to the platform where Artimus stood, trying to catch his eye, but his gaze was on Sev, mouth turned down in distaste. Across from us on the Court of Shadow's balcony, Umbrane was leaning forward eagerly, eyes gleaming with wicked delight as he waited for whatever he'd planned to unfold.

Ignatius picked at his nails, seemingly uninterested in what was about to go down, and Zepar sat, head bowed, goblet in hand, as if he just wanted it to be over.

The balcony allocated to the lords and ladies buzzed with excitement, though.

Sev sauntered into the center of what was obviously an arena and tipped his head up, scanning the balconies until he found Umbrane. He lifted a hand and gave the duke a mock salute, the corner of his mouth tipping up sardonically before he made a bow.

Umbrane's jaw ticked with rage.

I leaned forward and Sev must have caught the movement because his gaze whipped across to meet mine.

His cocky smile fell and something dark and hopeless filled his silver eyes.

I held his gaze, heart hammering against my ribs in fear. I was afraid, not for me but for him. I barely knew him, but…fuck…

Sev started, scampering backward, his attention dropping to a spot in the arena I couldn't see. He fell into a defensive stance. What was it? What was coming at him?

My question was answered a moment later as two huge beasts prowled into the arena. I thought helhunters were scary, but these beasts were next level. Muscled, wide shoulders rippled with power as they moved, sharp muzzles lowered, glowing red eyes on their target as their pointy ears twitched in excitement. They pulled back their lips in twin snarls, exposing an array of sharp fangs.

"Oh, God." Tristeene pressed her hand to her chest.

I glanced at her. "What? What are they?"

"Daimon born. Demibeasts. They're vicious, bloodthirsty, and those…those aren't even fully grown ones."

They split up to flank Sev, moving with a sinuous, lethal grace that smacked of confidence. They knew they had him. They knew there was nowhere for him to run.

"What's stopping them from turning on us?" Mallini asked. "You know, once they're done with him."

"See the cuffs on their ankles?" Tristeene said. "They allow Umbrane to control them somehow. He owns them. They say Prince Merihem brought a couple back from the abyss after the Chaos War and bred them. He gifted these to Umbrane when he took over the Shadow Court as duke. They don't play with their prey. They kill it."

"This is an execution," Mallini said softly.

"A public one," Tristeene added.

Oh, God.

Below us, the demibeasts attacked. A scream lodged in my throat as Sev leapt, sailing over the beasts to land on the other side of the arena.

"Did you see that?" Gus gripped the railing. "Did you see him leap?"

"Nightmares are agile and fast," Tristeene said. "But with his tail bound he can't balance. He won't be able to access his talons either. Severely limited, he won't last long."

Below us Sev ran, weaving between the beasts, jumping to avoid their jaws and their swipes, but his landings were sloppy and I caught him stagger several times. His center of gravity was compromised without his tail. Tristeene was right, it was only a matter of time before he slipped up.

This was unfair. This was wrong.

How could everyone just sit here and watch this happen?

One of the beasts caught Sev's shoulder with its claw and the nightmare's bellow of pain was a slug to my chest.

My chair fell back with a clatter.

"Nyx?" Tristeene stared at me in shock.

Yeah, I was standing up.

And now I had Ignatius's and Zepar's attention. "This is wrong!"

Ignatius narrowed his eyes and Zepar merely shook his head slowly as if to say, *don't make a fuss*.

Fuck that. "You have to stop this." I looked to Umbrane. "Make it stop. Now. Please."

Umbrane ignored me, his attention on the arena, where Sev stood bleeding and panting as the beasts readied themselves for another attack.

No one was going to stop this. No one was going to save him.

But... They'd save me.

My chest ached and swelled with the heat of indignation and rage. "Fuck you all!" I yanked up my skirt, retrieved my dagger, and slashed at the material, leaving me in a mini dress I'd be able to move in.

Sorry, Chesra.

Sev deserved a fighting chance, and he might have that with his tail unbound and his talons at the ready.

I grabbed the balcony rail, catching Zepar's eye. "You're my sponsor, right? So save my ass."

I vaulted over the balcony and into the arena.

The world whizzed by, and a wicked euphoria lit up my chest—the thrill that came before a fight. Before justice was served.

I'd missed this.

Falling was easy, it was the landing that'd break you if you did it wrong. Luckily for me, I'd had plenty of practice. I hit the ground in a neat crouch, one leg out to the side, one arm extended for balance, dagger pointed outward, the other with my fingertips touching the ground.

The beasts faltered, red eyes flicking from me to their target then back me. Yeah, I wasn't on the menu.

"What are you doing?" Sev hissed. "Get out of here."

I straightened slowly, my gaze locked with the nearest beast. "In a moment I'll make a dash for you and free your tail."

"You won't make it." His voice vibrated with hope.

"Just be ready to leap."

"I can't protect you."

I was distinctly aware of the commotion above. "Zepar will save me."

"Dammit, his protection won't begin till *after* the Custodia," Sev said. "They can't interfere with this."

Well, there went my clever plan. An eerie calm fell over me. "In that case, we fight." I dashed toward him and sliced the thick, ropy net that bound his tail.

The rope fell away. His tail whipped out and the beasts roared and lunged at us. He snagged me around my waist and launched us into the air and over the beasts. We landed on the opposite side of the arena. I clung to him for a heartbeat before he released me and shoved me behind him.

"Stay out of the way. Evade. Can you do that?"

"Sure I can, but—"

He charged at the beasts, talons extending from his fingers, tail whipping the air, increasing his speed somehow, until he was on the beasts, slicing, jumping, tearing, puncturing. He was fast as fuck. A beautiful shadow of death leaving a trail of blood in his wake.

His attack had the beasts in a frenzy as they attempted to counter, but the more they raged and snarled, the less coordinated their attacks became. Blood spattered the ground and the walls.

Sev had taken the upper hand.

Above me the world erupted in roars of encouragement. I caught sight of my fellow spawn practically hanging over the balcony to track the action, but it was Zepar who demanded my attention. He hovered in the air above the arena, wings beating every so often to hold him aloft, tawny eyes fixed on me with an intensity that made my throat hurt. Frustration was evident in every line of his body. He wanted to swoop down and pluck his investment out from the jaws of danger but was held back by the rules. And boy was he pissed.

I couldn't see Artimus from my position, just the base of the platform high above. But I could imagine the tongue lashing he'd give me later.

Sev's whoop brought me back to the arena. He bounced off one beast's head and onto the other's.

"Watch out!" The cry hit me from above.

I turned my head in time to see a third demibeast barrel into the arena. Sev hadn't seen it yet, and by the time he did, it would be too late. With a battle cry worthy of a warrior, I launched myself toward it, landed on its back, and jammed my dagger into its neck to anchor myself.

It roared and bucked, trying to throw me off, but I held on and swung my body higher so that I was straddling it. It shook its huge head from side to side, desperate to lose me. Damn it was strong, but I had some serious thigh grip game.

I caught Sev's eye for a moment, noting the flare of surprise followed by the flash of canines as he grinned.

But in the next moment he was back to the business of holding off the first two demibeasts while I kept the third occupied.

We could do this.

"NYX!" A collective warning cry from above alerted me to a fourth demibeast.

It rushed into the arena, running straight at me.

I released the dagger and dropped from the beast's back in time to avoid the snap of the fourth beast's jaws. Its momentum slammed it into the third beast.

They rolled across the arena, separated, and quickly came to their feet before turning their snarling snouts not toward me but toward Sev.

The nightmare had his claws buried in one of the

original demibeast's haunches with his back to the newcomers.

He was about to get ripped into.

"Sev!" I ran toward him without thinking, sliding between him and the third beast's maw in time to take the hit.

Teeth sank into my shoulder and upper arm. Blinding pain turned my vision white, then black. My scream burned my throat.

The beast released me, and I dropped to my knees.

"No!" Sev fell to the ground behind me, covering my body with his. "What did you do? You crazy fool." His tone was hushed with awe.

My arm was on fire, tears blurring my vision as the beast who'd bitten me whined softly and backed away.

The others joined him, putting distance between us, their heads down, ears going flat. It looked like...like they were bowing.

"End it now." Zepar's voice boomed above us. "Seneschal, give the word."

The cuffs on the beasts' ankles fizzed with power. They threw back their heads and roared as if in pain. They moved forward a few steps before checking themselves and backing up again.

"Umbrane, your beasts have made their intentions clear." Ignatius appeared in the arena. Up close he was huge, almost seven feet tall. Thick, powerful thighs encased in tan slacks, large feet pushed into open-toe sandals. He looked down at me with eyes like flame before addressing the audience above. "The entertainment is over. Duke Zepar and I claim Custodia. Now." His tone brooked no argument.

Zepar landed in the arena beside Sev and me. His wings snapped, then disappeared behind his back.

Above us Umbrane stood on his balcony, face contorted in fury. "The nightmare is meant to die." His body vibrated with rage. "He is sentenced to death!"

"And he will," Artimus said from above. "Unless Nyx of no family name wishes to claim him under law of blood debt."

Umbrane's chest expanded. "That old law? You dare to use it against me?"

"Laws apply to us all." Artimus's tone was cold. "You, as an extension of Prince Merihem, should recognize and uphold them."

Sev held me tighter. My head swam with pain; I could barely think.

"What does he mean?" I gasped out the words.

"The law works on abyssbloods. It means you can choose to own me." Sev's breath was hot against my ear. "You spilled blood to save my worthless life. I'm in your debt, yours to command if you wish it." His tone was tight, restrained, as if he was holding back a host of emotions. His grip was so tight now it was almost painful.

"You'll die if I don't."

"Yes."

I didn't want to own anyone, but I couldn't let him die either. "I'll do it." I raised my voice and pushed the words past the pain. "I'll claim the blood debt."

Sev sucked in a sharp breath and a fresh heat ignited in my shoulder, forcing a sob from my throat.

"It is done," Zepar said. "The nightmare now belongs to you."

Chapter Twenty-One

The pain was so bad, I couldn't focus, and my eyes kept closing as my body attempted to drag me into unconsciousness.

"Give her to me," Zepar demanded.

Sev hissed and held me tighter. I could feel his heart beating against my back, fast and steady.

"He's acting on primal instinct," Ignatius said coolly. "The bond is fresh. Let me try."

A scent like warm bread and honey filled my head and then Ignatius's cool, calm tone drifted over me. "Sev, listen to me. We need to heal her. A demibeast's bite needs special attention. Not even Lake Morbidus can heal her. But I can. If you let me."

Sev's chest heaved. "I stay with her."

Zepar made a sound of exasperation.

"Yes, you'll stay close," Ignatius said. "But you won't interfere with the treatment."

Sev's chest vibrated, and he nuzzled the back of my ear. "Don't die," he whispered, and then he let me go.

Unfamiliar arms gathered me up. That delicious smell enveloped me.

"*I* can take her," Zepar said.

"I'm sure you can," Ignatius replied, his voice intimately close.

He was holding me. I forced my eyes open, fighting the draw of unconsciousness to tip my head back and look up at his face.

He glanced down, thick, inky lashes swooping in a blink over eyes like embers. They seemed to heat as they settled on me, his jaw tightening and nostrils flaring. His biceps flexed around me.

"Sleep now," he ordered. "I have you."

My last thought as darkness surged up and dragged me down was to wonder if his words were a promise or a threat.

"Nyx, can you hear me?"

I surfaced to searing pain and Zepar's tense face. His eyes were dark with conflicting emotions.

"Fuck, it hurts." I'd been hurt plenty of times and my tolerance for pain was high, but I'd never had to experience it for long because I healed, but this...this was true agony. It made me want to curl up into a ball and die. "Make it stop."

"I can," another voice said from across the room. "But apparently I need permission."

"Damn right you do," another voice said gruffly.

Nugen?

I turned my head to find the weapons master standing by an elaborate dresser.

Where was I? Whose room was this? The muscles in my

shoulder spasmed so tight they stole my breath. Fuck it, who gave a shit where I was. I needed pain relief and fast.

"Nyx, will you allow Ignatius to heal you," Nugen asked.

"Yes, dammit."

"It involves skin-on-skin contact," Zepar ground out, eyes flashing.

My gaze flew to Ignatius, who stood by the door, arms crossed, expression unreadable.

"I'm no shrinking violet, Zepar, take off my damn clothes and get this done."

A ghost of a smile played on Ignatius's lips. "Do you hear that, Sev? Nugen? She's given her permission."

A shadow moved in the corner of the room. Silver eyes watching us. "Do it. Fix her." There was a snarl to Sev's tone that sent a shiver through me.

Zepar's jaw flexed. "I'm watching you, Ignatius."

"Good. In that case, you might learn something."

Zepar's hands curled into fists as he stepped back, allowing Ignatius to take his place.

"I'll be outside." Nugen retreated.

A door closed.

I was alone with a fallen, a nightmare, and an efreet. I should have been on my guard, but the agony made it impossible to care what they did to me as long as it stopped the pain.

"Hurry. Please." I implored Ignatius with my eyes.

He settled on the bed beside me and carefully peeled the remnants of my dress from my body, leaving me naked except for my knickers. Someone sucked in a sharp breath.

"Like you haven't seen tits before. Just fix me." My plea was now a glare of command.

"Do it," Zepar said.

Ignatius shrugged off his vest, leaving his golden torso

bare. His broad, muscular body blocked out the room as he lowered himself onto the bed beside me.

"This will hurt," he warned.

"Gee, now that would be a novel experience."

He let out a surprised chuckle and rolled me against his velvet-smooth body. His skin was warm, like he'd been baking in the sun. His arm settled around my waist, forearm pressing along my spine, hand cupping my nape to hold me steady.

The contact aggravated the wound in my shoulder. I moaned and angrily blinked back tears. I hated being vulnerable.

"Do it, dammit."

His body heated, hotter and hotter, until I was squirming and shoving at him, desperate to be free, but he held firm. The pain in my shoulder intensified, sharpening and burrowing into me until all I could do was scream. The fire ants burrowing into my skin turned tail and headed up and out. Pain exited my body like smoke off a sizzling steak.

I collapsed against Ignatius, gasping as I struggled to draw breath.

He massaged my nape. "I have you."

The intense heat ebbed and settled into a comfortable warmth, taking the final remnants of pain with it. A sob of gratitude clawed at my throat.

I rolled my forehead against his pectoral, relieved to be able to revel in the contact. "Thank you."

"Look at me." He used his grip on my nape to tip my head back. He was close. So close I could see the gold flecks dancing in his eyes and count the individual lashes framing those ember orbs. "I take care of what is mine."

My gaze dropped to his lips. Perfectly formed, golden

lips. What would they taste like? The corner of his mouth tipped slightly as if he could read my thoughts.

"Sleep now, little Nephilim. Sleep and heal fully. The trials will begin soon enough." He slid his hand down my back, fingers leaving an aching trail in their wake.

I bit back my moan of protest as he detangled himself from me and stood. He picked up his waistcoat and padded toward a golden door to my right. Light flashed when he opened it, and he was gone.

"What the—"

Zepar moved in and draped a blanket over me.

Oh yeah, I was practically naked.

"These are your new quarters," he said. "Nugen will explain everything. Rest." His gaze slipped to the shadows where Sev crouched. "Your nightmare will watch over you."

He headed to a white door, and just like it had with Ignatius, a light flashed, taking him away.

I sat up, clutching the blanket to my chest. "What just happened?"

Sev straightened and approached the bed. He climbed up and stretched out beside me, rolling onto his side to face me. "You saved my life." He looked almost angry about it. "But I suppose now I get to see how it plays out?"

I couldn't read him properly, couldn't figure out the emotions playing across his face. "How what plays out?"

His eyes narrowed, and I could almost hear his brain whirring. "Everything, Nyx. Everything." He touched the center of my forehead and the world dimmed.

We were still in the room, on the bed, but I knew instinctively that this wasn't real.

"I'm dreaming."

"Yes... and I owe you pleasure."

I'd been writhing in agony a moment ago, I shouldn't be

able to get horny so quickly, but my body begged to differ. I'd always thought my demon genes were the reason for my libido, but now I knew it had to be my fallen side.

I didn't stop him when he ripped away my blanket, leaving me naked beneath the moonlight that seemed to come from nowhere and everywhere. After the pain I'd just experienced, I was ready for some pleasure.

His fingertips trailed between my breasts and down my stomach to tease the edge of my panties.

I held my breath and watched as he slipped his fingers beneath the fabric and dipped into my heat. Oh...Oh, God. The fabric melted, leaving me exposed as he rubbed and circled my clit.

Heat built and blood rushed to places...oh. Perfect. He was perfect at this.

Something nudged my thigh. His tail. The arrowhead gleamed in the gloom, then morphed, becoming smooth and thick like the head of a cock.

"Yes." I parted my thighs.

It slid over me, past his hand and down to nudge my entrance. He continued to tease me with his fingers, working me until I was ordering him to enter me. I cried out as he obliged, pushing my hips up to meet the thrusts of his tail.

He moaned with me, and when I looked up, his eyes were black as night, mouth parted in pleasure as he fucked me. Could he feel himself inside me? Was his tail...Oh, fuck. I was about to come.

He cupped my jaw, tugging my mouth toward his.

"No." I pressed a hand to his chest, lips aching with the need to taste him. "No kissing."

"Maybe not these lips, but the others..." He pulled out of me and slid down my body to claim my pussy on the edge of an orgasm. I came hard against his mouth, crying out and fisting the sheets as he wrung every ounce of pleasure from my body there was to give.

When I opened my eyes, the moonlight was gone. Lamplight filled the room and Sev was crouched in a shadowy corner. But we were still in the dream. I could feel it.

I reached out to him. "Come back. I want to taste you."

"Soon," he whispered, licking his lips. "We'll make a new transaction soon. For now, you better answer the door."

I sat up with a lurch to a sharp rapping on the plain wooden door. The real entrance to the room.

The blanket was back over me and Sev watched me intensely from his spot in the shadows. No longer in the dream.

"Nyx? Hey, can I come in?" Tristeene called.

Shit. "One second." I looked about for clothes. Nothing. I climbed off the bed and headed for the dresser, yanking open the top drawer to find vests and shirts in silken material along with loose-fitting slacks. I grabbed a vest and a pair of slacks and tugged them on. No bra, but whatever.

I crossed the room and tugged the door open to find Tristeene in the corridor. But she wasn't alone.

She'd brought all the Satan spawn with her.

All of my siblings.

"I still think you're insane." Mallini plucked a fresh grape off the tray on the floor.

Nugen and Zinichi had decided to bring our supper to us in my chambers. They were large enough, and a few cushions and such made the rug in front of the wide hearth a comfortable spot to eat.

Sev was stretched out on my bed, fast asleep, his silver hair covering his beautiful, scarred face. Turned out that nightmares were nocturnal beings. The exertion, the almost execution, must have tired him out. He'd sleep until tomorrow night now.

"That was a brave thing you did," Tristeene said. "You saved him. Has he told you why he was sentenced to die?"

"No. We haven't had a chance to talk properly yet. Ignatius had to heal me and then I kinda... fell asleep." I speared a hunk of meat with my fork and popped it into my mouth. "Fuck, I'm hungry."

"Not surprised," Keelan growled with grudging respect. "You fought a demibeast and survived being bitten."

"What I want to know is why they backed off?" Charod said. "They could have finished you off, but they didn't."

I'd been wondering the same thing. "I don't know."

"Satan blood," Gus said. "It has to be something to do with it. They bit you and then they backed off."

"Makes sense," Mallini said.

"Of course it does." Tristeene nudged Gus with her shoulder. "Gus is a genius."

He blushed.

"Did you see Duke Zepar when she jumped in?" Charod said. "I thought he was going to blow a few blood vessels."

"Ignatius seemed pretty calm, for an efreet," Mallini said.

"They're certainly taking the custodia thing seriously." I sipped my juice. "If I hear the line *I take care of what's mine* one more time..." I shook my head.

"Fallen are extremely possessive," Tristeene said. "Duke

Zepar is known for being exceptionally particular about his bed partners."

"Bed partners? Whoa, what has that got to do with anything?"

She gave me a sly smile. "Oh puh-lease, like you haven't thought it."

I couldn't help but smile. "Fine, maybe for a second. But he's so overbearing. Not my type at all. I prefer to be in control."

Keelan made a low, gruff barking sound that it took me a moment to realize was a chuckle.

"What?" I arched a brow at him. "What's so funny?"

"You won't get to be in control with a fallen or a demon male," Keelan said. "We don't operate that way." He jerked his head toward Gus. "Even the imp males take charge in the bedroom."

My mind went to Sev, how he'd commanded my body. How he'd made me come while respecting my wishes. Maybe I didn't have to be the one steering to be in control.

"I'm not interested in a relationship with Zepar. I need his protection and that's all."

"And Ignatius?" Tristeene nudged me with her shoulder. "He carried you out of the arena like you were a long-lost lover."

The memory of the efreet's warm, silken skin rose in my mind. "Nope. Not interested."

I got the impression that those two males wouldn't be content in taking only a piece of me. They'd want it all, and that was something I wasn't willing to give.

We ate in silence for a few moments. My gaze flicked around the room, from face to face. But one was missing. Veena wasn't here. Her room was empty, but there was a doorway to the Shadow Court in her chambers just like I had mini portals to the Ivory Court and the Court of Flame. The dukes could come and go, and so could I, but no one else had access. Veena was probably with Umbrane. The thought made me feel sick, but there was nothing any of us could do about it. She'd made her choice.

Tristeene had a doorway to Zepar in her room, Keelan had one to Ignatius, and Gus to Lady Minera of House Lunar, which occupied an independent space on the edge of Shadow Court territory. Her lands were hers to rule, not Umbrane's.

Mallini and Charod were to remain in the residences.

"I don't like that we've been split up." I toyed with the food on my plate. "We should stick together."

"This is how it is," Mallini said, mouth turning down. "Truth is, Charod and I might not even live till the first trial."

I stared at her in horror. "Surely your mother can provide some protection. You're an Erinyes."

She smiled sadly. "The laws are clear. She can't intervene."

"Having a sponsor isn't always a blessing," Tristeene said softly. "Veena... Umbrane has no control when it comes to his playthings."

"She's Satan spawn. His custodia. He won't hurt her," Gus said.

"Won't he?" Mallini said. "And if he does, can you see Veena telling him to back off?"

We fell into silence.

"Why did she do it?" Gus pondered out loud. "Why accept him?"

I sighed, all hunger gone. "I don't know. But it's our job to keep her safe and out of his clutches the best we can."

Everyone murmured in agreement.

"I'll find her tomorrow, tell her that we're here for her and that she doesn't have to give him any control."

Keelan growled in agreement.

"Tomorrow is a free day anyway," Tristeene said. "We get to spend it however we like because after that the trials begin."

"They have a special guest coming to monitor the trials," Charod said. "No idea who."

But my mind was on tomorrow, on the fact I had one day to do as I wished? "Can we leave Morningstar?"

"No," Mallini said. "That mark they put on our heads may have vanished, but it did something that'll keep us here until the trials are over."

Not ideal but I could work with it. Orina needed to know where I was and what was happening to me, and there was only one person I trusted with a message to my best friend.

Tomorrow I'd take a trip to see Sin.

Chapter Twenty-Two

I crouched by Chase and stroked his head. Moving him while he was in his sleep phase wasn't a good idea, but I didn't want to leave him here alone either.

"I'll check in on him," Zinichi said from the doorway to my old room. "I'll bring him to you as soon as he wakes up."

I nodded. It was the best we could do right now. "Sev, my nightmare, is asleep in my room. If Chase does wake and you take him to the new residences, best to leave him in the communal lounge area."

"Ah, yes. We might have a territory dispute otherwise." She smiled warmly. "How do you plan to spend your day?"

I straightened and stretched. "I'm going to the market."

Her eyes went round. "You can't leave the keep."

"I was told it was a free day. *Free* being the operative word."

Her eyes grew round. "It's too dangerous."

"It is, without protection." Artimus appeared behind Zinichi. "Luckily you have me."

Zinichi ducked her head and scampered off, leaving Artimus to fill the doorway with his neatly tailored frame.

Today he was wearing a midnight-blue waistcoat over a sky-blue shirt open at the collar and black pants cinched into ankle boots. His dark hair was bed head today, falling across his forehead rakishly, even though his sapphire eyes were studiously serious. There was a controlled air about Artimus that needled me, making me want to unravel him or unbutton him to set him free.

"It's either me or a retinue of guards picked by your sponsors," Artimus continued, taking my silence for resistance. "Those are the rules, and you'd be wise to follow them if you want to survive."

I shrugged. "Sure. You can tag along if you like."

He arched a brow. "Tag along isn't how I'd phrase it."

"Then how would you phrase it?"

"Accompany. Escort. Guard."

"Like you guarded me when I was in the arena?" It was my turn to arch a brow.

His mouth tightened. "It wasn't my place to act. Although, might I say, your decision was foolhardy and reckless."

I bridged the distance between us so that I was standing directly in front of him, a mere foot between us. He tensed. "That foolhardy decision saved an innocent life, and I don't believe for a second you couldn't have stopped the event once I jumped down. You're the seneschal."

He inhaled through his nose, keeping his gaze on a point above my head as if looking at me was sensory overload. "It doesn't work that way. The laws, the rules must be followed. Not even the dukes are exempt. The event ended when the demibeasts conceded." His gaze dropped to me now, sapphire eyes bright with a revelation I wasn't privy to. "They conceded to you, Nyx."

Wait... "Did you know that would happen?"

He looked away. "How was I supposed to know that?"

"What is your game, Artimus? What do you really want from me?"

"The best you can give." This time when his gaze met mine it simmered with a heat and longing that stole my breath. He blinked and looked away. "Are you ready to leave now?" His tone was cool and impersonal once more.

I dropped back a step. "Yeah. Let's go."

Artimus was a conundrum, but there was no doubt in my mind that he held the answers to all my questions and probably more. If there was anyone that I needed to cultivate a relationship with, it was him.

Luckily for me I'd mastered the skill of turning an interrogation into a conversation.

It was time to test my skills.

THE CARRIAGE ROCKED GENTLY as we made our way over Lake Morbidus. I sat back, boots resting on the seat opposite, arms crossed as I studied Artimus's profile. He was busy looking out the window at the scenery, a landscape he probably knew like the back of his sexy hand, which led me to the logical conclusion that he was attempting to avoid looking at me.

"Do I make you uncomfortable, Arty? Can I call you Arty?"

"No. And no, you cannot."

I bit back a smile. "Then why won't you look at me?"

He sighed and sat back in his seat before fixing his stunning sapphire peepers on me. "Because I find you attractive, Nyx. I want to fuck you and drink your blood and fuck you some more."

My stomach flipped hard. He was kidding. He had to be? But no. His expression showed no hint of humor; if anything, his eyes were darker than before, pupils large with desire.

"Does that answer your question, Nyx?" he asked.

I swallowed hard and licked my lips. "Yes. It does. But I have another one for you."

He planted one boot on the seat beside me, knee cocked, elbow resting on it. "Go on."

"Is wanting to do those things bad?"

His eyes narrowed. "You have no idea how bad."

He had no idea how badly *bad* attracted me. "You think I can't handle you?" Why was I asking him that? Damn me and my inability to walk away from a challenge.

"I know you can't." He raked me over. "And even if you could, I wouldn't touch you. Not like that."

Okay, now I was even more intrigued. "Why not?"

"I made a vow to protect Satan's spawn. If I claim you, Erinea will find a way to end you. She doesn't like to share."

"Ah, yes, you're fucking Erinea. How is that?"

He shrugged. "Not awful. It's a means to an end."

"And what end is that?"

He gave me a crooked smile. "Your inquisitiveness will get you in trouble."

"My inquisitive nature has kept me alive."

"Not in Morningstar it won't. In Morningstar, poking your nose in places it doesn't belong will get you killed."

"So if I ask you about your relationship with Satan..."

He smiled and slow-blinked. "I won't kill you for that. Besides, I'm sure you've heard things."

"That he practically raised you."

His expression sobered. “He did. My parents were killed in the Chaos War and Satan took me in as his own.”

“So he adopted an incubus but didn’t bother to claim his blood spawn. Nice.”

His eyes narrowed. “You have a lot to learn about politics.”

“Then teach me.”

“What do you think would have happened to those innocent, vulnerable infant spawn if everyone had known who and what they were?”

“I thought spawn were protected?”

“That law activated when Satan died. While alive, his spawn would have been vulnerable. A target to be used for extortion, blackmail, whatever.”

“But you weren’t blood, so they left you alone.”

“I believe I was the recipient of all the love he would have given his blood spawn, if he’d had the opportunity.”

“But then he shunned you, right? Why was that?”

His expression shuttered. “Why did your mother abandon you, Nyx?”

After my recent dream visit to that very memory, his question landed like a sharp slap. I wanted to answer, to speculate, just to prove that his question hadn’t fazed me, but my throat was too tight.

Certain things were best left in the shadows of our mind. “Point taken.”

He sighed. “I like you, Nyx. I think you’ll make a fine leader in time, and I want to help you. Let me do that.”

His tone was sincere, and a warm feeling unfurled in my belly. My instincts told me to trust him, just as they had on our first carriage ride.

“Okay, Artimus. I’ll trust you. Just…don’t let me down.”

Artimus took the carriage right into the market, down the narrow streets, and parked it smack bang in front of Sin's workshop.

I climbed out and Artimus followed.

I turned and pressed a hand to his chest. "I don't want you coming in with me."

His brows went up. "What part of *it isn't safe for you to be unaccompanied* didn't you understand?"

"I'm safe in the workshop. Trust me. I've known Sin for years."

Artimus sighed. "I'll be standing outside the doors."

"Thank you." I ducked into the cool interior of the workshop and headed for the back, listening for the steady thump of hammer on anvil. But the space was silent and empty too.

No sign of Sin.

I checked the washroom and then walked over to the door that I was certain led to his living quarters. I knocked and waited.

Nothing.

I knocked again. "Sin! I need to speak to you."

Silence greeted me.

There'd never been a visit when he hadn't been here. He had to be close, the front door would have been locked otherwise, right? My gaze tracked to the other door, a metal obstruction fitted with several bolts, all of which were now open.

"Sin?" I approached the door and pressed my palm to it, suddenly uncertain.

Sin wasn't someone to be messed with. Encroaching on

his private space was a huge no, and I had no doubt I'd pay for it dearly if I did, but this was my last chance to get a message to Orina before the trials started. After that, goodness knew what kind of shape I'd be in...if I survived.

I couldn't leave her wondering what had happened to me.

I gripped the door handle and tugged. The metal door swung open on silent hinges to reveal darkness beyond. I stepped over the threshold. "Sin? Are you down there?"

A prickle raced over my skin, and a strange smell, metallic but with a hint of sweetness, hit my senses.

"Sin..." I took another step.

The air shifted and hands gripped my shoulders.

I let out a yelp as Sin hauled me off my feet and back into the workshop, kicking the metal door closed behind him.

"You dare to snoop?" He lifted me so we were almost nose to nose.

His midnight eyes swirled with stars and his chest expanded as he held me aloft as easily as a ragdoll. He could break me with a snap of his wrist, and fuck if that wasn't sexy as hell.

He inhaled deeply and pressed me to the wall. I wrapped my legs around his waist instinctively and his hand went to my throat, thumb stroking my jaw.

"You trespassed, Nyx." He slow-blinked and the outer edges of his irises bloomed crimson. I'd never seen them do that before. "You trespassed and now you'll pay." His grip tightened, and I caught movement by my eye where his index finger lay on my cheekbone. Oh, God, was that a talon growing out of his nailbed?

Sin was intimidating, scary, and growly. I'd always

sensed his potential for violence and danger, but I'd never been frightened in his presence.

Until now.

My stomach quivered. "I'm sorry…I—"

"Quiet. You'll pay, Nyx. You'll pay with something you prize dearly." His gaze roved over my face. "You'll pay with your heart."

My pulse burst into a canter. "What? You're going to rip my heart out for that? What the—"

He let out a cruel bark of laughter. "I don't need to tear it from your body to own it, Nyx." His gaze settled on my mouth and my lips parted in realization.

"No."

"Yes." He kissed me, swiping his bottom lip against my top lip, then brushing his top lip against my lower one before claiming my mouth fully.

It had been too long since my lips had touched another's with the intention of a kiss, too long since I'd allowed myself this vulnerability. A sob clawed up my throat, part anger part relief, because oh, God, to be claimed like this, to be devoured and plundered. I wrapped my arms around his neck and slid my fingers into his silken locks, tilting my head to give him better access as he stroked my tongue with his. He was hungry and I was his meal. My chest swelled with emotion as the need I'd supressed and denied for too long filled my head with a warm buzzing.

The kiss softened, retreating to something questing and aching and filled with longing before Sin broke it with a ragged sigh and pressed his forehead to mine. I clung to him, head reeling, his words ringing in my ears. *I don't need to tear out your heart to own it.* One kiss couldn't claim my heart, that was ridiculous, but one kiss with the right person could make me vulnerable, and I felt it now, because Sin...Sin was my guilty pleasure, permitted only because of the boundaries I'd set. A few days ago he'd asked for a kiss as payment. Asked and waited for permission. Waited for me to put up my walls and keep my boundaries intact, but today he'd claimed his prize. Taken me unaware. Claimed me when my walls were down.

Nothing would ever be the same.

"I should have barred you from my workshop a long time ago." His gravelly voice teased my sensitized senses. He moved his thumb back and forth against my cheek. "But I have a weakness for challenges and danger. You, Nyx, are both."

I didn't understand why he was saying this. "Sin…what are you talking about?"

"You need to focus on the trials, little Nephilim."

My heart stuttered. "You know? How do you know?"

He dipped his head and licked up my neck. "Your taste." He nuzzled the spot below my ear. "Your scent." He pressed his arousal against me, rolling his hips and making me gasp. "You shouldn't have come here, Nyx. You shouldn't keep coming back. It isn't safe for you or for me."

"What do you mean?"

He moved away and lowered me to the ground. "You need to leave."

My chest tightened in panic. He'd never asked me to leave before. "Sin… what did I do?"

I hated how lost and vulnerable I sounded.

He strode over to his anvil and picked up his hammer. "Nothing yet. But you will. You will."

He grabbed a sheet of hot metal and began to hit it.

I watched him for long seconds before walking away with a confused, aching heart because I was certain that one kiss had lost me a valuable friend.

Chapter Twenty-Three

Artimus waited for me, leaning against the imposing carriage. The massive equine beasts charged with pulling the contraption pawed at the earth and blew shadow and smoke from their nostrils, eager to be on the move.

"All done?" Artimus asked.

"Yes and no."

"Oh?"

"I needed a message sent to the mainland, to my best friend, but..." I glanced back at the shop. "It's not going to happen now."

He frowned down at me. "You came all this way to ask a blacksmith to send a message for you?"

"Yes."

"Can I inquire why you didn't think to ask me?"

I stared at him, dumbfounded. When I'd thought of contacting Orina, the only person who'd come to mind had been Sin. I'd known him for long enough to trust him. Asking Artimus hadn't occurred to me.

He pressed his lips together. "I'll get your message to your friend. Where is it?"

I pulled the note I'd written last night out of my pocket and handed it to him. "She lives in the Fringe. She works for the Order of Helsing."

"I'll make sure it gets to her." He tucked it into his pocket. "Now, how would you like to spend the rest of your day?"

I shrugged. "I hadn't thought that far ahead."

"Then allow me to do it for you." He steered me to the carriage. "I know this wonderful place by the Flumen Doloris, the River of Sorrow, where we can have lunch."

I climbed into the carriage. "Do all the rivers and lakes in Morningstar have such morbid names?"

"You think those names are morbid? You should hear the names of the five rivers of the demon realm."

We set off again, and as Artimus chatted, telling me about the demon realm and its woefully named rivers, the weight in my chest lifted a little.

Sin wasn't lost to me. What we had was simply on hold. For now.

Lunch with Artimus was a revelatory experience, telling me more about the man's personality than I'd been able to glean through conversation alone.

For example, women fawned over him, but it didn't seem to register. He was courteous and respectful, maintaining a polite barrier between himself and the servers at the inn. Strange for an incubus, because as far as I knew, his breed of abyssblood needed sex and blood to survive, which got me wondering where he got his fix.

Erinea? The thought grated and that bugged me. Artimus didn't belong to me. Heck, I barely knew the guy, but there was no denying that I liked what I'd seen and experienced so far.

By the time we got back to the keep, I was almost sorry to part ways with him.

He walked me to my new residences located on the floor directly above the old ones. Two of the demon guards provided by Zepar stood outside. Short, stocky demons with short horns and tusks. A breed of Minorax. They looked sulky and bad-tempered, as if being here was a chore, which it probably was to them.

One of them—I couldn't figure out which one because they looked almost identical—had insisted on escorting me to the basic residences this morning. If Nugen hadn't shown up to guard me, I was pretty sure I'd have been stuck with one of them, and I didn't do broody, unless I was the one brooding.

They glared at me now, as if I'd personally insulted them by accepting any other escort but theirs.

"I'll see you tomorrow at the trials," Artimus said. "Try and get some rest."

Yes, I'd pushed to try and get information out of him, but he'd been as tight-lipped as a cleric's ass.

"I will, and thank you for lunch and the company."

His eyes warmed. "Anytime."

The Minorax pushed open the doors and I clipped across cream marble floors woven with gold abstract patterns. Sunlight streamed in through tall, slender windows, cutting shapes on the ground and hitting the stone walls in such a way that they glittered with silver specks. Several doors lined the wall to my left. Rooms for the sponsored. Each had a portal to their chosen duke's domain. Temporary access created by a conji. Yep, I'd learned what one of those was. A wielder of elusive allure. A demon or devil who could harness allure that existed in the atmosphere and manipulate it into doing magic shit. To be honest, the technicalities went over my head, probably because it wasn't something I was interested in.

I passed Tristeene's door, then Keelan's, but stopped outside Veena's. I'd checked this morning and the zuni hadn't returned from her audience with Umbrane. Was she back now?

I moved toward her door just as Tristeene opened hers.

She stepped out, adjusting her shimmery tunic top, then looked up, saw me, and froze. Her gaze flicked from me to Veena's door. "You want some company?"

"Looks like you're off somewhere nice."

She gave me a sexy grin, her crimson lips parting to reveal neat white teeth. "Just a little charge-up before tomorrow. It can wait."

"In that case, please."

Her smile dropped as she joined me.

We were probably both thinking the same thing: that we weren't sure what condition we'd find Veena in.

I knocked. "Veena, it's Nyx and Tristeene, can we come in?"

The silence beyond the door was broken by a soft thud.

"Veena?" Tristeene rapped her knuckles sharply on the wood. "Open the door. Now."

The command in her voice had my back straightening. "Whoa, what was that?"

She shrugged a shoulder. "A little of my personal allure." She winked. "They don't call me a charmer for nothing."

"Have you used that on me before?"

She gave me a sidelong glance. "Not yet, sweetie. But if I do, you'll know, being Satan blood and all. Others, well, they won't."

She went to rap on the door again, but it swung open to darkness.

Another soft thud sounded from somewhere deep in the room. "No wonder she's falling over. It's pitch black."

"No..." Tristeene shook her head. "Zuni have the best night vison of all demons. The dark isn't an issue."

We shoved the door wide, letting the light from the hallway shine in.

"Don't," Veena said.

I scanned the room, making out the bulky form of a wardrobe, a dresser, the bed, and there, curled up on the floor beside it, was Veena, still in her pretty dress. Except the dress wasn't so pretty any longer. It was torn and dirty.

"Oh, God..." Tristeene hurried across the room and knelt by Veena. "Veena, sweetheart, let me see."

She gently tilted Veena's face to the light and sucked in a shocked breath. Veena's beautiful dark eyes were swollen shut, the skin black and bruised. Her lip was busted, and the front of her dress torn to reveal her breasts.

"Oh...Oh my..." Tristeene wrapped her arms around Veena and hugged her. "What did he do?"

"Not him," Veena said softly. "He watched."

"Did they violate—"

"No!" Veena shook her head, dislodging tears. "He just wanted to hear me scream."

Bile clawed up my throat, and rage burned my chest. "Why? Why did you accept him? Why?" My voice shook with rage at him, at the circumstances, at our impotence, and at the zuni for allowing him access to her.

Veena shoved Tristeene away. "You wouldn't understand. None of you would understand. You, with your status and your estate." She spat the words at Tristeene. "And Mallini and Charod with their high-born status. Keelan with his military background, and even Gus has noble origins. And you." She pointed her finger at me. "The Nephilim everyone is interested in. But me? I'm no one. Nothing. An easy target to pick off."

"And so you chose Umbrane?" Tristeene stared at her, incredulous.

Veena's smile was thin and bitter. "It's worth it for his protection. No one will dare touch me now. No one will hurt me." She let out a manic laugh that ended in a cough.

"Except him." I looked down at her pitiful form, unable to deny the empathy I felt for her. "I care about you, Veena. I would have protected you. We all would have if you'd given us a chance. You didn't need to choose him."

She let out a ragged sob and fell into Tristeene's arms.

My gut twisted and my heart thudded in anger, but I tamped down on it. Anger wouldn't help her now. Right now, she needed…She needed her sisters.

"I'll run a hot bath. Do we have any herbs for the pain?"

Tristeene nodded. "I have something."

"Good. Go get it."

She hurried off and I took her place beside Veena, gently tucking her hair behind her ear. "I promise you, Veena, whatever happens, I'll find a way to make him pay, I swear it."

We tucked Veena into bed an hour later and quietly left the room. Rage clawed at my insides and my voice was a ragged rasp when I spoke.

"He has to die, Tristeene. It's the only justice."

"There is no justice when it comes to Umbrane," she

said softly. "The Shadow Court is his world. It's his domain. Veena isn't the first creature he's hurt or violated, and she won't be the last. As Satan spawn she can stop him, if she has the strength to do so."

"But she won't. She's too afraid he'll withdraw his sponsorship." I lifted my chin. "It's up to us to help her find that strength. To show her she's safe with us."

Tristeene nodded.

"Will she heal by tomorrow?"

"Yes. Zuni heal fast."

"Good. The others don't need to know about this, not unless she decides to tell them."

Tristeene's eyes glittered. "Agreed."

"You better go and recharge for tomorrow."

She made to step away but then leaned in and gave me a hug. "I'm glad you're my…"

"Sister?" I smiled wryly.

She sighed. "Yes."

I swallowed the lump in my throat. "I'm glad you're my sister too."

And we'd take care of our other sister together. I'd keep my promise. I'd win that damn seat, and when I did, Umbrane would pay.

I headed for my room. I was done for the day.

The trials couldn't start soon enough.

Chapter Twenty-Four

Sev lay sprawled across the bed, one leg cocked, one arm thrown over his head. His mouth was slightly parted, silver hair cutting across his face. He looked like a wet dream, and he was mine.

Mine…

Where had that thought come from?

He didn't belong to me, even though technically he did. Still, I didn't believe in that growly ownership attitude when used on me, so using it on someone else was wrong. Why, then, did it feel right with Sev?

I kicked off my shoes beside the free-standing full-length mirror. The thing was a monstrosity, overly ornate and bulky and totally not my taste. In fact, this whole room was over-the-top opulence, with polished cherry wood, silk sheets, and golden candelabras. I felt like I'd stepped into a cross between a historical novel and a fairy tale.

I climbed onto the bed beside Sev and lay down with a sigh. He groaned softly and turned on his side, slinging an arm around my waist.

Was it wrong to touch him in his sleep? Probably. But I

couldn't resist running my hand up his arm, skimming my fingers over the corded muscle. His skin was smooth, cool, taut, and had a tough, almost abrasive texture, which made sense if his breed didn't wear clothes. I glanced down at his thigh, at the dark, thick skin that covered his lower body. He was built for action. A stealth fighter, and yet Umbrane kept the nightmares locked in stables and used them like cattle. Surely that was a waste of their skills.

A yawn ripped through me. Huge lunches always made me sleepy. I allowed my breathing to even out and closed my eyes. I couldn't remember the last time I'd slept in someone's arms. Too long ago to matter, that was for sure. It felt…nice.

I must have dropped off because when I opened my eyes the room was dark and Sev was awake, watching me sleep.

"Have you any idea how creepy that is?" I dragged a hand down my face. Shit, had I drooled?

"You snore."

"I do not!" I shoved his chest, but he held me tighter.

"You do. Like a feline purring." His gaze flicked from my eyes to my mouth, then back again. "It reminded me of a companion I had once…a long time ago…"

"Oh?"

"A lyncat, beautiful, powerful, and intelligent. She'd follow me everywhere. Hunt and bring me her kills as gifts."

"What happened to her?"

"She was my first kill." There was no emotion in his tone, and for a moment I thought I'd misheard him.

"Sorry, what?"

"I killed her."

I pushed up on my elbow and looked down at him, searching for any shred of sentiment: remorse, guilt, shame.

There was nothing.

He met my eyes, unfazed. "She didn't try and run," he said matter-of-factly. "She trusted me. Even as I held the knife to her throat, she still believed I wouldn't hurt her. But I did."

His words weren't a confession, just a recounting of an event, or a statement of fact, like telling someone what the weather was like that day.

Warning bells tinkled in my head. Had I been deluding myself in thinking Sev was a victim? "Why did you do it?"

"Because Umbrane ordered me to. My master, my duke, and the only father figure I'd known. He asked and I obeyed. It was a lesson. It showed me how easy it was to kill someone once they trusted you."

Umbrane. It was always that bastard Umbrane. "How old were you?"

"We don't age in years. We age in stages. I was pre-adolescent. The perfect age to be molded. He took me under his wing, taught me how to inflict pain until it was the only thing that could quench the hunger inside me. Until the fear found in nightmares was no longer enough."

I held my breath, not wanting to interrupt his train of thought. I needed to know him, to know more.

"I was his favored for over a century." His mouth twisted. "His plaything. His hands for every debauched act he wanted committed."

Would he have hurt Veena if ordered to? Oh, God. How many innocents had he tortured and killed in Umbrane's name?

His mouth curled in a bitter smile. "Are you still glad you saved me?"

I could read people well enough to read him now. He wanted me to despise him. To be disgusted by him, because he felt he deserved it. Maybe he even craved it.

Yeah, well, fuck that. "Do you regret the pain you inflicted in his name? The lives you took?"

He blinked in surprise and a slight frown furrowed his forehead as if he hadn't considered this question before. "No, I didn't regret it. I couldn't. I shut down my empathy. If I hadn't, I would have gone insane, starved, or both."

Survival instinct was a bitch. How could I look down on him for what he'd done? He'd been mentally and emotionally abused by Umbrane. He was a victim just as must as the beings he was ordered to torture. Thinking about Umbrane brought a sneer to my lips.

Sev tensed beneath me. "I'm no fool, Nyx. I know what I am. A murderer and a sadist. I know it and I own it."

He thought my sneer had been aimed at him. I placed my hand on his cheek. "You are all those things, Sev, but you're also noble, strong, and kind."

His throat bobbed. "You wouldn't say those things if you knew me before."

"Maybe not. But I know you now. You saved my life. You backed off when you could have violated and hurt me. You didn't do those things; instead, you protected me from your brethren. The Sev I know isn't a monster."

"I was. I was Umbrane's monster."

And Umbrane had ordered him executed. "Why did Umbrane order you executed?"

"Why did your mother abandon you?"

I snapped a blink at the abruptness of the question. The same question that Artimus had asked me mere hours earlier. "What's that got to do with anything?"

"Everything. Answer me and I'll answer you."

I hadn't felt comfortable talking to Artimus about this, but the question had festered in my mind for several hours and now the words came easy and without emotion.

"You want to know why I think my mother abandoned me? I think it was because she was afraid of me. She was afraid of my strength and what I might become. She wanted to protect her human children from me. So she got rid of me."

There was no sympathy in his eyes, no pity, and I was grateful for that. He touched my chin lightly with his fingertip.

"Now you. Tell me why Umbrane wanted you executed."

"For the same reason your mother abandoned you. He was afraid."

"Of you?"

"Of what I'd become and what I represented."

"I don't understand."

He rolled onto me, pinning me to the bed with his body. "You will. When the time is right."

"I don't like cryptic shit, Sev."

"And I live for it." He canted his head. "So I guess we're at an impasse, aren't we?" He rubbed himself against me.

I growled and shoved at his chest. "You can't distract me with sex."

"Can't I?" He dipped his head and grazed my neck with his teeth.

"Oh, fuck…" I closed my eyes, reveling in the sensation for a moment before pushing him off.

He rolled off me with a chuckle. "You best answer that."

"What?"

There was a knock on the door a moment later and Sev arched a brow.

"Don't tell me, you have supersonic hearing."

"Fine, I won't."

I climbed off the bed and crossed the room to the door.

A zuni I'd never seen stood on the doorstep. She handed

me an envelope and scampered away. I stepped out of the room to see Keelan standing in the hallway scratching his chin, an identical envelope in his hand.

He looked up and shrugged, then tore his open. I mimicked his actions and tugged out a white card with gold leaf writing scrawled across it.

You are cordially invited to the Atrium for an audience with the emissary at seven p.m. An escort will be provided.

I arched a brow at Keelan. "An invite to the Atrium?"

He made a rumbling sound. "Looks like we'll be meeting the mystery guest who'll be monitoring the trials."

"Any idea who it might be?"

"None. But I'm interested to find out."

"Me too." Me too.

Two Minorax guards arrived to escort us to our audience with the emissary at quarter to seven.

Veena was still healing, and we'd told Gus and Keelan she was feeling unwell. They hadn't questioned us further, thank goodness.

I'd asked Sev to keep an eye on her, and to check in with Zinichi over Chase too. Leaving him cooped up in my room all night was cruel, and as he wasn't permitted to come to the audience, giving him stuff to do seemed like a good idea.

We bumped into Mallini and Charod at an intersection. Nugen was with them, a spear clutched in his hand, his expression fierce.

I guess with no sponsors, he'd opted to be their escort.

They fell in beside us.

"How did your day go?" Tristeene asked them.

"In confinement," Mallini said. "Mother felt it best if we stayed in the residences for now." Her eyes flashed. "I hate this."

"It'll be over soon." I fell into step beside her. "We'll get these trials done and we can relax. Whoever gets the seat will make sure the others are taken care of, right?" I looked about at my siblings, and they all nodded in agreement, but Nugen wouldn't meet my eyes.

"Nugen? You have a shifty look on your face."

"*Pah*, you and your observations. Get away with you."

"No way. If you know something that affects us, you need to tell us."

"I know nothing. Just rumor and scaremongering."

"Okay, what rumors?"

"About another contract. Written and signed in blood by the three princes and Satan. Rumors say it will be revealed after the first trial, and the earth knows what could be in it."

"Whatever it is, we weather it together," Keelan said.

I looked across at him in surprise. "Aw, Keelan, I didn't know you cared."

He snorted. "You fools are growing on me."

I'd barely been paying attention to the décor as we walked, because so far it had been stone corridors hung with tapestries and marble floors, but then the timbre of the echo of our clipping boots changed. The floor was no longer marble. It looked like granite and the walls were sandstone. The corridors grew wider and the ceilings higher.

"This is the central keep," Gus said. "Home to the Erinyes and any dignitaries who come to visit."

Beautiful paintings hung on the walls and the ceiling was a mosaic of red and ochre hues. The whole place had a warm, chic vibe to it and natural light was key here.

Moonlight streamed in through huge windows hung with gauzy drapes, leaving the candelabras bolted to the wall redundant. I could imagine this space during the day, kissed by the sunlight, warm and alive.

"You're probably thinking the sunlight will ruin the paintings," Gus said.

I mean, I didn't really give a shit about the paintings, but the enthusiasm on Gus's face when he spewed facts was too delightful to miss. "Actually, I was wondering *exactly* that very thing."

Tristeene caught my eye, biting back a smile.

Gus's stunning blue eyes lit up. "It's no ordinary paint, it's made from crushed onyx and obsidian. Extremely hardy."

"Really..." I took another look at the paintings, noting the grainy, over-textured surface. "And who painted these?"

"The seneschal," Gus said.

"Artimus?" Surprise colored my tone.

"Oh yes. He's known for his art. Most courts have something created by him."

Now I wanted to stop and study these works of art, to look for pieces of my mysterious mentor in them. But the Minorax had picked up speed, hurrying us along to a door bracketed by pillars. They stopped and moved to stand either side of the door.

"Go on," Nugen said. "In you go."

The room beyond shimmered and wavered, as if heat was rising off the ground, making it impossible to determine the interior décor or pick out any figures inside.

"It's a middle ground," Gus said excitedly. "I've heard about these. Spaces designed to act as neutral spots. They exist on several planes at once and ensure no one occupant has an advantage there. They used them in the war a lot to draw up peace treaties and forge alliances."

"Which begs the question, who in the earth is this emissary," Mallini muttered.

I moved to stand in front of the group and threw a grin over my shoulder. "Let's find out."

I stepped into the shimmer and out into a brightly lit room. I felt the others enter behind me, but barely registered their gasps of awe because the man standing with his back to me had my breath stalling.

I recognized that powerful, wiry frame and the ink that raced up his bare arm to vanish beneath the hem of his dark shirt.

Turn around. Oh, God, turn around.

His shoulders bunched beneath the fabric of his shirt as if sensing my presence and then he turned to face me, dark eyes boring into me from across a room filled with people that no longer mattered.

His name sprang to my lips, but the warning in his eyes came quick enough for me to swallow it.

It blazed in my mind nonetheless.

Loke, the lover who'd vanished on me, stared at me impassively.

Loke was here.

Loke was the emissary.

Chapter Twenty-Five

Loke's gaze swept over me and flicked to my siblings as if he didn't know me. As if he hadn't pressed me to the mattress and claimed kisses that I'd surrendered willingly.

I'd caressed those tattoos, straddled those hips, willing to share my body with him. But he'd been ripped away, back to Tarrifel, and we'd never finished what we'd started.

I'd accepted that because he'd warned me. Explained that once he was gone he could never return, so what had changed? Why was he here looking at me like I was a stranger?

If I hadn't seen the flash of recognition in his eyes, the spark of heat, I might have thought I was going nuts. But it was obvious he was playing a part and our relationship needed to remain a secret for whatever reason.

I knew Loke well enough to understand that everything he did had meaning. The man always had a plan.

I'd find out what that plan was soon enough.

"These are our candidates for the Satan seat," Erinea said from across the room.

She was dressed in white. Tight slacks and a long-sleeve, thigh-length silk shirt fastened with two buttons at her breasts, leaving her taut stomach bare. Her dark plumes spilled down her back and the blue patterns lining her forehead shimmered as if she'd dusted them with glitter.

It was strange seeing her without her chainmail, but I guess there was a different outfit for every occasion.

I'd been so busy checking out Loke and Erinea that I'd almost missed the third figure in the room. Artimus made himself known now, sidling up to Erinea and placing an arm around her waist in a possessive move that made my throat ache for some inexplicable reason.

She tipped her chin up to offer him her mouth and he claimed it in a soft kiss that sparked indignation in my chest.

"Why are we here?" I crossed my arms. "I'm assuming it's not to watch you two suck tongue."

Tristeene made a strangled sound and Mallini snickered.

Erinea's posture went from relaxed to defensive in an instant. "You dare speak out of turn." Her voice vibrated with rage, and a few days ago I might have checked myself, but I'd learned a lot since then. Along with how valuable we, the spawn, were.

"I think you're the one forgetting your place." I narrowed my eyes. "Aren't you going to be working for one of us one day soon?"

Twin spots of color bloomed to life on her cheeks. She opened her mouth to respond but Loke beat her to it.

"I see we have an opinionated spawn here."

Erinea sniffed. "Indeed. Spawn, this is Loke from Tarrifel."

Loke sauntered toward me, hands in his pockets, head tipped to one side. "And what's your name."

Oh, God, his scent. How could I have forgotten his heady scent. "Nyx."

"Nyx..." He trailed off and canted his head, waiting for me to give him my full name.

My heart squeezed in my chest. "Just Nyx." I gave him a cocky smile. "You're not the only one allowed to have a singular name, Loke."

Erinea sucked in a shocked breath. "Loke, I apologize. She wasn't raised on this side of the bridge. She doesn't know who you are or what you represent."

"Then let me enlighten you," Loke said. "I represent the source of all supernatural power. It's my duty to monitor the trials and report back to Tarrifel to ensure that Satan's contracts are adhered to." He fixed his gaze on me. "You may be Satan blood, but none of you will be able to claim his seat of power unless the contracts are adhered to."

"Why does a seat matter so much?" Gus asked.

Loke frowned at Erinea. "Have you not explained it?"

Erinea looked to Artimus. "Did Nugen cover it?"

Artimus shrugged. "I have no idea, love." His eyes were on me as he uttered the endearment, and it made my gut twist. "Loke, would you care to do the honors?"

Loke sighed. "The seat of power is exactly that. When Satan's body died, his power didn't. It was pulled into the seat, ready for the next Satan. One of you. And to claim that power, you must follow the contracts. Do you understand?"

We all nodded. It was making more sense now. The importance of the throne...the feeling I'd gotten when I'd sat on it.

"An original fallen's power is immense," Loke said. "Imagine how much power it takes to kill a daimon thrice to make it stay dead."

Everyone mumbled in agreement, but he'd lost me.

"Excuse me? How do you kill a daimon three times? I mean…dead is dead."

Loke's jaw ticked and he slid a sharp look Erinea's way.

She threw up her hands. "The others know. Like I said, this Nephilim was raised outside of our world and our ways."

"Nephilim?"

"She's powerless," Erinea said quickly. "We made sure of that."

Loke slow-blinked. "Powerless or not, as Erinyes, it is your duty to ensure all spawn are equipped with the adequate knowledge to navigate and understand this world and their responsibilities should they become Satan."

Erinea pressed her lips together.

Loke fixed his attention back to us. "Who would like to explain how to kill a daimon?"

Gus's hand shot up.

Loke nodded toward him.

"A lower daimon has one life but a higher daimon has three. History tells us that some daimons actively gain power after they die, so in the war, as the fallen cut down daimon, those daimon then rose again, more powerful than before. The fallen had to fight these armies and kill them three times over to eliminate them."

Loke smiled. "Correct." His gaze skimmed over us one by one. "Tomorrow you'll be tested and your journey to becoming Satan will begin. What you don't know, you should learn." He looked at me pointedly. "The first trial will begin at dawn and not all of you will survive it. But know this, right now, in this room, you are all worthy of that seat. It's up to you to decide if you can remain as such."

He turned his back on us and crossed the room to a drinks tray.

Artimus said, "Sleep well. You'll need it."

We'd been dismissed.

I strode back through the shimmer, pulse fluttering with excitement, because there was no doubt in my mind that now Loke was here, he'd find a way to speak to me.

BACK IN OUR RESIDENCES, Tristeene and I checked on Veena to find her still asleep. Her bruises had gone and her eyes were no longer swollen, but the internal injuries were probably still healing. Tristeene opted to stay with her while I went back to my room.

Funny how a few days ago I might have been wary about leaving them alone, still debating on who the killer amongst us was, but now I couldn't imagine any of them being a murderer.

Sev wasn't in the room, which meant he was still a floor below checking on Chase. Maybe Chase was awake? I made a beeline for the door but stopped when movement in the periphery of my vision caught my attention.

What was that? There was something in the mirror. A shadow?

I approached the full-length monstrosity with caution and reached out to touch the surface.

The glass rippled.

I jumped back like a scalded cat. "Fuck you."

A low chuckle drifted out of the mirror. "You're adorable when you're spooked, you know that?"

My racing heart slowed. "Loke?"

"The one and only."

"Where are you? How are you doing that?"

"I'm in my room and I have skills. Want to join me?"

Damn, that was a loaded question. "How? And if you say by stepping into the weird rippling mirror, then—"

"Then what? You'll say no?" There was challenge in his tone.

I rolled my eyes and sighed. He knew I never shirked from a challenge. "I won't say no."

"In that case, step through the weird rippling mirror, Nyx."

"For the record, I hate magic." I gripped the ornate frame and pushed my leg through the shimmery glass. It felt cold and odd and the urge to back up was a visceral force.

"Would it help if I told you I was naked," Loke drawled.

"Bastard."

I closed my eyes and stepped all the way through into a lamplit bedroom that smelled of Loke—a fresh, airy scent like the outdoors and summer days. How could a creature bound to the afterlife smell so much like freedom?

In fact, how could a creature linked to the afterlife be so full of life? He stood bathed in the shadow of the flickering flames that danced in the hearth. Bare-chested, tatts on display and begging to be touched, bottom half covered in loose trousers.

"So much for being naked." I crossed my arms and shot him a mock glare.

His smile widened. "It's good to see you again, Nyx."

My heart lurched at his words, longing spearing me. Loke was the closest I'd ever come to emotional heart shit. He'd barreled into my life, knocked my good sense out of my head, and then vanished. Now he was back.

I had so many questions. Things I needed to say. "I

missed you." Motherfucker, what was wrong with me? "We made a good team."

Great save, Nyx.

His expression sobered and he took a step closer before checking himself. His throat bobbed. "I didn't want to leave, Nyx. I had no choice."

"I know. But you're back." I needed to temper the hope in my voice, dammit. It made me sound desperate, and I was a bunch of things, but desperate never made the list.

Shadows fell over his eyes. "Yes, I'm back. For now..."

It was a warning that this, him being here, was temporary. A warning not to get attached.

The burgeoning hope stabbed itself in the chest and keeled over.

I shrugged and smirked. "Hey, you know me. I fly by night. I don't do permanent."

His smile verged on the edge of humoring me.

I embraced the flash of anger it evoked. "God, you're so arrogant. What did you think, huh? That I was pining after you?"

He sighed. "No. You're not the pining type. But I'd hoped you'd miss me a little."

"I already told you I did. We made a great team."

His smile widened. "It was more than that." He took another step. "*We* were more than that."

A lump formed in my throat. "No. We never crossed that line, thank God. Because if we had, your leaving might have torn me to shreds." It was the first truly candid thing I'd said to him.

He let out an explosion of breath. "Nyx..." His expression softened, shoulders relaxing, as if my words had knocked the fight out of him.

"Just laying it out on the table, Loke. I knew you were trouble the moment I set eyes on you all those months ago. That hasn't changed. You're back, but you can't stay, so you'll keep your distance." I smiled, forcing it to reach my eyes. "No touchy-touchy."

A defiant spark lit up his eyes. "No?" He prowled closer, bringing his damn charisma and those flashing dark eyes with him. My body reacted instantly like a brainless moth to a sexy flame, knowing its wings would get burned and not giving a shit as long as it got to feel the heat.

Dammit. Shields up. I lifted my chin. "No."

We stood face to face, a mere meter between us, chests heaving with defiance against the attraction that drew us together.

"Why are you here?" I searched his face. "Did the source really send you?"

The source of all creation had been a myth until I'd met Loke. I'd learned she was very real and that she was his boss.

"Tarrifel has always had a vested interest in the Satan seat. It's my job to ensure these trials are run fairly and to the specifications of the contracts created by Satan and witnessed by the source centuries ago."

So he wasn't here for me. Why did that sting a little?

"Nyx, if I could have come back sooner, then I would have."

"I guess my poker face doesn't work on you." I smiled wryly.

"No." He padded across the room to a silver drinks trolley, poured two glasses of amber liquid, and carried them over. He handed me one. "A long time ago, I told you that you had a destiny."

"Yes, and I scoffed in your face."

"And yet, here you are."

"You knew?"

"Not the specifics. Not then."

"But you do now?" Oh, fuck. "Am I meant to be Satan?"

"It's not that simple, Nyx, and I'm bound by mystical forces so I can't tell you much. The only advice I can give is to follow your gut and to trust your instincts. There are forces at play here larger than us both, and lies and deceit are popular tools of the creatures bound by contracts. Listen to what's said, *really* listen, and don't trust too easily."

I sipped my drink and smiled. "Oh, believe me, I'm learning. I've had to be on my guard since getting here. Did you know that twelve of the spawn were murdered?"

He snorted softly. "I'm not surprised."

"Yeah, I still can't believe that one of my siblings is a killer." I frowned. "I've kinda gotten to know them. I like them. It'll suck to find out one of them is a murderer."

"They might not be," Loke said.

"It has to be one of them. The protection laws were in place when the murders occurred."

He rolled his eyes. "Means nothing if you have the skill and the power to cover your tracks."

What was he saying? "Are you insinuating someone high up ordered the assassinations?"

"Someone killed Satan. That same someone could have culled the spawn too."

I saw where he was going with this line of thought. "Culled them so that their choice of candidate had more of a chance..." Made sense. "So one of my dukes might be responsible."

He arched a brow. "Your dukes?"

I waved a dismissive hand. "I'm thinking."

He took a swig of his drink. "Hmmmm."

"The killer obviously wants control, so he wants a promising candidate, but one they'll be able to manipulate if they become Satan."

He smiled, pleased with my deduction.

"I could be that candidate, couldn't I? The outsider. The spawn with no clue..." I shook my head. "No. I got here *after* twelve spawn were killed. I wasn't even in the running." But someone had tried to kill me by sending helhunters to the Fringe. "Argh, this shit is convoluted. Any one of them could be the killer, or the puppet master." I took a swig of my drink and the alcohol went down smooth and easy. "Wow, this is good stuff."

"My personal stash." It looked like he wanted to say more, but instead he sighed.

"What? There's something else, isn't there?"

"I can't be with you," Loke said. "Sexually."

The jump from talking about murder to talking about *us* took a moment for me to process. "Didn't we already have this conversation?"

He slow-blinked. "Yes, and we had it the last time I was here too. But last time it was out of choice. This time, the source has forbidden me from engaging with you carnally."

"What? Why?" I was happy for us not to bang if it was on our terms, but I wasn't about to let someone else dictate who I fucked. Not even if she was the source of all supernatural power.

"I'm not a part of this world," Loke said. "I don't belong in your story."

"And yet, here you are." I didn't bother to keep the bitter edge out of my voice.

He pressed his lips together. "A punishment. A task."

"I don't understand."

"And you don't need to. Just...don't die tomorrow."

My heart skipped a beat. "You know what the trial entails, don't you?"

"Yes."

"But you can't tell me."

"No, I can't. But I'm here if you need to talk, I'm here as support if you need me. You can use the mirror anytime. Just touch it and say my name."

Yes, the creepy mirror...Wait. "I saw a shadow in a couple of mirrors before. Was that you?"

He tensed. "No. I arrived today. But mirrors can be used as doorways if you know how. Be wary and—"

A knock sounded on his door.

I arched a brow. "Expecting someone?"

"Morningstar hospitality," Loke said with a sardonic smirk. "You should go now."

The knock came again.

I didn't need to ask, didn't need to wait to see, to know that there'd be a female on his doorstep come to service him.

My chest burned as I turned away. "Have fun."

He grabbed my elbow and spun me to face him, yanking me toward him so our bodies collided.

"If I had a choice..." His tone was a breathless rasp, our lips almost touching, breath mingling. He released me abruptly and stepped back with a smirk. "I'll be thinking of you."

My stomach twisted in a mixture of anger and desire. I allowed my lips to curve in a smirk of my own. "And I'll be thinking of you when I fuck my nightmare."

His eyes widened as I gave him a jaunty salute and stepped backward through the mirror into my empty room.

Of course, I wouldn't be as petty as to use Sev to get back at Loke, but right now, I could do with...a cuddle. Oh. My. God. What the hell was wrong with me? And where the heck was Sev?

Chapter Twenty-Six

SEV

This hound doesn't look like it will be waking up anytime soon. At least the female demon who let me in to the residences has stopped watching me with her eagle eyes.

Maybe she thinks I'll eat the creature?

My stomach rumbles.

I am hungry but not for flesh. For blood. I lick my lips and Nyx's face comes to mind. I haven't tasted her yet, but soon...She's bound me to her in a blood debt and I'm hers to own, and feed, and fuck. Ah, yes, that part will be my favorite, even better if I can make her scream. The tip of a blade pressed to her soft flesh, a bead of blood, her gasp of pain.

I'm hard.

But is that what she wants?

Does she want me to hurt her?

I've never considered the needs and wants of my

playthings before, but Nyx...Is she a plaything? I'm not sure what I'm feeling.

I absently stroke the hound's head. He belongs to her too. Maybe we will be friends?

A shadow falls over me, and I bite back a sigh of exasperation. "By the moon, woman, what do you—" I stare unblinking at the drably dressed zuni. "What do you want?"

"Umbrane demands an audience," he says.

"Well, Umbrane can go fuck hims—"

The zuni leaps at me and the world shatters before spitting me onto a cold stone floor in a dank, musty-smelling room. The fucking zuni must have used a transfer crystal, the kind of conji magic that holds a portal that can be used anywhere.

I know this place. It's been my home for as long as I can recall. I'm back and I've brought Nyx's hound with me.

Panic gnaws at my mind, but there's no time to dwell because I'm not alone.

I slowly raise my head and lock eyes with the fallen who raised me.

Umbrane looks down his nose at me. "Hello, Severin. Are you glad to be home?"

Curses come to mind, but I swallow them on instinct, trained to do so by years of pain. Defiance invites agony, not on me but on my brethren. I've seen nightmares flayed and left to bleed, healing achingly slow, only to be flayed once more because of my defiance.

Umbrane knows it's the only way to hurt me. He's learned that I've come to revel in any agony inflicted on me directly.

He's come to know who I truly am.

Large shadows enter the room, moving to flank him.

Daimon dogs.

"Did you think a blood debt with a dirty human blood would prevent me from carrying out your execution?" Umbrane says.

This, bringing me here, taking me from Nyx, is against the rules, but Umbrane dances to his own tune whenever he can.

By the time anyone finds out what's happened to me, it will be too late.

I crouch, one hand on Chase's neck. The portal that brought me here is still active, shimmering behind Umbrane. Has he left it there to taunt me?

Still, I can't help but take the bait and wonder *what if*? What if I get to it? I can find my way back to Nyx. But that will mean leaving Chase behind. I can't do that. He belongs to Nyx, and I won't allow him to be harmed.

"It's time to finish what was started in the arena," Umbrane says.

I hiss and bare my teeth in a show of defiance. The daimon dogs growl low in their throats.

They'll tear me to shreds and my plan will remain unfinished. Indecision wages a war inside me. Old loyalties battling new.

Umbrane steps back with a smug smile. "Finish him. I don't want a scrap of evidence left. Same goes for that bitch's pet."

He takes another step back and vanishes.

The daimon dogs move toward me, ready to act on their orders. I prepare to fight, talons extending, tail whipping up, arrowhead at the ready. Three of them and one of me, not great odds, but at least I'm not bound this time.

My chest aches as I think of Nyx, of the possibility of not seeing her again. She's under my skin, burrowing, familiar, because we're the same.

After all this time there's hope, and I won't be there to see it come to fruition.

Chase shifts beneath my hand. I don't dare tear my eyes from the threat, but I can hear his growl.

He's awake. Good, now maybe we can make it to the portal together.

I drop my hand from his fur. "Chase, I belong to Nyx just like you. We have to get back to her." His growl deepens in timbre. "We have to get to that portal."

He stops growling and chuffs once.

The daimon dogs falter in their advance, and wait... What is this?

They're backing away. Ears flattening, heads coming down. I risk a glance at Chase to find him on all fours, stance wide, lips peeled back, a rumbling growl of warning vibrating his chest, and...the daimon dogs obey.

They fucking obey.

Chase walks forward and they make a path for him.

I don't question, simply falling into step behind him as he leads me to the portal and freedom.

NYX

I was about to drop off when Sev sauntered into my room, Chase in tow.

"Chase!" I climbed out of bed and fell to my knees to give him a cuddle. "I missed your soppy face."

Okay, so his face was far from soppy, he had an *I will tear you to shreds and eat your entrails* kinda face but his huge brown eyes were always soppy and filled with love for me.

He pulled away and fixed those warm brown eyes on me before looking up at Sev as if to prompt him.

"Umbrane grabbed me and Chase," Sev said. "Although I doubt he meant to take Chase. I just happened to be touching him when some zuni used a portal crystal on me."

"Whoa, back up. Umbrane *took* you? Where? Why?"

"Back to the stables. To kill me."

"What!" I shot up, pulse pounding. "Are you hurt?" I moved toward him, scanning his body for injuries.

"I'm fine." He looked down at Chase. "Because of Chase. The daimon dogs backed down for him."

Chase had scared off the daimon dogs? Just like he'd scared off the helhunters. At the time I'd thought the beasts had backed off of their own accord, but now it made sense that Chase had been the one to scare them off. But how?

"What are you thinking?" Sev asked.

"I think the same thing happened with the helhunters when I was attacked in the Fringe."

"You were attacked before coming here?"

"Long story, but I think someone here knew I was Satan spawn before I did."

"And they wanted to cull you." He nodded as if it made complete sense. "The question now is, what is Chase?" Sev studied my hound speculatively.

"I'm beginning to think that's a question we need to look into."

Chase chuffed, as if to say, *that's enough speculation for one night*. He padded to the door and lay across the threshold before closing his eyes.

I stood hands on hips. "Are you serious right now? You *just* woke up."

He opened one eye and lifted his lip in what I called his doggy grin.

"Fine." I climbed back into bed. "Go back to sleep."

"Is that it?" Sev followed me to the bed. "You're leaving it at that?"

I pulled the covers up over me. "Yep. Chase and his ability to cow bigger beasts will have to wait. I have a trial tomorrow, and I need my sleep."

The bed dipped as Sev joined me, sliding his arm around my waist. "Just sleep?"

I smiled into the dark. "Has your almost-death experience made you horny?"

"Hungry." His fangs scraped my jugular, and I resisted the urge to arch into him.

"I have to feed you now?" I turned to look at him.

"I'm yours," he said softly. "Don't you take care of what's yours?"

I felt his hunger like a yawning chasm and the urge to fill it swelled inside me. I'd bound him to me in a blood debt. I still didn't fully understand what that meant, even though I felt it as a connection between us, as a protective instinct, like what I felt for Chase but more evolved because Sev was a person. My person.

I needed to understand. "What is it, Sev? What is this blood debt really?"

"An ancient contract, one not even the fallen understand fully. One not everyone can claim, even though they believe they can."

"What does that mean?"

"It means that the world is changing." He ran his thumb over my bottom lip, and heat licked at my core. "And you and I are in for an intense ride."

He smiled, flashing wicked canines, then pressed a kiss to my jaw. "But for now, you rest. You need your strength for tomorrow. I can wait to claim what I'm owed." The hunger died and I allowed him to pull me close. "Let's dream together, Nyx."

I fell into slumber, taking him with me.

I woke to a hand on my throat, glowing eyes glaring at me. I opened my mouth to scream but something cold was pressed to my nose and mouth. My eyes bugged and the world went dark.

When I next came to, I was lying on a wooden floor. I pushed myself up onto all fours, waiting for my head to clear. Where was I? The sound of crashing waves filled the air.

I was in a wooden cabin. Mismatched furniture dotted the room. A table, two rocking chairs, a footstool, and... Keelan? I crawled across the floor toward his prone form, not trusting my legs to hold me upright just yet. Whatever drug they'd used on me was still making its way out of my system.

"Keelan?" I rolled him onto his back and patted his cheek. "Hey, big guy, wake up."

He groaned and cracked open an eye. "Too early."

I bit back a smile. "It's Nyx. Get your shit together." I looked about the room and spotted a pair of legs sticking out from behind a couch.

I took a deep breath and slowly stood, then tested my balance with a step or two before making my way to the couch. Gus lay on his side, hands tucked beneath his cheek.

"Gus, wake up!" I shook him. "Hey. Up!"

He groaned and then stretched.

I heard Keelan waking Tristeene across the room.

"Where the fuck are we?" Mallini asked.

I spotted her on the far side of the cabin with Charod.

It looked like a cross between a lodge and a hunting cabin. A large space with wooden log walls. An old-fashioned hearth made up the back wall. It had a huge pot hanging over it and a cabinet to the side filled with cooking things. An herb rack sat on the mantel. Someone liked to cook. Rugs covered the floor and nondescript paintings hung from nails on the wall. The end of a bed peeked out from behind a screen at the far side of the room. Veena appeared from behind it. Her bruises were gone, her skin smooth and unmarred once more, dark eyes wide as she took in her surroundings.

"Where are we?" she asked.

The crash of waves filled the room. I strode to the nearest shuttered window and flung it open. Cold sea air smacked me in the face and the sound of crashing waves grew loud. I stared out at the epic view of angry gray skies, then down at a dark sea that stretched on forever. A small boat was moored to a narrow dock, bobbing precariously on the choppy waves.

"What the fuck?" Keelan said.

I stepped away from my window and joined him and Gus at the window on the other side of the lodge, where a landscape of snow and ice filled the view.

"Um, everyone..." Tristeene swept a hand toward the view from a third window. Mallini was looking out to sea, but she joined me in crossing to Tristeene's view of a lush, humid forest landscape that buzzed with life.

"What's happening?" Veena asked softly. "Where are we?"

Tristeene smiled kindly at her. "Honey, it looks like the trial has begun."

Chapter Twenty-Seven

We were all dressed in our sleepwear, which in Keelan's case was a pair of boxers. We had no weapons, and no direction on what the fuck we were meant to be doing.

Yeah, the trial had begun.

There was no door to exit the lodge, only the three windows, each large enough for us to climb through if we wished. "I think we have to pick a landscape."

"Yeah, but which one?" Mallini said from the seascape window. "That boat could carry us all."

"The frozen landscape has snow buggies," Keelan pointed out.

"Which'll be great if we want to freeze our testicles off," Gus said.

"Good point," Keelan agreed.

"There are probably a host of nasty bugs in the jungle one." Tristeene shuddered. "I'm not a fan of bugs."

My mind was whirring. "We have to choose a route, so there has to be a clue in here as to which route to choose, right?"

"Makes sense," Gus said. "Let's split up and look for clues."

"And clothes." I smiled. "There have to be clothes in here, maybe even some weapons."

"Now you're reaching," Charod said with a smile.

I shrugged. "A woman can hope, right? Even a pointy stick will do."

"Or we can make our own..." Keelan moved to the hearth and plucked a poker from the basket.

"Nice." Mallini grabbed one too.

There were enough pokers for us all to take one.

I scanned the room, gaze tracking over the rugs, contemplating using them as clothes and discarding the idea. We didn't even have shoes, for fucksake. They must have hidden proper clothes in here somewhere.

My attention fell to the footstool, to the overhanging top that looked like a lid. I hurried over and tried to lift the stool. It was stuck fast. Heart hammering, I ran my fingers along the top until they hit a snag, a small button. I pushed it in and the top of the footstool lifted with a click.

"What is it?" Veena joined me as I lifted the lid back to reveal a stash of items.

"Clothes." I tugged out a tunic.

"Boots." Veena pulled out a pair of leather boots.

The others crowded around as I reached into the space and pulled out item after item. There was enough for three outfits each. An outfit perfect for each terrain.

"Dammit." I sat back on my heels.

"What?" Keelan looked confused. "We have clothes. That's a good thing."

"Yeah, but I was hoping the kind of clothes we got might clue us in to what window we needed to take."

"I think I found something," Gus said from across the room, standing in front of a row of framed paintings.

I joined him and the others followed. "What is it?"

There were two seascapes, a photo of two guys standing beside snow buggies doing a thumbs up, two framed certificates written in some language I couldn't understand, and a battered, yellowing, framed letter.

He pointed at the letter. "It's a diary entry about an expedition in the Langua Jungle. He mentions the path to freedom." Gus frowned and gently unhooked the picture. "Maybe..." He turned it over and undid the clasps at the back, then tugged off the thick cardboard holding it in place. "Yes!"

The back of the letter was a map. "X marks the spot." Gus tapped his finger on an ink X marked on the map of the jungle.

"Great work, Gus." I patted his back. "Let's gear up for humidity."

"Is there any insect repellent in that box?" Tristeene asked.

"No." I scanned the room, zeroing in on the herb rack I'd spotted on the mantelpiece. "But maybe we can make some? Gus, don't insects hate the smell of lavender?"

His eyes lit up. "Lavender, peppermint, rosemary..." He tracked my gaze. "Yes, we can totally make our own."

I smiled. "Let's get to work, then."

A HALF HOUR later we had a homemade insect repellent that Tristeene made sure to lather on.

Keelan shook his head. "Insects won't be able to penetrate my hide."

The rest of us applied the ointment. We had no clue what kind of toxic and poisonous bugs were out there, and the last thing we needed was to be taken down by a bite.

Veena filled up the seven water bottles that came with the jungle outfits and handed them out. There were seven packs also, each containing provisions of what looked like dried-up strips of meat. There was also flint to make a fire.

I used a belt from the winter gear to make a makeshift holster for my poker and strapped it to my waist.

"How did you do that?" Mallini asked.

I helped her and Charod make one.

"I'll keep mine in my hand," Tristeene said.

Veena struggled with her poker, which was almost the same height as she was.

I yanked open the cabinet and rifled through the cutlery until I found a filleting knife. It came with its own sheath. "Here you go."

She took it with a grateful smile.

"We ready?" Keelan stood at the jungle window.

I joined him. "Ready."

He climbed out into the humid air, and we followed, one by one.

"I don't get it," Mallini said. "What's the point of this?"

We'd been walking through the lush green jungle for almost an hour now. My body was beaded with moisture, my loose cotton shirt and pants kept sticking to my skin.

"To make us lose weight?" Charod said with a grin.

I chuckled. "It's working. I think I've lost at least three pounds."

Veena stumbled and Tristeene grabbed her arm to steady her. The zuni looked like she was about to pass out.

She was small, having to work twice as hard to keep up with us, but maybe… "Keelan, do you think you could carry Veena for a little while?"

Keelan's brows shot up. "No one rides me."

"Maybe if they did, you'd be less of a grumpy ass," Tristeene said dryly.

Gus snort-laughed.

"Huh?" Keelan looked confused.

"It's okay," Veena said. "I'm okay."

"No, you're not." I needed to use a different tactic to get Keelan on board. "You're slowing us all down."

Veena flinched like I'd slapped her.

I kept my tone firm and my eyes hard. "It'll be dark soon. If we want to get to the shelter marked on the map, we need to keep a good pace."

"I-I'm sorry." Veena's lip trembled.

My heart squeezed but I kept my expression cold. "Maybe we should just leave you behind." I shrugged. "I mean, there can only be one Satan, right?"

Keelan growled and came to a halt. He scooped Veena off her feet and set her on his shoulder. "There can only be one Satan," he growled. "But he doesn't have to be a dick."

I bit back a smile and Veena caught it, her eyes widening. *Thank you*, she mouthed.

I nodded.

We were back on the move and it was five minutes later before Keelan spoke. "You weren't going to leave her behind, were you? You just wanted me to carry her."

"Yep."

He chuckled. "I like you, Nyx, even if you are weak and powerless."

"Gee, thanks, big guy."

"But you should know, when it comes down to it, I'll do whatever it takes to be Satan."

"Duly noted."

"No one answered my question," Mallini said. "What could this trial be testing us for?"

"Teamwork," Gus suggested.

"No," Charod said. "There is only one Satan. No need for teamwork. He makes the decisions."

"Decision-making, then," Mallini said. "We had to decide what window to take."

"And what items to take with us," Veena piped up.

"They said not all of us would survive this," Tristeene pointed out. "So far we haven't been thrown in any real danger. Unless you call my hair frizzing up and threatening to blind me dangerous." She pushed her frizzy locks back off her face.

"I think I've sweated half my body weight," Mallini said.

"My vision keeps blurring," Gus added.

"My balls are hot," Keelan said.

Silence fell and was broken by Veena's manic giggle.

"What?" Keelan snapped. "I thought we were sharing."

I patted his bicep. "Too much information, big guy."

The group fell into an easy banter as we continued down the narrow track. I used my poker to knock aside the heavier foliage from time to time as Gus navigated, using the map to take us toward our first stop.

I was beginning to lower my guard when my hackles rose, signaling danger.

The group fell silent, sensing it too.

"What is it?" Veena whispered.

"I caught movement to the left," Mallini said. Her poker was at the ready, gripped in two hands like a sword.

Charod had fallen into a crouch, poker up and ready to swing.

The world fell silent. Not a buzz or a hum.

We moved stealthily, falling into a circle, backs to each other, eyes on the foliage and the shadows.

Something moved along the ground and shifted in the trees above and around us. My skin pricked and crawled with awareness.

Large black snakes dropped from the trees and slid out from behind huge, leafy plants to surround us. Their eyes glowed with hunger in the gloom.

"Does insect repellent work on snakes?" Veena's voice was a trembling whisper.

I backed up. "I think we're about to find out."

Chapter Twenty-Eight

The snakes surrounded us, blocking off our exit.

"These are Rondine snakes," Gus said. "They paralyze with a bite, then swallow their prey alive, and they have no aversion to insect repellent."

"They don't look big enough to swallow us," Mallini said.

"Trust me," Gus replied. "They're big enough."

"What do we do?" Charod asked. "There are too many of them."

But they weren't attacking. Why? "They're waiting for something."

"What?" Tristeene sidled closer to me. "Whatever could they be waiting for?"

Her question was answered a moment later when the wall of bushes to our left parted to admit a snake's head larger than Keelan's whole body.

Ice replaced the hot blood in my veins as the monstrosity slid into our path, head rising up to peer down at us. Its slanted emerald eyes roved over our party with intelligent perusal.

"Well, well, well, intruderssss in my foressst."

It could talk. Why was I surprised?

Her tongue flicked out to taste the air and her pupils dilated. "Too long since I tasted the blood of a fallen. Much too long."

She could smell the Satan blood in our veins.

"But I have inssstructionsss. I may take only one of you. You must decide who that will be." Her gaze fell on Keelan. "I would prefer someone sssubsstantial. But the choice is yoursss. Decide quickly before my children become impatient. I will not be ressssponsible for their actionsss. Take too long and you all shall die."

"Nyx, what do we do?" Charod asked.

My mind whirred. Submit and pick a sacrifice and six of us would walk. Refuse to choose and we'd end up in a fight that we wouldn't win. Maybe a couple of us could make an escape, but the rest would die.

"Nyx?" Tristeene urged. "Nyx, do something."

Her tone created pressure at the back of my mind. The need to act. To fix this.

Motherfucker!

I turned to her and grabbed her hand. "*You* fix it."

"What?" Her eyes flew wide. "What are you talking about?"

I leaned in, my eyes hot with the fervor of my idea. "*Make* her let us go."

She shook her head with a frown. "How can I make her..." The confusion melted. "Oh..."

I nodded.

"I don't know if I can do that on a snake."

"You can try."

"What are you two whispering about?" Mallini snapped.

"I swear if you're plotting to sacrifice one of us, then I'll kill you both myself."

The snakes hissed and slid closer.

"Time'sss running out," momma snake said.

"Fuucck." Tristeene wrung her hands.

I nodded encouragingly. "You can do this."

She took a deep breath and closed her eyes for a long beat. When she opened them, her eye whites were completely black and a sexy smirk painted her lips. She turned toward momma snake and sashayed toward her.

"You and I need to talk." Tristeene's voice was like honey and silk, washing over us with throbbing allure.

"Are you kidding me," Charod whisper-hissed. "Is she seriously gonna try to seduce the snake?"

"No," Gus said with a proud grin. "She's going to try and charm it."

The snake dipped its head toward Tristeene. "Are you my meal?"

"I'm sure you'd love that," Tristeene said. "But you know what you'd love even more?" The air was suddenly thick and heavy with power.

"What?" the snake asked.

"The warm feeling of letting us all go."

The snake's pupils dilated. "Let you go..."

"Yes." Tristeene stepped closer. "It's what you want to do." She reached out and placed her palm on the snake's nose area.

It hissed softly and closed its eyes. "Yessss. Sssso good to let you go."

Motherfucker, it was working.

Tristeene threw a glance over her shoulder and jerked her head in a get-moving gesture.

I nodded and ushered the others past the huge beast.

"You feel so good about your decision," Tristeene continued.

I stopped when I was behind the reptile and looked back at Tristeene. Her eyes were still black, but her jaw was tense, as if it was taking everything she had to hold the monstrous snake in her thrall.

I turned back to the rest of my siblings. "Move. Get ready to run if need be."

Keelan picked up the pace, vanishing into the foliage. Gus hesitated, then hurried after him. Charod looked torn.

I waved him away. "Go."

He ducked into the shadows, but Mallini shifted closer to the snake, poker at the ready.

I locked gazes with her and nodded.

I held my hand out to Tristeene. "Come on."

She shook her head. "You're happy with your decision... You...you don't want to hurt us..."

The snake shuddered. "I...I don't...I'm...hungry..."

Her head jerked back, breaking contact with Tristeene's hand. My succubus sibling let out a scream as the snake's maw hurtled toward her, but I was already in motion. I slammed into her, knocking her out from beneath the snake's trajectory.

Its fangs hit earth.

I rolled, taking Tristeene with me, and sprang to my feet, yanking her up with me.

We ran past the beast.

Its head whipped toward us, jaws snapping and missing us by a hairsbreadth, then it screamed.

"Hurry!" Mallini yanked her poker out of the snake's tail and joined us as we ran.

Branches snapped and cracked behind us as the beast followed. I dragged Tristeene with me. Mallini was fast, matching my stride as we wove and leapt through the underbrush. The air grew cooler, fresher, the foliage sparser, then the angry rush of water filled the air.

I caught sight of the others up ahead. "RUN!"

"There *is* nowhere to run," Charod yelled back. "River and waterfall up ahead."

"Then jump!" Mallini yelled.

The air behind us was thick with danger. The snake's angry hiss much too close. We broke cover, boots beating moist earth as we rushed toward the rapid river. The others caught sight of our pursuer and turned toward the water. We leapt into the rapids as one entity, trading one danger for another.

For a moment the world was upside down, ice biting at my skin, drawing all the heat from my body, grabbing hold and dragging me forward in an unbreakable current. I was swallowed, submerged, and then spat up again long enough to take a desperate gulp of air before being sucked down once more.

I broke the surface again, finally taking control and treading water. I spotted Tristeene to my left. She had her arms around Mallini's neck, holding on for dear life as the Erinyes kept them afloat.

Keelan was up ahead, Veena clinging to his back. Where were Gus and Charod?

The world was too loud, too bright, the rush of blood in my veins matching the rush of water around me and it was getting louder.

Someone was shouting.

What were they saying?

My stomach dipped and then the world rushed out from under me.

My scream was swallowed by the elements, and for a

moment I was suspended in the air with nothing but foamy water and the sky for company, and in the next moment gravity grabbed me by the ankles and pulled.

I hit the water so hard my lungs shot into my throat, and in the next instant I was kicking water beneath the surface with inky blackness below.

I needed to breathe.

Now.

I kicked out, forcing myself toward the light, and broke out of the water, sucking in lungfuls of crisp, cool air.

"Here!" someone yelled.

I treaded water, turning my body toward the sound.

Gus stood on the shore, waving his arms above his head. Charod sat on the ground beside him, his plumes flat against his head.

I looked about and spotted Keelan already headed to shore with Veena clinging to him like a drowned rat.

"Where is she?" Mallini cried. "Can you see her? I lost her when we fell. She can't swim. She can't fucking swim!"

It took a moment for my brain to process what the hell she was talking about, but when she dove under water, realization hit me.

Tristeene was gone.

I bobbed up, took a deep breath to fill my lungs, then exhaled and dove. My eyeballs ached with cold, but I forced my lids to stay open, scanning the darkness below for movement, going as deep as I could before having to swim to the surface again.

I hit the surface and exhaled before taking sips of air, inhaling deep, exhaling fully, and diving again.

Shit, shit, shit. Tristeene, where the fuck are you?

I caught movement to my left, the flash of a pale hand. I swam toward it, reached for it.

It grabbed me.

Tristeene. I pulled, but it pulled back.

What the fuck?

Another hand joined the first, this one scaly and green.

Hell no!

I fought, lungs burning as I struggled to get free of the grip. I needed to breathe. I needed to fucking breathe.

Was I going to die here?

A thick arm wrapped around my waist and pulled. The hands lost their grip, and I shot to the surface. My head hit the air. Sweet oxygen filled my lungs, but a cough racked my frame, bringing tears to my eyes.

"It's okay." Keelan held me above the water. "I have you."

"Tristeene?"

"Mallini has her. She's fine."

He swam me to shore and all I could think was he came back for me. The big lug came back for me.

Chapter Twenty-Nine

The fire crackled and spat warmth, drying out our clothes bit by bit. I kept sneaking glances at Keelan.

"Stop it," he growled.

"You saved me. You didn't have to. It wouldn't have been murder, just one less spawn to compete against."

"And believe me, I'm regretting my decision."

I smiled sweetly at him. "Admit it, I've grown on you. We all have."

"Like nasty fungus."

Tristeene laughed softly. "We make a good team, don't we?" Her tone was almost wistful.

"We do," Gus said.

"We can survive anything if we stick together," Veena said softly. "Maybe it doesn't matter who Satan is, as long as we promise to look out for each other." She looked around the fire at us, her expression hopeful.

Mallini sighed. "That won't happen. Once this is over, whoever wins will have obligations. People... *their* people to take care of. If Keelan wins, the Minorax will come first. If Gus wins, the imps will have his ear, and if Charod and I win…" She sighed.

"The Erinyes will have all the power," Tristeene finished for her.

Mallini nodded.

"It's politics, Veena." Gus smiled sweetly and stroked her hair. "This here, these trials, are probably the only time we'll get to be…siblings."

A thick silence descended, filled with the musings of what could have been if the Satan seat didn't stand in the way of being a family.

I'd been dragged into this race for the seat because of a heritage I hadn't asked for. Determined to claim the title of Satan to prove to everyone who looked down on me that I could. I'd planned to keep the other Satan spawn at arm's length. To know my enemy but not build relationships with them, but here I was, misty-eyed because somewhere along the line, these bitches had become my family.

There was no point fighting it.

"How much further?" Veena asked.

"Another mile," Gus said. "The map's unclear on the terrain between us and the X, but it's another mile."

I looked up at the sky, at the dipping sun. "If we leave now, we can make it before nightfall."

Keelan stood and kicked dirt on the fire to put it out before holding his hand out to Veena. "Come, I'll carry you."

We set off in silence, each of us lost in our own thoughts. The terrain was woodland, cooler, and less threatening than the jungle. Or maybe I'd just reached my adrenaline threshold for the day.

An hour passed and we found ourselves in a narrow

valley flanked by rock walls, and from what I could see we were headed toward another rock face.

A dead end.

I jogged to catch up to Gus, who had his head bent over the map. He blinked up at me. "Nyx?"

"Are you sure this is the right way."

He frowned and nodded. "The X is up ahead."

"Dead end," Keelan said.

"There has to be a passage through," Gus insisted.

"I see it," Veena said. "A cave up there." She pointed toward a ledge in the rock face.

"I see it now," Keelan said.

"Yay for being tall," Mallini muttered.

"Looks like our rock-climbing skills will be tested now," Charod said.

We reached the foot of the wall. Keelan went first, climbing up easily for someone so huge and bulky.

I followed with Mallini and Tristeene close behind. Keelan got to the ledge, then reached down to haul us up one by one.

The ledge was wide enough to hold us all easily, and a dark cave waited for us to enter.

"This has to be the way to the X," Gus said.

"We've been assuming this X is the way out. The end of the trial," Charod said. "But what if we're wrong."

Gus looked thrown. "We have a map. It was the only clue."

"We can stand here dithering or we can find out for sure." I shrugged. "I vote we find out."

"It's pitch black in there," Mallini pointed out. "What's everyone's night vision like?"

I looked to Veena. "You can take point. You have the best night vision."

She looked up at me in surprise. "You want me to lead?"

"I'll be right behind you," Keelan said. "You'll be fine."

She nodded. "Okay."

We ducked into the cave, leaving the remnants of a dying sun behind us to embrace the chill of stone walls.

I expected a smell, but the air was dry and odorless.

"No water running through this cave," Gus said from behind me.

"How do you know?" Mallini asked.

"A wet cave with running water would have fresh, cool air. There may even be an undertone of mud. If there was no running water, then there might be a moldy smell, but the air is dry with no odor. Dry cave."

"Maybe this is simply a passage?" Mallini said.

"I think so," Veena's voice echoed back toward us. "No intersections."

It was so dark now that I could barely see the hand in front of my face. "We need to link up."

I tapped the air until I found a shoulder and squeezed.

"Ouch," Mallini said.

A slender hand landed on my shoulder. "Got you." There was a smile in Tristeene's voice.

"We're so close," Gus said.

"How do you know?" Charod said. "You can't see the map."

"I have it in my head now. We're almost there."

"I see something," Veena said excitedly.

"Me too," Keelan added.

The world turned gray. There was light up ahead.

"What is it?" Tristeene asked from behind me.

"A portal," Veena said.

The cave brightened and I dropped my hand from

Mallini's shoulder. The cavern widened, allowing us to stand almost shoulder to shoulder in front of the portal.

"What now?" Veena said.

"This has to be the way out." Gus pored over the map again. "It's the X."

"So we go through." Keelan took a step toward the portal and slammed into the air. He staggered back, clutching his face. "Motherfucker."

"Congratulations, spawn," a male voice echoed around us.

Artimus?

"You have completed the first trial. The portal will open to admit you back to the keep momentarily."

Mallini and Charod whooped. Keelan made a sound of satisfaction and Gus grinned at me before tucking the map into his pocket, but my stomach knotted in foreboding, and when I met Veena's gaze I saw my doubt reflected in her eyes.

"Then open it," Tristeene said. "What are you waiting for."

She felt it too, and now all of them did. They fell into silence. Waiting.

"When I call your name, you will step through the barrier and stand by the portal."

"Keelan of the Minorax, son of Briatzu."

Keelan took a wary step forward, shoulders relaxing when he didn't get knocked back.

"Lady Tristeene of House Moray."

Tristeene joined Keelan. This time I saw the air ripple as she stepped through.

"Gustus of House Solar."

"Shit... okay." Gus stepped past the barrier.

My stomach grew tighter, heart pounding harder, and I had no idea why.

"Nyx of no family name."

For a moment, my name didn't register. When it did, I made to step forward but something in my gut stopped me.

"Why are we doing it like this?" I lifted my chin, talking to the disembodied voice of my secret mentor. "Why one by one?"

"Nyx of no family name, please step forward now." There was steel in Artimus's tone.

I looked back at Mallini, Charod, and Veena. "Is this in some kind of order?"

"Cross the threshold or be trapped on the other side," Artimus said. "Choose. Now."

Fuck. There was no way I was risking that. I stepped through the invisible barrier and stood beside Tristeene.

"Something's not right," Tristeene whispered.

"I know."

I felt her hand reach for mine and allowed her to take it.

"Mallini el Erineas of House Furorem."

Mallini looked to Charod, who grinned and nudged her. "Go on, I'm right behind you."

Mallini gave him a quick hug and joined us on the portal side of the barrier.

"Veena Zuni."

Veena hurried forward to join us, leaving Charod the last man standing.

Long seconds of silence followed before Artimus spoke again.

"A trial tests for certain aspects and although you all completed the trial, you did not all meet the standard of expectation."

Oh, shit. I knew what was coming. I'd sensed it in the back of my mind, ignored it, pushed it aside, but here it was.

"No." I turned to the portal. "You can't do this."

"What," Mallini said. "What's going on?"

"Silence!" Artimus's voice was a booming command that shook my teeth and made me want to bow in submission.

"Fuck." I clutched my abdomen and gritted my teeth. "Don't do this..."

"Charod al Erineas of House Furorem, you did not meet our expectations. You will be eliminated."

"Did he just say eliminated?" Gus said. "As in...banned from the trial?"

My stomach quivered. "No. Oh, God... No!"

Mallini's eyes flew wide as she realized what Artimus meant. She rushed toward the barrier only to be knocked back. "Charod! Charod, come on."

Charod stood stunned. "I...Eliminated?"

"Come on!" Mallini cried.

Charod seemed to snap out of his daze and his eyes flared with comprehension. He rushed toward the barrier only to be knocked back.

"The portal is open for those who passed expectations," Artimus said.

Behind us the portal changed from white to green.

"I suggest you leave now to avoid seeing the elimination," Artimus said.

"This can't be happening," Gus said. "It has to be another test."

Charod looked lost and confused.

"We have to do something," Tristeene said.

"Even if we could bring down that barrier, I'm pretty sure the portal will reject him." Movement behind Charod drew my attention. "What's that?"

Veena let out a scream as the cavern behind Charod erupted in a flurry of movement. A multitude of legs and eyes.

"Watch out!" Keelan bellowed.

Charod spun to face the onslaught of mammoth spiders scuttling toward him.

"No!" Mallini shook her head, dislodging tears. "No!" She battered her hands against the barrier, digging in her heels to stop herself being propelled back on contact.

Veena screamed again.

I turned to Keelan. "Get her out of here!"

He scooped her up and leapt through the portal.

"Go!" I shoved Gus.

Tristeene pressed her hand to her mouth, eyes shimmering with tears.

I nodded, releasing her from having to witness this.

She backed up and stepped through the exit.

Beyond the barrier the spiders screeched and attacked. Charod swung his poker, knocking them back again and again.

"You can do it!" Mallini cried. "Charod, you can do it."

He fought, slashing and stabbing, taking them down one by one, but for each one he took down another one appeared.

He wasn't going to make it. "Open the barrier, dammit! He doesn't deserve to die." My voice cracked. "Please. Please don't do this."

I felt the air shift behind me, and for a moment I thought my plea had been answered, that they'd dropped the barrier, but when I turned to look, my heart leapt into my mouth at the fresh onslaught of spiders.

Charod cried out, his blows weakening as he realized there was no way he could win this.

"Nyx, get her out," he bellowed. "Get her out now! Please..." His voice broke on a sob.

I grabbed Mallini around the waist and dragged her away from the barrier. She kicked and cursed but adrenaline gave me the strength to plunge through the portal, taking her with me, Charod's gurgling scream echoing in my ears.

Chapter Thirty

We landed in the Conventus Locus, in the spot where the arena had been less than two days ago. It was covered now. The dukes, Artimus, and a few Erinyes stood in a semi-circle before us.

I searched them for Loke, but he wasn't there. I was relieved to find him absent; it meant he hadn't taken part in Charod's murder. It meant I didn't have to direct my rage at him.

No, my fury would be reserved for these fuckers, standing here, faces impassive and unmoved by Mallini's heart-wrenching grief.

I held her tight, rocking her until her sobs petered out and she fell silent. Her body went limp as if the loss of her sibling had ripped out her soul.

"Keelan..." My voice shook with suppressed rage.

He crouched and gently took Mallini from me, freeing me to turn my burning ire on the bastards watching the spectacle.

Zepar's jaw was tight, his tawny gaze on a spot behind us, as if he couldn't bear to look at us. Ignatius watched with curiosity, as if intrigued to see what was about to happen. There were two Erinyes I didn't recognize, but my attention zeroed in on Erinea. Her mouth was pressed in a thin line and her eyes were bright.

She'd just lost her son. Why hadn't she stopped it? Why let this happen? How could she stand there so unmoved by his loss?

My gaze flicked to Artimus, the speaker, the voice, the one who'd ordered Charod killed.

"Why? Why did you have to do that?" My voice trembled with rage. "What possible purpose did it serve, hmmm?" I advanced until I was a couple of feet away from him. "Why did you have to kill him?" My voice rose.

Artimus stared down his nose at me. "The first contract is clear. The weakest spawn are to be eliminated after each trial."

Something inside me snapped. I lunged at him, slamming my fists into his chest over and over. Part of me realized how ineffectual and childish the move was, but the other part, the part that needed retribution and craved the violence, didn't give a shit.

"You bastard, you fucking bastard!"

Artimus didn't try to stop me, taking the blows stoically until someone grabbed my wrist and yanked me away.

"Enough!" Zepar glared at me. "You've had your say."

I bristled and tore my hand from his grasp. "Who the fuck are you to tell me I've had my say, huh? You have no fucking idea how much more I have to say."

"Nyx…" Tristeene grabbed my hand with a soft sob, pulling me away from the line-up of officials.

I resisted, my eyes on Erinea. "How could you let him die? Your son…" My voice cracked again. "He was your *son*."

My chest swelled with emotion, eyes blurring. "You could have stopped it. You *should* have stopped it."

Erinea lifted her chin. "There *is* no stopping this."

"The contracts are unbreakable and must be followed," Artimus said. "The first contract states the weakest spawn from each trial will be eliminated. The second contract states the chosen be given the seat and Satan's power. And we have just opened the final contract."

Another contract? Nugen had mentioned rumors of this.

Artimus's expression was blank as he spoke. "The final contract states once the two previous contracts have been adhered to, once the new Satan has claimed the throne, the remaining spawn are to be executed."

Executed?

My heart stuttered as my siblings let out soft cries of alarm behind me. I stared from Artimus, cold, unmoved Artimus, to Zepar, who watched me warily, and then to Ignatius, who merely slow-blinked as if Artimus had quoted a weather report, not just revealed that at the end of this process, only one of us would be permitted to live.

A fresh wave of anger surged inside me, momentarily cutting off my breath, but when I found my voice, it was cold and filled with venom.

"Fuck you, Artimus. Fuck you all. We quit."

Artimus frowned, the first emotion he'd shown this whole encounter. "You can't quit."

"Says who?" I narrowed my eyes. "You can't force us to run your trials. You can't force us to be Satan. *You* need *us*, one of us at least, and if we don't play your game, you don't get a Satan. So, fuck you. We quit."

His jaw ticked. "You *will* take part in the trials, the contracts—"

"Can go fuck themselves too. We didn't sign a damn thing."

"Your blood did," Zepar said. "You're bound because you're Satan blood. If you refuse the trials, the resistance will kill you all."

"Then burn it." Silence greeted my statement. "Burn the first and final contracts in the Svarog flame. No one has to die for a Satan to be chosen."

More silence followed as they digested my demand.

"It doesn't work that way," Artimus said finally. "We cannot allow there to be any contest for the seat once Satan has claimed it. Other blood-claims to the throne would mean Satan would always be at risk of assassination."

"You can't kill people based on a potential scenario. You don't know us. You have no idea what we may or may not do."

"I would never hurt my siblings," Tristeene said. "Not for any seat of power." She squeezed my hand and my throat tightened.

Gus stepped up beside me and took my free hand. "Me neither."

Keelan came up behind us, Mallini cradled in his arms. Her soft, shuddering breaths made my heart hurt.

Veena pushed between Gus and wrapped her arms around my waist.

"Burn the contracts," Keelan growled.

Something passed across Artimus's face, a brief emotion I couldn't catch or identify, but it gave me hope that the man I'd come to know was still there, buried under the mantle of authority, listening, wanting to help even though his hands might be tied by red tape.

"Artimus...please..."

His jaw ticked and I realized my tone had come out too familiar, almost intimate.

"They can't be burned," Erinea said matter-of-factly. "These contracts are written in the blood of the princes, which makes them indestructible, even in the Svarog flame. If they could be destroyed, we'd have burned the first and last already." She tucked in her chin. "There is no other way but to follow the edicts laid out in the contracts."

My heart sank.

"Not necessarily," Ignatius said. "Blood contracts can be altered by those who bled to pen them. *We* may not be able to burn them, but one of the original authors might."

Zepar's head whipped up. "What are you suggesting? That we stroll into the demon realm and ask the princes to destroy a contract that they created after much deliberation and thought? Have you met the princes?"

Ignatius shrugged. "I'm not suggesting that *we* do anything, I was merely making an observation that may aid the spawn." The embers in his eyes danced as they settled on me. "What they do with that observation is up to them."

The ball was in our court.

Morningstar needed a Satan. The princes might punish a duke for asking them to destroy a contract, but they'd think twice about hurting a Satan spawn.

There was only one thing to do.

"I'll go and see whichever prince I can get an audience with." I set my jaw and locked gazes with Artimus. "Make it happen or lose us all to resistance." I was bluffing about the resistance, because the survival instinct in us all was too strong for us to curl up and just die, but they didn't need to know that. "Right now, I have a grieving sister to take care of."

"YOU CAN'T KEEP HER HERE." Nugen followed as we carried Mallini onto our special residence floor.

He'd been waiting for us outside the arena room along with two Minorax guards, ready to escort us back to quarters. But no way was I leaving Mallini alone in the basic residences.

I ignored him and continued walking. "There's a spare room here."

"That is not the point."

I rounded on him, fists balled in rage. "That is *every* bit the point. She stays with us and if anyone has a problem with that, they can go through me."

"And me." Sev appeared beside me.

Nugen held up his hands. "Fine." He nodded. "I'll send Zinichi up to tend to her. She's just lost her twin. The torn bond will take time to heal. She'll need rest and herbs and care."

My throat pinched and my anger melted. He wasn't the enemy here. "Thank you."

He hurried off and I followed Keelan into the spare room where Tristeene was turning down the sheets on the bed.

We tucked Mallini in and smoothed her plumes off her face. Her eyes were closed, her breathing even, her cheeks tearstained and raw.

"I'll stay with her for a bit," Tristeene said.

Keelan, Gus, and Veena retreated, but Sev remained in the doorway, breathing deep, his silver eyes glowing softly. My gaze dropped to his crotch to find it bulging, and realization hit me like a fist to the chest.

"Are you feeding on her pain right now?"

He gritted his teeth. "Hard not to. It's…delicious."

Hard not to? Disgust twisted my gut. I advanced on him, fury turning my vision red.

"Get out. Get out. Get out!" I shoved him into the corridor.

"Nyx." He held up a hand. "Stop."

I shoved him again, tears blurring my vision. "You do not get to feed on this. You don't, you—"

He grabbed my shoulders and slammed me into the wall. "What the fuck did you think I was, huh? A fuzzy pet like your hound?" His lips curled in a sneer that exposed a fang. "Did you think I was something that would follow you around and do your bidding?" I stared at him, my breath twisting in my lungs. "I'm a killer, Nyx, a torturer who thrives on pain. I would have claimed it from the fuckers who came to take you for the trial if they hadn't used Evershade to slow me down. I need pain like you need oxygen. That's the nightmare that *you* claimed by blood oath. I need to be fed. You need to let me fucking feed."

"Then feed on me." I yanked the collar of my shirt down. "Feed on my blood but don't feed on her pain. Just don't…" I blinked back tears.

He inhaled sharply, then pushed away from me, spinning on his heel and striding away.

I sagged against the wall as the world seemed to close in. I needed to walk.

The upper residences were just as much of a maze of corridors as the basic ones below us. Enough to take turn after turn, stride after stride, until the knots in my chest and belly eased. Until I could breathe again. Think again.

Charod was gone. We couldn't change that, but I was damn well going to make sure that I didn't lose any more siblings. This was about more than the damn seat, this was about family. My newfound family. And I'd do whatever it took to protect them.

I came to a halt just before the next intersection, hands on hips, and exhaled away the twisted emotions churning inside me, centering myself for what was to come.

I'd been too hard on Sev. He was what he was and yelling at him wouldn't change that. I needed to go back and apologize. I needed to feed him.

I needed him.

Fuck.

I made to turn back.

"No, I mean it..."

I paused, cocking my head to listen. I knew that voice.

"You'll do what we say," a gruff male voice replied.

"But you don't understand. We don't need to do this anymore. Everything has changed. She's brought us together. We're a family now."

Veena?

"*We* are your family. The zuni. The downtrodden. The persecuted."

"I know, and I did everything you said. I even accepted Lord Umbrane as my sponsor. I allowed him to..." She let out a soft sob.

"Yes, you did well. Umbrane thinks he can control the seat through you, a weak zuni. He has no idea how strong we truly can be."

"My siblings will protect us. They'll give us the status we—"

"Enough! You'll continue to pick them off to ensure your victory. The Satan seat *must* be yours or else..."

"Please..."

"You know what you have to do, Veena, and you know why."

I backed away from the intersection, blood rushing to my head as I hurried back the way I'd come, an awful new knowledge blooming in my mind.

I didn't want to accept it. I didn't want to think it, but it etched itself into my mind regardless.

Irrefutable.

Undeniable.

Veena, my sweet zuni sister, was the spawn killer.

Nyx's story continues in Demon Gambit.

Other books by Debbie Cassidy

The Gatekeeper Chronicles (Gatekeeper World)

Marked by Sin

Hunted by Sin

Claimed by Sin

The Witch Blood Chronicles (Gatekeeper World)

(Spin-off to the Gatekeeper Chronicles)

Binding Magick

Defying Magick

Embracing Magick

Unleashing Magick

The Fearless Destiny Series

Beyond Everlight

Into Evernight

Under Twilight

The Chronicles of Midnight (Chronicles World)

Protector of Midnight

Champion of Midnight

Secrets of Midnight

Shades of Midnight

Savior of Midnight

Chronicles of Arcana (Chronicles World)

City of Demons

City of the Lost

City of Everdark

City of War

Chronicles of Deadworld (Chronicles World)

Deadworld

Dead City

Dead Sea

Dead End

For the Blood

For the Blood

For the Power

For the Reign

For the Hunt (novella)

Heart of Darkness

Captive of Darkness

Bane of Winter

Fate's Destiny

The Nightwatch Academy (Nightwatch World)

Shadow Caster

Shadow Weaver

Shadow Warrior

Shadow Master

The Nightwatch Series (Nightwatch World)

Ghost of a Chance

Give up the Ghost

Ghost at the Feast

Lay the Ghost

Deadside Reapers Series (Deadside World)

Reaper Unexpected

Reaper Uninvited

Reaper Untamed

Reaper Unveiled

Reaper Undone

Reaper Unhinged

Reaper Unleashed

The Thirteenth Sign (Deadside World)

Witch Unexpected

Witch Undecided

Witch Untold

Witch Unbound

Wolves of Hawthorne Cove (Accords World)

A Shifter's Sin

A Shifter's Trial

A Shifter's Heart

A Shifter's Curse

A Shifter's Choice

Demons of Morningstar (Accords World)

Demon Throne

The Iron Fae Series

Taste My Wrath

Feel My Power

Dragon Guard Series

Dragon Trial

Dragon Rising

Dragon Ashes

Eldritch Blues (New Blood World)

Aberrant Monsters

The Monsters Among Us

When Monsters Lie

Survivor's Heart (Planet Athion World)

Novellas

Rogue

Rebel

Survivor

Standalone Novellas

<u>Blood Blade</u>

About the Author

Debbie Cassidy lives in England, Bedfordshire, with her three kids and very supportive husband. Coffee and chocolate biscuits are her writing fuels of choice, and she is still working on getting that perfect tower of solitude built in her back garden. Obsessed with building new worlds and reading about them, she spends her spare time daydreaming and conversing with the characters in her head – in a totally non-psychotic way of course. She writes Urban Fantasy Romance, Paranormal Reverse Harem Romance and Sci Fi Romance. You can find Debbie on Facebook, Amazon, Bookbub, Goodreads and on her website, debbiecassidyauthor.com.

Printed in Great Britain
by Amazon

41465768R00169